MURDER BY PAGE ONE

A PEACH COAST LIBRARY MYSTERY

OLIVIA MATTHEWS

Print: ISBN: 978-1-952210-12-9
eBook: ISBN: 978-1-952210-13-6

www.hallmarkpublishing.com

DEDICATION

To My Dream Team:
My sister, Bernadette, for giving me the dream.
My husband, Michael, for supporting the dream.
My brother, Richard, for believing in the dream.
My brother, Gideon, for encouraging the dream.
And to Mom and Dad, always, with love.

I'd also like to express my sincere thanks
to Maria F. and Toni B. for their invaluable
help and insights on Georgia culture.

CHAPTER 1

"I WAS PROMISED CHOCOLATE."

I directed the reminder toward my new best friend, Jolene Gomez, after entering the bookstore. I threw my gaze into every visible nook and cranny of To Be Read in search of chocolate-covered pecan clusters.

Jo owned To Be Read, an independent bookstore on the southeast side of Peach Coast, Georgia. It wasn't that I needed the food bribe to come to her bookstore—or any bookstore—especially when a bunch of authors were signing their books. It was just that, well...promises had been made.

"Marvey." The tattooed businesswoman's tan features warmed with a welcoming smile. Her coffee-colored eyes shifted to my right. "Spence. I'm glad you both made it."

Jo seemed relieved, as though she'd worried we wouldn't come. Why would she have thought that? I kept my promises, especially those made to another book fanatic. Jo and I had bonded over our love of books, our newcomer status—she was from Florida and

I was from New York—and chocolates, which reminded me today's stash was still conspicuously absent.

"Of course we came. We're readers. On top of that, we're here supporting our friend." I nudged Jo's shoulder with my own.

"The others are on their way," Spence said, referring to the members of the Peach Coast Library Book Club.

Spence and I had walked over from the library after our Saturday afternoon meeting. It was about a fifteen-minute walk, and the weather on this May Day had been comfortably warm. As geographically challenged as I was, I'd been glad to have Spence with me. On my own, I probably would've still been circling the library's parking lot.

Spencer Holt was a local celebrity, although he'd deny it. The Holts were the richest family in Peach Coast and one of the wealthiest in Camden County. They owned a bed and breakfast, a hotel, a local bank, and the town's daily newspaper, *The Peach Coast Crier*. It was considered required reading among the residents, and Spence was the publisher and editor-in-chief.

The family was also philanthropic: Peach Coast's answer to Gotham City's Wayne Foundation. Spence's mother, for example, served on the board of directors for the Peach Coast Library—which technically made her my boss.

For all his money, prestige, power, and good looks—think Bruce Wayne with a slow Southern drawl—Spence was very humble. He was more interested in listening than talking about himself, and he seemed to prefer comfort over fashion. I once again noted his brown loafers, faded blue jeans, and the ruby-red polo shirt that showed off his biceps and complimented his warm sienna skin.

Spence shifted his midnight gaze to mine. "If you want pecan clusters, we can get some at the coffee shop after the signing."

After the signing? "It wouldn't be the same." Translation: that would be too late. Far too late. I continued scanning the store, my mind rejecting the truth my eyes had confirmed.

"I haven't put the chocolates out yet, but I'll get you some in a minute." Jo waved a hand as though the treats weren't important. The right sleeve of her citrus-orange knit sweater, which she'd coupled with leaf-green jeans, slipped to reveal the University of Florida Gators logo inked onto the inside of her small wrist. Jo was a proud alumna. "First, let me introduce you to Zelda Taylor. She's the president of Coastal Fiction Writers. The authors who're signing today are members of her group. Zelda, you know Spence."

"Ms. Zelda, it's nice to see you again." Spence's greeting rumbled in his Barry White voice.

"Mr. Spence, it's always such a pleasure," the redhead gushed. Her porcelain cheeks glowed pink. "How is your mama?"

"She's very well, ma'am. I'll tell her you asked after her." Spence's smile went up a watt. The poor woman seemed dazed.

I tossed Spence a laughing look. "Is there anyone in this town you don't know?"

Spence's smooth forehead creased as he pretended to consider my question. "Well, nearly one thousand people reside in Peach Coast. I'm sure I've yet to meet one or two of them."

Jo gestured toward me. "Zelda, this is Marvella Harris. She moved here from New York—the city—four months ago. She's the library's new director of community engagement."

Zelda tugged her attention from Spence. Her appearance was flawless: well-manicured nails, perfect makeup, and salon-styled hair. She was camera-ready for a photo spread in a Southern homes magazine.

"Oh, yes. I read the article about you in the *Crier* a couple of months back." Her voice was now imposing, as though she were reading a town proclamation. "Welcome to Camden County. What brings you all this way, Ms. Marvella?"

Referring to the county of residence instead of the town was taking some getting used to. I supposed it was like New Yorkers saying we were from Brooklyn, The Bronx, Queens, or Staten Island. Only people from Manhattan said they were from "the city."

"Just Marvey, please." The Southern custom of adding a title to a person's name was charming, but it was a lot to say before getting to the point. "I want to help the library increase its outreach and services. Do you have a library card?"

Zelda's eyes widened. "Why, yes." Her commanding tone had faded. "Yes, I do."

Although suspicious of her response, I gave her the benefit of the doubt. "Excellent. I look forward to seeing you at the library. You should join our book club. We meet the first Saturday of each month."

"Oh. That sounds nice." Zelda smoothed her silver cotton dress in a nervous gesture. I sensed her casting about for a believable excuse to get out of the meetings.

Spence offered an incentive. "Marvey serves Georgia

Bourbon Pecan Pie and sweet tea after every meeting—but you have to stay till the end of the meeting for the refreshments."

Panic receded from Zelda's eyes to be replaced by interest. "Oh, well, now. That would be nice indeed."

I turned my attention from Zelda to survey To Be Read. I loved the store. It was like a giant welcoming foyer, flooded with natural light. Closing my eyes briefly, I drew in the scent of crisp new paper from thousands of books and magazines. Fluffy furnishings in pale earth tones popped up at the end of aisles and in quiet nooks. A multitude of blond wood bookcases stuffed with stories offered the promise of adventures and the thrill of knowledge.

A couple of Jo's employees were setting up for the book signing. They'd already arranged the wooden chairs and matching tables. The twenty-somethings transferred books from wheeled metal carts to each author's assigned table. Jo's third employee processed purchases at a checkout counter while engaging each customer in conversation as though they were lifelong friends. Every now and then, a burst of warm laughter rolled across the store.

But there still wasn't a single chocolate-covered pecan cluster in sight.

"I'm sorry I missed the meeting." Jo's gaze swung between Spence and me, twinkling with curiosity. "How was it?"

"It was great," Spence said. Slipping his hands into the front pockets of his jeans, he turned to me. "I'm impressed you were able to get the club up and running so quickly, within a month of your arrival."

"We librarians are known for our efficiency." It was a struggle to keep the smugness from my tone.

Spence's compliment filled me with a massive sense of achievement—and relief. Even though it was only our third meeting, I'd known the book club would be a success. We'd already attracted twenty-five book lovers, all from diverse backgrounds and each strengthening our argument for a bigger budget. *That* continued to be my motivation.

Leaving my parents and older brother in Brooklyn to relocate to Peach Coast with my cat had been hard. My roots were in Brooklyn. I'd lived my entire twenty-eight years in the New York borough, but I'd grown increasingly frustrated by my lack of opportunities to shine in my public library system. There, I was just one of many small fishes in a very big pond. I couldn't generate any waves. Not even a ripple. But I'd been confident that, if given a chance, my ideas for growing the community's interest in and support of the library could make a big splash. Here, in this small town, I'd finally be able to try. The library's success would make at least some of my homesickness worth it.

Jo grinned. "So who came in costume, and what did they wear?"

Spence ran a hand over his close-cropped hair. His voice was devoid of inflection. "Mortimer painted himself blue and called himself Aquarius."

This month's member-selected read was the latest paranormal fiction release by Bernadine Cecile. I loved paranormal stories. This one featured a world in which meta-humans used the power of their zodiac signs to defeat villains—hence Mortimer's costume. He wasn't the only one who'd gotten carried away. Most of the members hadn't wanted to read *Born Sign*, but the first rule of book club was to keep an open mind. To my relief, the novel had been a hit.

Zelda spoke over Jo's laughter. "Marvey, if you don't mind my saying, that's a lovely pendant." Her gaze had dropped to my sapphire cotton T-shirt, which I wore with cream khakis and matching canvas shoes.

"Thank you." I touched the glass pendant. I'd suspended it from a long antique silver chain. It held a silver-and-black illustration of the cover of Lorraine Hansberry's *A Raisin in the Sun*, the version depicting the Younger family's dream home.

Jo inclined her head toward me. Her long raven ponytail bounced behind her narrow shoulders. "Marvey makes those herself. And the matching hair barrette. She draws the pictures and puts them in the pendants and barrettes."

Zelda glanced at my shoulder-length, dark brown hair, but she couldn't have seen my barrette, which gathered my hair behind my head.

"You're very talented." Her eyes glinted with admiration—and longing. "Do you sell them?"

This question came up a lot. Each time, I stood firm. "No, it's just a hobby. I'd like to keep it that way."

I'd been making those pendants and barrettes since high school. The craft fed my love of art and jewelry making, and allowed me to pay homage to great works of literature. It was the kind of activity I could do while listening to an audiobook. Although I often gifted sets to family and friends for birthdays and holidays, the hobby was something I did for enjoyment, not for money. If I mass-produced them, it wouldn't be fun anymore.

Jo's dark eyes twinkled with mischief. "With all the

interest people have shown in your pendants, you may have to break that rule."

Spence flashed his silver-screen smile. His perfect white teeth were a dentist's dream. "Maybe you should give a class. That way, you can teach people how to make their own pendants."

"That's a great idea. The course could be a fundraiser for the library." New books. Updated software. Additional periodical subscriptions. Every little bit would help. I shelved the idea to consider in depth later.

"Ready for another great idea?" Spence's lips twitched with humor. "Run the Cobbler Crawl with me."

The man was relentless. I responded to his winning smile with a chiding look. "For the fourth time, no, I will not."

The Peach Coast Cobbler Crawl was an annual three-and-a-half-mile race to raise money for the local hospital. Each two-member team had to stop and eat a large, heaping spoonful of peach cobbler at the one-, two-, and three-mile points. The first team to cross the finish line together won.

"I can't enter the Cobbler Crawl without a running partner." Spence had been trying to convince me to form a team with him almost since the day we'd met.

I was running out of ways to say no. "Why don't we both just give a donation and watch the event from the sidelines?"

Jo laughed. "You should do it, Marvey. You run six miles every day. Three and a half miles will feel like nothing."

Now they were ganging up on me. "If we only had to run, I wouldn't hesitate. But I don't think I can run *and* keep down the cobbler." I shuddered to think of the consequences.

Zelda came out of her spell, dragging her attention from my pendant. "I'm the exact opposite. I could eat the cobbler, no problem. But I couldn't run a mile in a month of Sundays."

Determined to change the subject, I turned to Zelda. "How many members of the Coastal Fiction Writers are published?"

"We're a small group, but we're growing. At the moment, there are twelve of us. Four of our members are published."

"Five." Jo lifted the requisite number of fingers. "I ordered books for five members. I think you're missing Fiona." She addressed Spence and me. "Fiona Lyle-Hayes just released her first book, *In Death Do We Part*. It's a mystery, and it's gotten great advance reviews."

Spence sent me a look before switching his attention to our companions. I could tell he wasn't giving up on the Cobbler Crawl. "We ran a piece about her book in the *Crier*."

"Oh, yes. How could I have forgotten Fiona?" Zelda clutched her pearl necklace. Her smile seemed fake. That was curious.

"Fiona helped coordinate the signing." Jo glanced at her employees who were setting out the books before returning her attention to Spence and me. "She's also the writing group's treasurer."

"Yes, Fiona manages our money. She's good at that." Zelda flashed another tight smile, then looked away. Tension was rolling off her in waves. I really hoped it didn't bubble over and ruin Jo's event.

I glanced toward the entrance again to see more of

our book club members arriving, as well as quite a few strangers—each one a potential new library cardholder. Four of the newcomers made a beeline for Jo, who identified them as the local authors who were signing today. I concentrated on the introductions, but keeping names and connections straight strained my brain. Of course, Spence knew all of them. I resolved to stick to him like gum on his shoe.

The authors dressed up their displays with promotional postcards and trinkets. Jo's employees put the finishing touches on the arrangements, which included the bowls of the long-promised-but-seemingly-forgotten chocolate-covered pecan clusters. Jo and I had only been friends for four months, but I'd known she wouldn't let me down. I began drifting toward the signing area—and the chocolates—when Jo's voice stopped me.

"I wonder what's taking Fiona so long?" Jo checked her silver-and-orange wristwatch. A frown cast a shadow over her round face. "The signing starts in ten minutes. I thought she'd have her books out long before now."

Zelda scanned the store. "Fiona left our writers' meeting early, saying she needed to get ready. Where is she?"

Jo jerked her head toward the back of the store, sending her ponytail swinging. "She's been in the storage room. She wanted to examine her books and bring them out herself."

Weird. "Why?"

Jo shrugged nonchalantly, but I saw the aggravation in her eyes. "She didn't say, but I suspect it's because she thought my staff and I would damage her books."

Zelda's smile didn't reach her eyes. "Fiona can be a pain in the tush. Bless her heart."

Bless her heart. That was a Southern phrase I'd heard before. It didn't mean anything good.

CHAPTER 2

WHILE I HUNG OUT WITH Spence and Zelda, Jo checked on the authors who'd taken their seats on time.

Spence's voice drew my attention from the bowls of chocolate. "Nolan, I'd wondered if you'd make it to Fiona's first signing."

Nolan was a few inches shorter than Spence—perhaps an even six feet—and fit. Despite his graying close-cropped brown hair and tired brown eyes, he seemed youthful. It could've been the casual clothes he wore: powder green jersey, dark blue jeans, and blue sneakers. That's right, sneakers.

Southerners—and admittedly, much of the rest of the country—referred to "sneakers" as "tennis shoes," but that felt wrong to me. Not all sneakers were tennis shoes. Some were running shoes or cross trainers. To me, it was like referring to all carbonated soft drinks as "Coke." Yes, Georgia was home to The Coca-Cola Company, but New Yorkers called it "soda." You could take the woman out of Brooklyn, but you couldn't take Brooklyn out of the woman.

Spence made the introductions. "Nolan Duggan, I'd like for you to meet Marvella Harris. Nolan's the co-owner of Lyle and Duggan CPA, along with Fiona. Marvey is the director of community engagement with the Peach Coast Library."

Nolan regarded me with an odd combination of welcome and wariness. "I read the interview with you in the *Crier*. You're from New York." I swear it seemed like he'd said, "You're an alien."

"It's nice to meet you, Nolan." I tilted my head and gave him my best nonthreatening smile. "Do you have a library card?"

Nolan gave me a blank stare. "I've never needed one. I'm at the bookstore all the time." His gaze drifted to Jo and lingered before returning to me.

"Everyone needs a library card, Nolan." I increased the wattage of my smile. "Why don't you stop by the library Monday? I'll help you with the application."

"All right." Nolan dragged out the two-syllable consent as though hesitant to make the commitment.

"Great!" Another customer. Another step toward a bigger budget.

An older woman and two younger men entered To Be Read. The woman marched with purpose, leading her contingent toward the signing area. If this had been New York, I would've suspected the trio was out to start something.

The woman's face flushed as she brought her posse to a stop in front of Jo. "Where's Fiona?"

I didn't like her tone. Not one bit. All of my protective instincts toward my friend went on high alert. I glanced at Spence. "Who is she?"

Spence lowered his voice. "That's Betty Rodgers-

13

Hayes and her son, Bobby Hayes. Bobby is Fiona's step-son. I don't know who the other man is. I don't think he's a local."

Nolan solved the mystery. "That's Willy Pelt, Fiona's friend from Beaufort, South Carolina. I met him when he was introducing himself to Ms. Betty and Bobby out in the parking lot."

Now I was even more confused. "It's nice of them to attend her event, but why are they so angry?"

Concern for Jo made me want to get a closer look at the wannabe mob. And I couldn't deny myself the clusters any longer. I wandered over to stand behind Jo and reached for one of the individually wrapped candies.

"Wow!" Jo's shout distracted me from my goal. She'd gestured toward Bobby's right arm. Her voice was reverent. "Who did your ink?"

My attention shifted from the candy dish to the bold rendering of a large, well-fed, and vicious-looking snake drawn onto Bobby's tanned arm. The orange, black, and brown serpentine illustration extended from his thick wrist, past his elbow to disappear beneath the sleeve of his faded red T-shirt. I suppressed a shudder. Snakes. I disliked them. A lot.

Bobby smiled shyly. As he turned his arm, I noticed several scratches on the back of his hand. "I got it done at a place out in Vegas."

But...a snake? I had to ask. "Why did you choose a snake?"

He shrugged. "I like 'em."

Why? But I let it go.

Betty's sniff was unfiltered maternal censure. "Well, I'm sure I don't know what got into his head to do such a crazy thing. It makes him look like a ruffian! And a *snake*? It's evil."

"Snakes aren't any more evil than humans, Mama." Bobby's voice was quiet and respectful.

But Betty was on a roll. She continued as though her son hadn't spoken. "Of course, he works in a hardware and repair shop full of ruffians. Well, I told him it's a good thing he does. Otherwise he wouldn't have any kind of job with filth like that covering his body."

Bobby gave a long-suffering sigh. "They're good guys, Mama."

"Your body is a *temple*, Bobby. *A temple*." Betty was breathless. Her brown hair fluttered above her sturdy shoulders with indignation. "Well, he can't ever get a decent job working in a decent place, now can he, looking like *that*?"

Bobby shook his head, never once raising his voice. "Just let it alone, Mama."

Jo pushed up the left sleeve of her sweater to reveal the silver, black, and gold sketch of a decorative cross inked onto her forearm from wrist to elbow. "If he ever wanted to try a new career, I'd hire him here at the bookstore."

Betty's brown eyes stretched wide. "Well, yes…" As Betty appeared to struggle to contain her true reaction, her son studied Jo's cross with avarice.

If the older woman had asked me first, I would've warned her that Jo was the absolute wrong person to turn to for a sympathetic ear on the topic of tattoos. But she hadn't asked me. And for the record, yes, I was amused by Betty's predicament.

Personally, I wouldn't get a tattoo. I couldn't fathom withstanding that much pain. But if I were to—and the odds were slim to none—it would be an image of Batgirl. I'd always admired the superhero. And—bonus!—Batgirl's alter ego, Barbara Gordon, was a librarian.

"It's nice that you've all come to support Fiona." I turned to Fiona's friend. "Especially you, Mr. Pelt, coming from South Carolina."

Willy glanced up from his wristwatch. He seemed surprised that I knew his name, then he noticed Nolan. Willy inclined his head in a silent greeting to Fiona's business partner, the expression on his pale, square face pleasant but vague. He drove his fingers through his shock of thick auburn hair. "I've known Fiona's family for years."

"I wonder what Fiona will do now?" Nolan's attention bounced from Jo to the rest of the group. "Will she give up her share of the business to write full-time?"

It was a good question, although I knew most authors continued to work full-time. Popular media's depiction of fiction writing as a lucrative career was greatly exaggerated.

Betty snorted. "Well, she doesn't *need* a job, now does she? Not like the rest of us. When Buddy died, he left *her* well provided for. The rest of us have to *work* for a living."

The bitterness in her voice seemed to come from far more than envy of another person's good fortune—literally and figuratively. Then I made the connection: Fiona Lyle-*Hayes*. Betty Rodgers-*Hayes*. There was a story there, one that could explain Betty's hostile disposition.

"I was wondering the same thing." Willy crossed his arms over his chest. His brown jersey and tan slacks were slightly wrinkled, as though he'd recently pulled both from a suitcase. Had he just driven into town from

Beaufort? How long that had taken? "Her late uncle left her his vacation property. The house's in good shape, and the land is pretty. It's in a quiet area on the out-skirts of town where she could write without being disturbed."

Bobby shoved his broad hands into the front pock-ets of his navy blue cargo pants. "She'll probably go on a lot of tours." He sounded disappointed, as though he was going to miss Fiona's company.

"This is ridiculous." Jo's words ended the discus-sion. Her eyes flashed with irritation as her gaze swung to the back of her store. Her ponytail arched behind her. "The signing has started, and Fiona *still* hasn't brought out her books. Now, I'm going to have to hustle to help her set everything up."

"I'll help." I hurried to follow Jo as she whirled to-ward a book aisle.

"So will I." Spence's voice came from behind me.

Jo stopped long enough to give us a grateful look. "Thank you, but I can't ask you to work for me. You're here as guests."

Spence arched a thick black eyebrow. "We're also your friends. Let us help."

"Okay, since you've twisted my arm." Jo turned to continue her agitated march down the aisle. Her pony-tail swung back and forth in a tsking motion. "I wish she'd let me and my team handle her books from the beginning. Unloading them now will be disruptive to the other authors who got here early and actually set up."

I struggled to both keep up with Jo and speed read the titles on the passing shelves. We were in the young adult section. I loved young adult fantasy novels. I hesitated in front of a newly released title. Spence nudged me along.

I caught up with Jo. "This won't endear her to the other members of her group." I remembered the way Zelda had acted, as though Fiona was She-Who-Must-Not-Be-Named.

"I don't think Fiona likes them, either." Jo's tone was dry.

"What makes you think that?" Spence asked.

Jo glanced at us over her shoulder. "It's just a feeling I got from her when we were organizing this signing."

Jo crossed into the storage room. Spence and I were right behind her. The room was dimly lit in comparison to the main part of the store. Empty boxes stood to the side, waiting to be flattened for recycling. Step ladders and carts were stored in a corner for easy access. Shelving affixed to the walls held office supplies such as paper, printer inks, packing tape, markers, and box cutters. In the center of the room, two matching dark wood tables balanced open boxes of books still to be shelved. On the far table, Fiona's books had been unpacked, only needing a cart to carry them out. But who would operate the cart?

Was I the only one feeling uneasy? "Where's Fiona?"

In front of me, Jo frowned as her store owner's attention seemed to catalog the room's contents. To my right, Spence appeared to be scanning the room, searching for the source of the disquiet. I stepped forward.

"Marvey, wait." Spence's voice stopped me.

But not before I saw the body, lying in a pool of blood on the far side of the rear table.

I must have rocketed a foot into the air before landing on semi-solid ground. Spence's large, strong hands gripped my shoulders to steady me.

Jo gasped. "Oh, my God. Fiona."

CHAPTER 3

"**D**on't touch anything." Every mystery I'd ever read came crashing back to me. "We have to call the police." My voice was sharp, pitched loud enough to be heard above the blood rushing in my ears.

On the outside, I may have appeared to be keeping it together. On the inside, I was screaming. The stench of death was a sour taste in my mouth. I wanted to spit it out, but that would contaminate the crime scene.

"The police. Yes, you're right." Jo was in shock. We all were. Fortunately, we'd been together when we'd found Fiona. I would've hated for Jo to have discovered this tragedy on her own.

My muscles shook as I helped her to the door. I tugged at her as I called over my shoulder to Spence. "Do you have a handkerchief?"

He pulled a plain white cloth from the back pocket of his jeans and held it out to me. "Why do you need it?"

"Oh, my God." Jo was mumbling to herself. "I can't believe this. Fiona."

I pressed my palm to the small of her back. She was

shaking even more than I was. I was afraid she'd come apart. I turned to Spence. "We need to secure the room, but I don't want to leave prints on the door." My voice sounded so far away. I had to get out of here.

"I've never seen a dead body before." Jo looked at me. Her eyes were blank.

Spence pulled the handkerchief from my reach. "Help Jo. I'll close the door."

"Ever," Jo whispered.

Neither had I. Using both arms, I steadied her. I half-carried, half-dragged her from the room as I made myself put one foot in front of the other. The door clicked behind us as Spence shut it. If only I could slam a door against the image of Fiona's corpse, but it was burned into my skull. With deliberate steps, I led us to Jo's office, away from that chamber of death. A sinister presence still weighed on my shoulders like a backpack stuffed with encyclopedias.

What happened? Who did it? And why?

I settled Jo on a green cushioned visitor's chair, then collapsed onto the one beside it.

Since Jo wasn't in any condition to call the sheriff's office, Spence circled her desk to use her phone. He reached past her orange University of Florida coffee mug for the receiver and punched in nine-one-one. "I'm calling to report a murder."

It felt like hours, yet took less than ten minutes for sheriff's deputies to arrive, accompanied by an ambulance. The piercing screams in my head had quieted to a low whine, but the virtual backpack of encyclopedias still clung to my shoulders.

The deputies had announced the murder before the emergency medical personnel had appeared with the gurney carrying Fiona's body under a thick white sheet. Shock had filled the store, thick enough to break with a jackhammer.

Jo had declared the book signing over. She was slowly recovering from her initial devastation. The glass of water one of her staff had pressed into her hand was helping. She'd flipped the *Open* sign in the front door to *Closed*, but the deputies had directed everyone on the premises to remain for witness interviews.

There were at least twenty people in To Be Read, including Jo, Spence, me, Jo's employees, and the authors participating in the book signing. Three deputies were conducting witness interviews in separate parts of the store. A fourth was watching over us. Was he there to comfort us during this time of distress, or to prevent us from coordinating our stories? The New Yorker in me dismissed the idea of Southern hospitality and went with option two.

Since Jo, Spence, and I had found Fiona, the deputies interviewed us first. Jo led a tall, baby-faced lawman to her office. A petite female deputy escorted Spence to a sitting area near the magazines.

An older deputy brought me back to one of the reading spaces in the children's book section. He was going to conduct the homicide interview in the company of *The Cat in the Hat*, *Curious George*, and *Madeleine*. My stomach took a tumble. Would I ever reminisce over those stories again without the memory of Fiona's murder?

The deputy waited for me to sink into the overstuffed mint green armchair before plunging into the orange one beside me. He cleared his throat. "I'm Deputy Jed Whatley, ma'am."

"Marvella Harris." I gripped my clammy hands together on my lap and shifted my shoulders to release some tension.

He looked at me askance. "How'd you spell that?"

As I spelled my name, I absently took in his uniform: short-sleeved white shirt and olive-green pants. He hadn't removed his green campaign hat.

Jed lifted cool blue eyes and caught my gaze. "And you're one of the people who discovered Ms. Lyle-Hayes's body in the storage room. Is that right, ma'am?"

Peach Coast residents spoke so slowly compared to New Yorkers. I could've made a pot of coffee and two slices of toast—buttered—before Jed finished asking his question.

"Yes." I kept my answer short to compensate for lost time.

He scanned his surroundings, taking in the section's bright yellow walls and kid-sized bookcases as though seeing them for the first time. "I didn't know they were having a signing here today."

That was disappointing, considering all the work Jo had put into promoting the event, including the fliers and posters in the library. His admission silenced the screams in my head once and for all.

I flexed my shoulders again. "I'd never met Fiona, but I understand she was excited about the signing." I rubbed my eyes to erase the nightmare-inducing image of the deceased woman. Her wounds. Her sightless sea-green eyes. Her blood.

Jed recorded my remark in his notepad, then followed with seemingly routine questions about the events proceeding our discovering Fiona's body. Where had I been? Who had I been with? Had I noticed anything out of the ordinary? Finally, he lowered his pen and paper.

He sighed as he stared across the store. "I wonder why Ms. Gomez would let Ms. Lyle-Hayes back there in the storage room by herself? Are non-employees allowed to go poking around in the storage area? I'd think only employees could do something like that. Wouldn't you?"

I shrugged. "You should ask Jo."

Jed's attention meandered back to me. His eyes narrowed as though he didn't like my response. "Why do *you* suppose Ms. Gomez let her back there?"

Knowing Jo and her empathetic nature, the answer was obvious to me. "I'm sure Jo understood that Fiona would be nervous about her first-ever book signing. She probably gave Fiona time alone to prepare so she'd feel more confident when the event started."

Jed wrote that down. "Did you see anyone near the room, either walking away from it or loitering in the area, before you went in, ma'am?"

"No."

He nodded as he made another note. "Did you observe any of the customers acting strangely? Did anyone ask after Ms. Lyle-Hayes?"

"Her friends and family. And I didn't notice anyone acting strangely." Then a hint of a memory asserted itself, seeming to contradict my statement. "Although Nolan Duggan, Willy Pelt, Betty Rodgers-Hayes, and her son, Bobby, all kept checking the time."

Fiona's business partner, Nolan, and her friend,

Willy, had frequently consulted their wristwatches while we'd waited for Fiona. I'd noticed Nolan's silver-and-gold Gucci watch and Willy's stainless steel Movado. They were attractive—and expensive—accessories. Betty also had repeatedly checked her peach Timex, and Bobby had looked at his black cell phone more than once during the brief period I'd been with them.

At first, their obsession with the time hadn't registered with me. Maybe they all shared the same nervous tic. I'd been distracted by the idea of asking Nolan and Willy, in particular, to become library patrons. But in retrospect, their behavior made me curious. It was as though they'd all been anxious to leave To Be Read, when they'd literally just arrived. If they hadn't wanted to be there, why had they come?

Jed didn't write down my tip about their frequent time checks, though. Perhaps he didn't find it as curious as I did. With nothing more concrete to contribute to the investigation, I felt helpless. Whether Fiona was well-liked or not—and I was beginning to think she wasn't; call it a hunch—she deserved justice.

"Where was Ms. Gomez before Ms. Lyle-Hayes's body was found?"

The question stirred all of my protective instincts toward my friend. Was Jed focusing on Jo? She had nothing to do with this. My voice was firm. "Jo was in the front of the store. She was either with me or within my line of sight the entire time."

"Are you sure about that, ma'am?" Jed rubbed his upper lip.

"Positive. Spence can confirm it too." I returned Jed's steady stare through several beats of silence.

The deputy made another entry in his notepad.

"Those are all the questions I have for you. For now. I may have a few follow-up questions later. Thank you for your time, Ms. Harris."

I wrote my home phone number on my business card and handed the card to Jed.

The deputy studied it. "You work over at the library?"

"Yes, I'm the director of community engagement."

He grunted. "I haven't been to the library in years."

Why was I not surprised?

Jed escorted me to the front of To Be Read just as Spence returned with the female deputy. Jo was already back, waiting with two members of her staff. Jed's suspicious gaze scrutinized her before moving on to the rest of the room.

"Excuse me, folks," he said loudly. "If I could just have your attention for a bit. Now, we understand y'all probably want to go home. Get back to your families. Try to enjoy what's left of your weekend. Believe me, we understand. You can do all of that once you've given us your statements. But just so you know, we may have some follow-up questions for y'all down the road. All right now."

He gave Jo another considering look before inviting one of her employees to join him in the children's book section. Spence's deputy took the other.

Jo was nursing the water one of her employees had given her earlier, or perhaps she'd refilled it. Still visibly shaken, she stared into the mug. "I told my team they could leave after they spoke with the deputies, but they said they'd stay to help close the store."

"Good." I glanced at Spence. He was regarding Jo with concern as well. "Is there anything I can do to help?"

"No, thank you." Jo's smile was a weak impersonation of her usual dazzling expression. "I appreciate everything you've both done already, taking charge of this...tragedy." She drew a shuddering breath. "I'm just sick that someone was murdered. But that someone would do something like this in my store... It's like they murdered a guest in my home."

I gave her shoulder an empathetic squeeze. Jo's analogy was perfect. She spent long hours at the store, tending to it as though it was her home. Vases of fresh flowers, bowls of potpourri, and plates of candy were scattered around the floor plan. And she treated her staff like family. I couldn't imagine how Jo must feel. Fiona's murder was a heinous act. How much more devastating would it be to have this crime committed in a place she loved so much?

"I'll stay and drive you home when you're ready to leave." Spence's voice was gentle.

"I'll wait with you too." I followed Spence's gaze.

A young deputy carried out what appeared to be evidence kits. Had she found the murder weapon? I cautiously searched my memory. There hadn't been anything resembling a weapon near Fiona's body.

"Thank you." Jo shook herself as though trying to shrug off the same helpless feeling that threatened to paralyze me. "The store's closed Sundays. I'll keep it closed Monday too, out of respect for Fiona."

"That's very thoughtful of you." I examined Jo's delicate features. She looked tired.

"Do you think the deputies suspect someone here killed Fiona?"

Spence raised his thick eyebrows and lowered his deep voice. "That doesn't make sense. The killer would've been covered in blood."

That same thought had crossed my mind.

I scanned To Be Read, settling on the front doors. The *Closed* sign hung in the window. "That's the only way in or out of the store. Whether you're a customer, an employee, or a delivery person, you use those doors."

Jo glanced over her shoulder toward the entrance. "That's right."

I frowned. "Question: how did the killer, covered in blood, get past a store full of people without being noticed?"

CHAPTER 4

THE NEXT MORNING, I WENT for my usual early jog along an idyllic path I'd found in a park a few blocks from home. Only the faint chirrup of birds singing and memories of finding a murder victim kept me company.

I came to the short weathered wooden fence that separated the dirt trail from the swamp line. Sweat stung my eyes. I wiped them and focused on my black Apple Watch, a gift from my brother. It read a quarter to six a.m. I'd been running for thirty minutes, three miles. I turned toward home to finish my six-mile run.

A faint breeze cooled my heated skin. Each deep breath drew in the sharp scent of dew-laden grass and the musky smell of compost from the swamp. It beat the exhaust fumes that had kept me company on morning jogs through my old Brooklyn neighborhood. I emerged from the park and turned toward home. The sleepy streets allowed me to get lost in my own thoughts instead of playing chicken with the New York traffic. I did, however, miss the energy of the city that never sleeps, and the silent solidarity with other joggers. There was always a trade-off.

But another bonus: I'd been able to buy a house. It was a simple little A-line cottage with a white wood façade and a gray gable roof. Sugar maples and sweetgum trees lined my sidewalk, and black-eyed Susans waved from my front yard.

I jogged up the four steps to my little front porch and turned off my stopwatch. I collected the Sunday edition of *The Peach Coast Crier* from my doormat before letting myself in and deactivating my security alarm.

Carrying my newspaper and my running shoes, I went in search of my cat. "Phoenix?"

The name suited him. When I'd adopted my four-year-old gray tiger rescue tabby a little more than a year ago, he'd been thin and weak. After a month and a half, he'd gained weight and strength, rising from the ashes like the phoenix of Greek mythology.

In New York, Phoenix would meet me at my front door after my morning run. Since resettling in Peach Coast, he seemed to have given up his security detail. I walked through my living room and down the hallway to my yellow and white kitchen.

Phoenix's food bowl stood about two-thirds empty near the side door. My shoulders slumped. It used to be that he wouldn't leave even a crumb behind. The vet had said Phoenix might not have much of an appetite until he got used to his new home.

I passed through the doorway that separated the kitchen and dining room, dropped the newspaper on the table, and then turned to find Phoenix in the foyer. He'd stretched out in front of the French doors that opened onto the wood deck. His new favorite spot.

"Are you still having trouble settling in? It's not easy for me, either. I'm homesick too." I lowered myself to the hardwood floor beside him and stroked his soft, warm fur. "It's quieter here, though. No sirens from emergency vehicles in the middle of the night. No neighbors, blaring their sound system or TVs. Don't you like that? I do." *Mostly.*

Phoenix gave me the side-eye as though I was missing the point. But after almost sixteen weeks, he still wouldn't tell me what the point was. He'd always been moody, but this silent treatment was next level.

"I could use a little help, pal. We've gone to the vet twice. He doesn't seem to know what to do, either."

Still nothing. Even as I stroked him, he didn't meow. He didn't purr. He didn't even stretch. He just ignored me as he stared through the French doors toward the Chinese privet bushes that edged our lawn. The real estate agent had taken pride in telling me those were the same hedges that surrounded the University of Georgia football stadium. She'd been offended I hadn't been impressed.

I pushed to my feet. "I'm hitting the showers. Hang tight."

Within the hour, bathed and dressed, I hustled back to the kitchen. Phoenix remained in front of the French doors, where he continued to ignore me. Pretending not to notice, I brought my cinnamon-flavored oatmeal, coffee, and orange juice to the dining table. I opened *The Peach Coast Crier*, shaking it more vigorously than necessary in an effort to get Phoenix's attention. No dice. We usually read the news together, but after our relocation, my cat had stopped keeping up with current events. Maybe he missed *The New York Times*.

"Fiona Lyle-Hayes's murder's on the front page." I shared the information over my shoulder. No reaction. "It's sad. I'm sure she'd planned to celebrate her first book." I shook my head as I sipped my coffee. The scent of the medium roast slapped my senses. Cream, four sugars. My sweet tooth imprisoned me.

The story went into detail about Fiona's debut novel, *In Death Do We Part*. It was being hailed as an *"engrossing mystery with twists and turns sure to keep readers breathlessly engaged."* Impressed, I made a mental note to ask if we had copies for the library.

The article didn't reveal many personal insights about Fiona beyond her first publishing credit. It noted she'd been married to Buddy Hayes, who'd died a year earlier. She'd had a stepson, Robert Hayes, from Buddy's previous marriage. Thinking about Betty Rodgers-Hayes, I shook my head. Who attended their ex-husband's new wife's book signing? Was that a Southern thing?

I arched an eyebrow at Phoenix's back. "I wouldn't go to my ex's new wife's signing on a bet." Not so much as a flick of his ear in response. I returned to the paper.

The story quoted Deputy Jedidiah Whatley. *"Ms. Lyle-Hayes's murder is a terrible tragedy for our community. We're determined to find justice for her and to ensure the safety of our community."*

The only personal quote in the article was attributed to Zelda Taylor, the Coastal Fiction Writers president. *"Fiona had been our group's treasurer for almost a year. She managed our money. She was good at that. Our condolences to her family and friends."*

Zelda had used the same phrasing about money

during the book signing. Was that really all she'd had to say for the article, or had the reporter run out of space?

I glanced toward Phoenix. "There was no love lost between Zelda and Fiona."

Phoenix cut me a dismissive glare before returning to his surveillance. That hadn't been a pleasant response, but at least he'd given me something. I crossed to the foyer and gathered him to me. He melted in my arms when I stroked his forehead.

I carried him back to the dining table with its matching chairs. "It's like I told you yesterday: I wish I could've given the deputies more information. I wish I'd seen or heard *something*, but I'd been with Jo and Spence in the main part of the store the entire time."

I froze beside the rectangular table. "Phoenix, why *didn't* I hear anything? Why didn't any of us hear anything? If someone was stabbing me multiple times, people would hear me in Atlanta. Why didn't anyone hear Fiona from just across the store?"

Atlanta was three hundred forty-two miles from Peach Coast. I'd looked it up. Driving sixty-five miles an hour, it would take five hours and twenty-six minutes to travel between the locales.

"Oh, well. The deputies will figure it out." Shaking my head, I reclaimed my seat.

Phoenix started to purr. Was I finally getting through to him after all these months?

"There's my boy." I gave him a brief squeeze before continuing to stroke his forehead.

I scanned the other news stories. One was a preview of the next town council budget planning meeting. Hopefully, council members would look kindly on the library. Another article revealed plans for the annual

Independence Day parade, still two months away. The paper also carried an announcement of an upcoming readers-and-authors event to be held at one of the beachside hotels. I felt a rush of excitement.

I'd started reading about the event when my cell phone rang. The screen displayed Jo's name.

"Hey, Jo." I switched hands so I could continue petting Phoenix. "How's your Sun—"

"They think *I* did it." She was frantic. "They think *I* killed Fiona."

CHAPTER 5

FIFTEEN MINUTES LATER, JO WAS sitting at my dining table. "The deputies interrogated me." Her voice squeaked with panic.

Phoenix gave her a startled look before running from the room. His claws clicked against the honey wood flooring. Jo's anxiety had been too much for him.

I'd offered to go to Jo's house, but she'd insisted on coming to mine. Perhaps she'd needed distance between herself and her latest encounter with law enforcement. I brought out the big guns: chamomile tea, meant to soothe her. I nudged the rose porcelain mug across the table toward her with one hand and gently pushed her fingers away from her mouth with the other.

"Start from the beginning—and stop biting your nails." I took my seat at the head of the table.

Jo took a deep drink of the herbal brew. "The deputies came to my house around eight o'clock this morning. I was on my way to church."

I'd attended the Saturday evening Mass and lit a candle for Fiona. "Which deputies?" I asked.

"The older one who questioned you, Jed Whatley, and the tall one who questioned me, Errol Cole."

"Go on." I sipped my coffee. For me, it was still too early for tea.

"They asked me tons and tons of questions. How well had I known Fiona? Had we had any disagreements? Can anyone confirm I *hadn't* checked on her while she was in my storage room? Well, of course I hadn't checked on her! And if she'd been as rude to the deputies as she'd been to me, *they* wouldn't have checked on her, either."

Tension seized my shoulders. "Did you actually say that to them?"

"Of course not," Jo grumbled. "They would've taken it as a confession."

"Probably. The deputies questioned you again, but what makes you think you're a suspect?"

"When I asked them if I was a suspect, they said yes." Jo pushed herself up from the table and paced the width of the room. Thank goodness Phoenix had left. Her agitation would've given him a coronary. "They said, 'Well, ma'am, the murder did take place in your store.'" Jo deepened her natural cadence to impersonate the male deputies.

Although I was starting to share her concern, I made a good faith effort to be the voice of reason. "This is only the second day of the investigation. Right now, everyone's a suspect."

Jo stopped and stared at the black-and-white picture of the New York Public Library, my previous place of employment. I'd mounted the photo in a thin black nine-by-twelve-inch metal frame to display on my wall. Odds were Jo wasn't seeing Patience and Fortitude, the marble lions that greeted the library's guests. Instead, images from her disturbing early-morning visit from the deputies were surely playing on a loop in her mind.

"As I told the deputies, I was in the storage room with Fiona for probably less than ten minutes. From there, I went straight to check on the event setup with my team. I was helping them arrange the tables and chairs when Zelda showed up, and then you arrived with Spence."

What a relief. "You have people who can corroborate that you didn't return to the storage room until you, Spence, and I went to get Fiona."

Jo turned to me. "Yes, but as the deputies pointed out, that means *I* was the last person to see Fiona alive."

"No, you weren't. The killer was."

"And the deputies think *I'm* the killer." Jo dragged both hands through her hair. Freed from the ponytail she wore at work, the thick raven tresses tumbled halfway down her back. "I'm scared, Marvey. I don't have money for a lawyer."

"You won't need one." I needed to believe that was true. We both did.

"Oh, yes, I will." Jo resumed her pacing. "I'm not convinced these Bulldog fans will do an unbiased investigation."

What, now?

Jo had caught me off guard. Don't get me wrong—New Yorkers were avid sports fans. But college football wasn't a thing in New York. It was a thing in the South, though. A very big thing.

I regarded Jo with mild concern as I tracked her journey back across my dining room. Connecting a murder investigation to a college rivalry sounded insane. "I read the *Crier*'s article on Fiona's murder. The deputies are taking this case very seriously. This is about justice for Fiona, not a college prank."

Jo stopped with her back to me. "I've never felt so isolated."

"The investigation's just started. You didn't have a motive to kill Fiona, nor did you have the opportunity."

"Then why do I feel like I'm going to wake up tomorrow and be served with a warrant for my arrest?"

What was it about the deputies' behavior that had made Jo so paranoid? "That's not going to happen."

We were silent for several moments. Jo paced while I sat, holding my pendant like a talisman. Today's image was an orange-and-black illustration of the cover of Maya Angelou's 1969 classic *I Know Why the Caged Bird Sings*.

I monitored Jo as she wandered past me again. "The deputies will get on the right track in a day or two. I'm sure of it."

She stopped beside the table. Her knuckles showed white as she gripped the back of the chair. "I can't sit around and wait to be railroaded. I need to do *something*. Now. I need someone on my side." Her gaze locked onto me. "Marvey, *you're* on my side."

"Of course. I know you didn't do this."

"Help me prove it."

My mind went blank. "How?"

Jo pulled out the chair and sat. "By helping me find proof that clears me. All I'm asking for is reasonable doubt."

"You *have* reasonable doubt." I leaned into the table, anxious to convince her. "Your team, Zelda, Spence, and I all saw you outside the storage room after Fiona had arrived. If you'd killed her, you would've been covered in blood."

Jo was shaking her head. "I need something more to get the deputies to stop focusing on me."

"Jo, I'm a librarian, not a crime fighter."

"Please, Marvey. There's no one else I can turn to."

Urgh. I squeezed my eyes shut to escape the plea in Jo's wide dark stare. What did I know about investigating murders, coming up with motives, suspects, timelines, and evidence?

But...Barbara Gordon/Batgirl was a librarian. And so was I. At its core, an investigation was research, learning about people, tracking down clues, and putting together the results of your inquiries. I could do that.

Couldn't I?

"All right." I exhaled the words before I could change my mind.

Jo popped off her chair and wrapped her arms around me. "Thank you, Marvey! Thank you so much!" She straightened and stood back. Her relief was palpable, making me glad I'd agreed to help—even as I had no idea what I was doing.

"I can't make promises."

"Of course not." Jo waved her hands. "I understand."

I rose to my feet, collecting my empty coffee mug for another refill. "First, I'll need some supplies."

"Like what?" Jo followed me into my kitchen.

"Laptop, paper, pencils, and my emergency bag of chocolate-covered peanuts." I couldn't handle stress without it.

"Are you going to share?"

"Of course."

"Okay. And then what?"

"We start with one of the many things librarians do best."

"What's that?"

I pulled the bag of chocolates from my hideaway bin. "Research."

"We've been going in circles for almost two hours." Disgusted, I dropped my pencil on the writing tablet. The top sheet was almost filled with notes. "What do we have?" Feeling the onset of a sugar high, I nudged away the bag of chocolates. Jo and I had started on our second pot of tea.

"We don't have much." Jo sounded as frustrated as I felt. The foot of her right leg, crossed over her left, tapped a frantic though silent beat. "Fiona talked a lot while we were planning the signing. I hadn't realized until now that she hadn't really said anything substantive."

"Her social media's a void. There aren't photos of family or friends." I once again clicked through her Facebook photo albums. It was a desperate move. I wasn't going to see anything I hadn't seen before.

We'd been able to navigate her Facebook, Twitter, and Instagram pages because Jo had connected To Be Read's social media accounts with Fiona's while they'd planned the signing. Fiona had posted photos of herself at author conferences and workshops, as well as book fairs. There were pictures of her with other published authors and images of her book cover.

"Maybe none of her friends or family had wanted

their pictures on the internet." Jo scanned the notes we'd taken.

Through scrupulous digging online, we'd learned Fiona had been born in South Carolina forty-one years earlier. Most of her past remained a mystery. Where had she gone to school? Why had she relocated to Georgia? Did she have living relatives?

"Why was Betty at the signing?" I asked. Jo was Southern. If it was a regional thing, I figured she could explain it to me.

She made a humming noise. "I'd wondered about that too. Maybe she came because of her son."

It still didn't make sense. "Fiona married Buddy Hayes only six months after moving to Peach Coast."

"Talk about your whirlwind romance." Her tone was dry. "She blew into town and broke up a marriage."

Not wanting to judge Fiona, I brought the conversation back to the signing. "Imagine you're Betty. Would *you* attend Fiona's signing?"

Jo shrugged her slender shoulders. "Maybe Betty's moved on."

I couldn't imagine moving that far on. It would be like changing time zones. I clicked through more photos. "Fiona had posted a lot of images of her book cover. She must've been excited."

"She was, and I was happy for her. But she was obnoxious about it all."

"I can understand why." I pointed to Fiona's posts on the computer screen. "She was getting fantastic advance reviews for her book from reputable sites: *Publishers Calendar*, *Suspense/Mystery/Thriller Magazine*, *Librarians Periodical*." I was especially impressed by that last one.

"That's one of the reasons I was happy for her. But it didn't give her license to be a witch to me and my team. She pushed back the event so we could include her book."

"I can understand that too. If she's going to act as a liaison between her group and your store, she should get something out of it for her time and trouble."

"I agree. *That* was the least objectionable thing she did. I'm working my way up." Jo shifted on her seat to face me. "She made demands on the store as though I worked for her."

"I'd have a problem with that too."

"She wanted to approve all of our publicity materials. She said her book had to appear first on the listing because it was being released by a big publisher. Her words, not mine."

I blinked. "*That's* the kind of information we need, not this sanitized social media stuff." I waved my hand at my laptop. "If we're going to find the motive for her murder, we need to learn who Fiona really was."

"How do we do that?" Jo looked hopeless.

"By talking with people who knew her and knew about her: associates, friends, family. But they may not want to speak with us. You and I are outsiders—"

"A New Yorker and a Gator."

I ignored her college football reference. "We need someone on the inside who can give us validation with the locals."

Jo and I had our epiphany at the same time. "Spence."

CHAPTER 6

"WE SHOULD LET THE DEPUTIES do their job." Spence's baritone voice came through my cell phone Sunday afternoon. Jo and I had him on speaker. "The deputies can't build a case against you, Jo. There isn't any evidence linking you to Fiona's murder."

"The deputies are using the fact that she was killed in my store to link me to her murder." Jo blinked rapidly as though struggling against tears.

Her fear was a tangible presence between us. My heart was breaking for her. What would she tell her team on Tuesday? How would she answer the inevitable questions from well-meaning—and in some cases, purely nosy—neighbors? I could imagine her stress and anxiety. Putting myself in her place, I was even more committed to doing everything I could to help, including persuading Spence to help us.

"Fiona's murder occurring in your store isn't enough to bring a case against you to court." Beneath Spence's easy Southern speech, I heard the pinging of metal on porcelain. It sounded like he was stirring a spoon inside a mug. The hushed voices in the background must be from the portable radio that stood on his kitchen counter. I recalled the room from the few times Jo and I had visited Spence's home. The spotless black, white, and silver space was a culinary artist's dream.

"It shouldn't be enough to get Jo on the suspects list, but that didn't stop the deputies from putting her there." My fingers itched to dive back into my bag of chocolate-covered peanuts. "I'm not confident they're experienced enough to handle this case. The town's last homicide occurred less than two years ago. Do you remember it? A tourist was strangled in his hotel room. The murder's never been solved."

"I do remember that case." He probably recalled details from his newspaper's coverage. "How do *you* know about it?"

"We researched murders in Peach Coast." I dismissed Spence's question. We needed to stay on topic. "The point is the sheriff's office won't want to rack up another cold case. To save face, they're going to have to close this one and quickly, which is the reason they're rushing to identify suspects. They put Jo on that list despite their inability to link a motive or an opportunity to her. They don't even have the murder weapon. Does that seem reasonable to you?"

"I agree it's not a promising start to their investigation." Spence was beginning to sound concerned. The hushed voices in the background abruptly went silent.

I shrugged a shoulder. "Based on the true crime novels I've read, it seems like they're being irrational."

"But what can *we* do?" Spence asked. "The deputies may not have much experience with murder investigations, but we don't have any."

"You're right." I gripped my pendant as I searched for the words to change Spence's mind. "But this is a big story for Peach Coast. Wouldn't you like to dig into it?"

"I'd rather give the deputies room to do their job." Spence's words floated up from my cell phone on the dining table. "They have resources we don't have access to. We also risk aggravating them, and they might take their frustration out on Jo."

Jo's eyes widened with additional fear. "I didn't think about that."

I bulldozed over both objections. "This is a small town. Everyone will know the deputies are investigating Jo. The negative attention will do serious damage to her, personally and professionally."

Jo appeared to be persuaded back to our original course of action. "I need your help, Spence."

"All right. What can I do?"

I exhaled a breath of relief. "We need to identify a motive someone would have for killing Fiona. Jo and I spent a couple of hours this morning searching the internet for information about Fiona. There's little to nothing to go on."

Jo chimed in. "It barely gives her name, birthplace, and residence. She's either really private or really boring."

"A third possibility is she was too smart to put personal details on the internet." Spence's tone was wry. "More people should follow her example."

He had a point. Fiona had been cautious about what she'd shared on her social media pages. Was it possible some of the information on her profile wasn't even accurate? Swallowing a sigh, I set that fear aside to deal with later, if necessary. "We need to talk with people who could give us personal information on Fiona. The librarians seem to know a lot of the residents."

"They're well-liked in town." Spence was contemplative.

Jo's eyes brightened. "We're hoping they'll have information that could help us."

"But why do you need me?" Spence asked. "They'll speak with you."

Jo chuckled without humor and her hand returned to hover near her mouth. "I'm not so sure about that."

I lowered her arm to keep her from biting her nails. "Although I work with them, I think they still see me as an outsider. I don't think they're ready to share any insider information with me yet. That's where you come in."

"I didn't know Fiona well." Spence's response was hesitant. "And what I do know is sketchy at best."

"I get that." I nodded although he couldn't see me. "But if we add your sketchy information with information from the librarians, we may be able to better identify where to start our investigation."

"So you want to set up some kind of emergency meeting?" Spence still sounded puzzled.

"Not a *meeting*." Jo leaned closer to the cell phone. "We want you to host one of your dinner parties and invite us, Corrinne, Viv, Floyd, and Adrian."

"I can do that. When?"

"Monday," I said.

There was a pause. "As in tomorrow?"

I looked to Jo. "Yes, tomorrow evening."

A longer pause. "I can't do that."

"Spence, we've got to do this tomorrow. Time is of

the essence. The killer could be destroying evidence as we speak, if they haven't already." The deadline clock was ticking in my head.

"This isn't New York, Marvey." Spence's tone struck a balance between amusement and incredulity. "I can't pull together a dinner party in a day."

I frowned. "Why not?"

His sigh whispered down the phone line. "For one thing, I don't have supplies."

Jo gave me a pleading look.

I squared my shoulders and mentally rolled up my sleeves. "If we start now, we'll have more than twenty-four hours to prepare. Not counting the hours we'll be at work tomorrow. And I'll help."

"I'll help too." Jo sounded determined.

I shook my head. "Jo, it would be best if you skipped the dinner party. People will speak more freely if you're not there."

"I have to miss Spence's dinner party?" Jo looked crestfallen. "But they're one of the biggest social events in this town."

Did I look as disbelieving as I felt? "Are you serious right now? You're serious. Jo, I really need you to focus. This won't be a social event. It's an investigation to clear you as a suspect in a *murder*. I promise to update you right after the dinner."

Spence sounded amused. "Jo, once your name is cleared, I'll host a special dinner party in your honor."

"I'll hold you to that." She practically sang her response. Waves of excitement rolled off her. I couldn't believe it.

Was I the only one still focused on the *murder* part of

this murder investigation? "If we're done here, Spence, when can I pick you up?"

He sighed again. "Marvey, we don't have enough time to plan a dinner party for tomorrow evening."

I thought fast. "If you do this for us, I'll make it worth your while."

"How?" He sounded dubious.

I closed my eyes and reminded myself that my sacrifice was for the greater good. "I'll be your partner for the Cobbler Crawl."

Another pause. "I'll pick you up in twenty minutes."

"Your usual, Marvey?" The greeting came from Anna May Weekley, the owner and operator of On A Roll. The neighborhood café and bakery served as the unofficial Peach Coast community hub. Time seemed to slow here.

"Yes, please, Anna May." I returned her smile as the scents of warm rolls, sweet pastries, and hot coffee led me across the brown-and-gold tiled flooring to her counter. Along the way, I stopped to exchange greetings with the other regulars, which was pretty much everyone in the crowded café. Most of the circular tables were occupied.

I'd known as soon as I'd seen the little gathering spot that it would be the best place to get to know the residents—and to let them get to know me. Making the café part of my morning routine on my way to work had sped up my acclimation to the town. It also was a great place to help raise the Peach Coast Library's profile in the community. I hoisted my American Library Association tote bag a little higher on my shoulder. Its tan canvas material prominently featured the slogan *Read, Renew, Return.*

When I arrived at the cash register, I handed Anna May the exact amount for my order. "And some of your delicious peach cobbler to go."

Anna May's T-shirt this Monday morning read *Coffee: The Right Answer to Any Question.* Her cherubic peaches-and-cream features glowed and her periwinkle eyes twinkled with what I considered the Anna May Weekley Seal of Approval.

Experience had taught me not to reject Anna May's cobbler. The first time I'd strode into the café to order what had become my usual—a small café mocha with fat-free milk and extra espresso—the café owner had tried to press the dessert onto me. I'd declined. In my defense, I'd still been full from breakfast. Suddenly, the air had filled with the smell of condemnation, overpowering the little shop's other far more pleasing aromas. I'd quickly learned my lesson. Now every weekday morning on my way to the library, I stopped in for my doctored mocha *and* the pastry. I gave the pastry to Floyd Petty, the reference librarian. The gesture had earned me the status of Floyd's Favorite Coworker. I also suspected it had delayed the lovable curmudgeon's retirement.

I exchanged greetings with a few familiar customers as they left the shop and nodded to others as they joined the line behind me.

"So, Marvey." Anna May spoke over the music of the coffee bean grinder. It had taken her three weeks to stop giving me the side-eye for requesting fat-free milk.

"News is you found Fiona Lyle-Hayes's body. May her soul rest in peace."

Silence covered the little café like a pie crust. I sensed the other patrons holding their breath in anticipation of my response. Those customers who also were on their way to work appeared to linger for my reply.

It felt like performing in front of a live studio audience. I pretended to ignore them. "Spence Holt and I were with Jo Gomez when she found Ms. Lyle-Hayes's body."

Anna May shook her head as she stirred the hot cocoa syrup. Overhead lights played on the reddish-blond curls escaping the white cap that covered her hair. "It's a terrible business, something like that. Murders just don't happen in Peach Coast, although being from New York, you must be used to it."

My eyebrows knitted at the misperceptions in Anna May's statement, starting with murders not happening in Peach Coast. Fiona Lyle-Hayes's spirit would disagree. "I've never seen a homicide before."

"Really?" Her question was thick with skepticism.

An overexcited male voice carried from one of the tables behind me. "The story in the *Crier* said Fiona had been stabbed. Wonder whose buttons she pushed this time?"

I turned in the direction of Dabney McCoy's voice. I estimated the tall, slender retiree to be in his late seventies. His companion, Etta Child, appeared close to his age. She also looked queasy as she set down a forkful of her peach cobbler.

Sending the grandmotherly woman an apologetic look, I responded to Dabney. "Who do *you* think could've killed her?"

Anna May added the espresso to the hot cocoa syrup, then poured the milk. "Not many people got along with Fiona. God rest her soul."

I remembered Zelda's disposition had cooled when Jo had mentioned Fiona on Saturday. Had that been a common reaction around Peach Coast to the now-deceased woman? If so, my list of alternative suspects for the deputies was going to be really long.

Dabney barked a sarcastic laugh. The creases fanning from his blue eyes and bracketing his thin lips deepened. "Stop tap dancing. People couldn't stand the woman."

Etta gasped and bowed her head as though in prayer. Her lips moved quickly and silently before she raised her chin and pierced Dabney with a glare. "You shouldn't speak ill of the dead." Her dark blue gaze scanned the café as though she expected Fiona's spirit to manifest and dump Dabney's hot coffee over his bald pate.

He snorted. "What's the difference? People spoke ill of her while she was alive." He picked up his spoon and jabbed it in the air above their table. "Obviously, the killer didn't think much of her, either."

Etta lowered her spoon and shoved her peach cobbler aside.

Dabney's sharp gaze bounced between Etta, her dessert, and back. "You goin' to eat that?"

Etta's narrowed gaze promised retribution. "No. It's all yours."

It wasn't the first time in my memory that Etta had given up her dessert to Dabney. Sometimes it was hard to remember the couple wasn't married.

I accepted my mocha from Anna May, lowering

my voice to keep the conversation limited to our small group. "Why didn't people like Fiona?"

Dabney grunted and spoke around a mouthful of pastry. "She was a stuck-up—"

Etta interrupted, speaking in a stage whisper. "It's not proper to speak ill of the dead, but since you asked, Fiona had broken up a happy family. Everybody knew she was only interested in marrying Buddy Hayes for his money. Fiona Lyle-Hayes was a home-wrecking gold digger."

I blinked at Etta's vehemence. "Well, I did ask."

Anna May put my warm peach cobbler in a small cardboard box. "Rumor is the deputies suspect Jo Gomez may have killed her." Her eyes scanned my face as though searching for a tell.

That stirred my protective instincts. "No, that's not possible. Jo was with her employees preparing for the book signing when Fiona was killed. Spence and I both saw her."

"That's what she wants us to believe." Dabney finished off Etta's pastry.

I started to respond to Dabney's comment, but Etta spoke first.

"Imagine, a murderer running around loose in Peach Coast." Her nervous gaze inspected the other coffee shop patrons. "It's very upsetting."

"Only if the killer's going to kill again." Dabney's tone was trivializing. "Chances are he was only after Fiona."

"What makes you think that?" I asked.

"This isn't the big city." Dabney waved a hand as though to encompass the town beyond the shop. "People don't go around willy-nilly killing each other. The killer must've targeted Fiona for a reason."

His reasoning seemed to further clear Jo. I lowered my voice again. "Who do you think would have the strongest motive?"

Dabney grunted, adding a shrug for good measure. "Who wouldn't?" he whispered back.

CHAPTER 7

A s I walked to work the next morning, the wide red brick sidewalk was sprinkled with other pedestrians. Cozy businesses and quaint shops were preparing for the day in their own Peach Coast style. I was growing to love the little town with its towering sweetgum trees and easy approach to time.

A cheeky feminine voice hailed me from the other side of Peach Blossom Boulevard. "Happy Monday, Marvey!"

The broad asphalt street was a major thoroughfare in the small town. Five vehicles comprised this morning's rush hour. I waited for them to roll past before responding to June Bishop. "Happy Monday, June. Your display windows are gorgeous."

The owner of Petals Palooza, the local flower shop, glowed in response to my praise. The vibrant rose and whimsical flower arrangements posing in the front windows were striking. I sensed they had a story to tell.

"Thank you!" June's laughter bubbled up, shortening the distance between us. Her thick blond braid swept her shoulder blades as she split her attention between me and the windows. Her floral-patterned dress floated around her. She hooked her hands on her hips. "And thanks again for the book recommendation. I had no idea I'd enjoy romantic comedies."

Ah, but I had. "I'm glad you enjoyed it." With a final wave, I continued on to the library.

"Marvey, good morning!" Lonnie Norman popped out from behind the signage he was arranging in front of his pet store, Paw Babies & More. He ran a hand over his thinning dark brown hair. "How're you today?"

"Lonnie." I lifted a hand in greeting. "I'm so glad I ran into you. Could you recommend another vet for me?"

Lonnie adjusted the waistband of his baggy beige pants over his stocky hips. His pale round features tightened, and his light brown eyes behind his rimless glasses widened with concern. "Is Phoenix still feeling poorly?"

"He's just not himself. The first vet you referred us to has already examined him twice. He insists Phoenix is fine. But something still seems...wrong."

Lonnie crossed his arms over his matching beige shirt with its Paw Babies & More logo on its upper right pocket. After a moment, he pulled his wallet from his front pants pocket, dug out a business card, and offered it to me. "Doctor Dahlia Sensor has a popular practice. She's not taking new patients, but tell her we're friends. I'll give her a call too. She may be able to fit Phoenix in for an examination."

Relief and hope eased the pressure from my shoulders. I tucked the card into my purse for safekeeping. "Thank you so much, Lonnie."

After promising to keep him apprised of Phoenix's condition, I continued on to the library. Strolling to work along the spacious Peach Blossom Boulevard sure beat commuting on the packed-in number five train.

The renovated building that housed the Peach Coast Library had once been a bus depot, arranging for residents as well as tourists to travel around town and along the coast. This seemed absolutely perfect, since books themselves had the power to transport readers to other locations, real and imaginary, past, present, and future.

As I entered the library Monday morning, the low heels of my black pumps tapped across the marbled gray linoleum. I took in the modest space with affection. The head librarian and my immediate supervisor, Corrinne Carpenter, had explained that very little restructuring had been needed to transform the decades-old depot into the five-year-old library. There was charm in the aged woodwork that molded the doorways and windows. The smell of freshly printed pages spun around the room, playing with the scent of lemon wood polish that lingered from the building's past.

The large picture windows allowed plenty of natural light. They framed the library's landscaping like living pictures. The spacious waiting area now featured a reference librarian's desk, displays of new materials, and modern silver metal shelves full of books, magazines, compact discs, and digital video discs.

It tickled me to know the intricate weathered oak circulation desk had once served as the counter where customers had purchased their travel tickets. Offices for the library's managers and the little staff breakroom were secreted in the area beyond the desk.

I'd just left a message with Dr. Sensor's office about an appointment for Phoenix when Vivian Lui, our circulation librarian, and Adrian Hobbs, our librarian assistant, rushed into my office.

"Oh, my goodness, Marvey. We read about Fiona Lyle-Hayes's murder." Viv's ebony eyes were wide with shock. She stood with Adrian behind my matching gray cloth visitors' chairs.

Adrian seemed to vibrate with excitement. A flush warmed his pale complexion. "The newspaper said you were one of the people who found the body."

Viv's curtain of raven hair swung above her shoulders as her head swiveled from Adrian to me. "That must've been horrible. Do you have any idea what happened?"

I straightened from securing my heavy purse and tote bag in my bottom desk drawer. "I don't know anything more than what the *Crier* reported." It was a little white lie, but I wasn't going to help the deputies damage Jo's reputation.

"I reckon there was blood *everywhere*." Adrian's blue-eyed stare locked onto me as though waiting for details—the gorier, the better. Horror was his fiction genre of choice.

The memory of Fiona's lifeless body still haunted me. I gripped the back of my black cloth executive chair. "Yes, Adrian. There was a lot of blood."

"But you're probably used to seeing that, I reckon, bein' from New York and all." The recent college graduate's smile faded at my expression.

I circled my desk, growing desperate in my need

to put space between me and the news story stalking me. How was Jo handling this attention? "Contrary to the impression popular media gives of New York, there aren't dead bodies on every street corner."

"Aw, come on now." Adrian waved his right hand nervously. "I was just pickin'."

I turned to Viv. The native Georgian was kind enough to serve as my Southern language interpreter.

Viv gave me an empathetic look. "He was teasing you."

I retrieved my cell phone from the right front pocket of my slacks and launched my Note app to add this latest phrase to my Peach Coast to New York dictionary. I inserted it alphabetically after both "aight now," which translated to either "hello," "goodbye," or "I'm going to beat your behind"; and "nem," which referred to a group of people.

Viv and Adrian accompanied me on my rescue mission to the employee breakroom. In this case, I was rescuing my coworkers by getting a second cup of coffee. Was it wrong to pour another cup while the memory of my café mocha was still so fresh?

"Good morning, Floyd." I greeted our reference librarian as I strode past his workstation in the library's main area. He'd been away from his desk when I'd delivered his peach cobbler.

"Morning." The older man grunted his response as he joined us.

With his buzz-cut salt-and-pepper hair, winter-blue eyes, and querulous demeanor, Floyd was like a Bad Attitude Santa Claus. At first, I thought he was curt with me because I was new. Then I realized Floyd was curt with everyone. Period. His decision to work in a public library fascinated me, considering how much of our time was spent interacting with people.

At the coffee station in the breakroom, I fixed my second cup of java. To my right, Floyd shuffled his feet. I could feel his impatience. To my left, Viv and Adrian plied me for details I didn't have about Fiona's murder. I stepped aside, giving Floyd plenty of room to pour his cup o' joe. The reference librarian drank his black.

The tap of sensible pumps across the linoleum announced our boss's arrival. In her powder-pink skirt suit, accessorized with understated pearl earrings, and matching necklace, Corrinne Carpenter, the head librarian, looked like she was hosting a summer tea party. Not one strand of her chin-length, honey-blond hair was out of place.

Corrinne's attention dipped to my pendant. Her green eyes shone with appreciation of the cover of Walter Mosley's 1990 mystery *Devil in a Blue Dress*. It was the original image depicting a woman in a blue dress, not the reprint version, which capitalized on Denzel Washington's starring role in the story's film adaptation. I didn't think my artistic skills could do justice to Denzel's perfection.

"Marvey, how are you?" Corrinne's forehead creased with concern. "I didn't expect you'd make it in today after the horrible tragedy at To Be Read on Saturday."

I liked Corrinne. She seemed genuine, but I'd only been working with her for four months. We were still in the honeymoon phase of our workplace relationship. "Yes, it was terrible, but I'm fine. Thank you. In fact, I'm looking forward to Spence's dinner party tonight."

Viv's face lit up. "So am I. His dinner parties are one of the biggest social events in town."

"So I've heard." I wrapped my hands around my warm black porcelain mug. Printed in bold, white block letters was the statement *Keep Calm & Read a Good Book.*

Floyd gestured to the group with his mug. Coffee leaked from a hairline fracture in its plain white surface. "Kind of short notice, isn't it? He's hosted at least two of these things for us, one right before we opened and one when Viv came on board. He usually sends the invite at least a week in advance."

"Yes, that did seem unusual, but even if I'd had plans for tonight, I would've canceled just to attend." Corrinne shrugged elegantly as she approached the coffeepot.

I caught a whiff of her perfume, a light powdery scent. Smell was the sense most closely linked to memory and emotion. The right fragrance could get people to remember you favorably. In that context, Corrinne's perfume was the perfect scent for someone in a leadership position for a nonprofit organization. It would be a very pleasant memory.

"What're these things like?" Adrian's shaggy brown hair fell across his eyes as his gaze darted from one library team member to another. He exuded excitement and anticipation.

Floyd grunted. "Bring your appetite." In terms of Floyd-speak, that was an effusive compliment.

Corrinne stirred French vanilla creamer and four packets of sugar substitute into her oversized coffee mug. The head librarian's sweet tooth was even stronger than mine. "Spence cooks the meals himself, and they're fabulous. There are usually multiple courses.

His home is lovely, and he's a gracious and generous host."

I braced my hip against the counter. "What's the dress code? Is it formal?" I should've asked him yesterday.

Viv waved a negligent hand. "Oh, no. It's nothing like that. Spence Holt is very laid-back. Business casual is perfectly fine." She cocked her head, scrutinizing my sapphire blouse and black slacks. "What you're wearing now would be fine."

That was a relief. I had a few dressier outfits in my closet, but I wouldn't have time to change before getting to his home to help with the dinner preparations.

Corrinne took a sip of her coffee. "I can't emphasize enough how important it is that Spence is hosting another dinner party for us. The support of high-profile influencers like him will be incredibly helpful in getting the budget we need to continue to provide our community services—and hire a computer support specialist."

That's the reason Corrinne had hired me for the newly created position of director of community engagement. My role was to raise the library's profile in the community, increase financial donations, and build a solid argument for growing our annual budget. In short, this was my dream job and the reason I leaped out of bed every morning.

Viv nodded in agreement with Corrinne. "It'll also help distract us from Fiona Lyle-Hayes's murder."

"Oh, I don't know if anything could do that." Adrian's eyes gleamed with morbid fascination. *Note to self: introduce Adrian to other fiction genres beside horror.* "I heard the deputies are looking hard at Jo Gomez."

"It's not just the deputies." Viv sounded concerned.

"I heard some customers at On A Roll talking about the murder. They were speculating about Jo too."

My shoulders tensed. If Jo was being tried in the court of public opinion, then the situation had already run away from us. "Why would people think *Jo* murdered Fiona? What's her motive?"

"It's not about motive." Floyd slurped his coffee. "People want quick-and-easy answers. Fiona was killed in the bookstore. Jo owns the bookstore. What's easier than that?"

I was struck by his answer. The person who didn't seem to like people sounded like a student of human nature. "I don't know much about Fiona. What kind of person was she?"

There was a tangible pause. I'd expected it. As the newcomer, the locals were still taking my measure, wondering if they could trust me. This was the reason I needed Spence's endorsement if I was going to help clear Jo's name.

Corrinne lowered herself onto a silver cushioned chair with the grace of a dancer. Her tone was cautious as though she weighed every word. "Fiona didn't come into the library much."

Adrian made a face. "She was so stuck up, she'd've drowned in a rainstorm."

Corrinne gave him a scolding look. "It's not kind to speak ill of the dead, Adrian."

He endeavored to look chastened. "Beg pardon, ma'am."

"Fiona was a very private person." Viv cupped her coffee mug in both palms. Her fingernails gleamed with a black polish that complemented her trim pantsuit. "You could tell from the way she carried herself. She was very aloof. Even though she'd been married to Buddy Hayes, who'd been a prominent resident, she never made an effort to get to know people or to let people get to know her."

Floyd grunted. "Not until she got that big contract with that fancy New York publisher. Then she was running all over town, telling people she knew and people she'd never said a word to, to buy her book when it came out."

Over the course of my six-year career, I'd met many first-time and veteran authors. Some were so shy you could have an entire conversation without learning they'd been published. At the other end of the spectrum were authors who'd give you their book's title and plot within the first few minutes of meeting you. Apparently, Fiona fell into the latter category. But why would a previously private person start running around town, opening up to people about her book? Had it been pride over her accomplishment? Or had she been concerned that in a town where she hadn't had many friends, her sales would suffer?

"I remember seeing her at On A Roll a couple of months ago." Corrinne crossed her right leg over her left and smoothed her skirt over her knee. "She referred to her story as a water-cooler book."

Adrian cocked his head. "A what now?"

"It's the kind of book that sparks discussion." Corrinne gave me a thoughtful look. "Fiona and I had moved in similar circles for almost two years, yet that was the first and last real conversation we'd ever had."

Interesting. What discussion had Fiona hoped her book would spark? "Have you started her book?"

Corrinne shook her head. "I bought it. And we have

several copies in the library, but I want to finish the book I'm reading now first."

Fiona had been excited at the thought of people talking about her book. Instead, everyone was preoccupied with her murder. Maybe the timing of her death wasn't a coincidence. Maybe someone envied the attention she'd been getting because of her book. Jealousy was a strong motive.

CHAPTER 8

THREE MINUTES AFTER I RETURNED to my office, I looked up from my desk to find Deputies Jed Whatley and Errol Cole standing at my door. Adrian, who'd escorted them, gave me a wide-eyed stare before drifting out of sight.

I gestured toward the two guest chairs in front of my desk. "What can I do for you, deputies?"

The bemused expressions the deputies exchanged reminded me that Peach Coast residents didn't conduct business in a New York minute. Here, business transactions seemed to last a Georgia afternoon.

Jed removed his green felt campaign hat, revealing his balding pink pate. "Mornin', Ms. Harris. Deputy Cole and I have a few more questions for you."

I folded my hands on my desk. "What do you want to know?"

Errol set his hat on his lap as he took the chair beside Jed. He opened his notepad. "Ms. Jolene said you'd been with her from shortly after she left the storage room until you, Mr. Spence, and Ms. Jolene had found Ms. Fiona's body. Is that right, ma'am?"

It took me a moment to untangle all of those Misters and Ms-es. "Is Jo a suspect in your investigation?"

Jed pinned me with a cool stare from his ice-blue eyes. "Now, could you maybe just answer our questions, please, Ms. Harris?"

I shifted my attention back to the junior deputy. "Yes, that's right."

Errol wrote something in his notepad. "And she stayed with you the entire time?"

"Yes." Errol and Jed stared at me as though expecting something more. "Yes, she did."

"You sure about that, now?" Jed pressed. "There wasn't any time she left you alone or you wandered away from her, even to go to the bathroom?"

"She was always within my sight, and neither of us had gone to the restroom." I wasn't comfortable discussing my bladder habits with law enforcement.

Errol cocked his head. "Had Ms. Jolene ever discussed Ms. Fiona with you or mentioned her at all, ma'am?"

"Not before Saturday." I was certain of that.

Jed pounced. "What'd she say to you on Saturday?"

His reaction startled me. In my peripheral vision, I noticed Errol poised to record my response. "She told me Fiona was in the storage room, collecting her books for the signing."

Jed stared at me. "Is that all?"

I spread my hands. "Have I disappointed you?"

Jed scowled. "What was Ms. Gomez's relationship with Ms. Lyle-Hayes?"

The older deputy was asking me the same question in a dozen different ways. Did he think I hadn't noticed?

"As I've said before, Jo didn't *have* a relationship with Fiona. She was only working with her on the signing."

Jed watched me closely. "What was Ms. Gomez's demeanor prior to finding Ms. Lyle-Hayes's body?"

My eyebrows knitted as I sat back on my chair, searching for the words. I had the impression Jed didn't believe anything I was saying. "Jo was energized about the event. She was very social and introduced me to several people."

Errol continued writing in his notepad as he spoke. "And then when she found Ms. Fiona's body, how would you describe her reaction to that?"

"She was deeply upset." Jo's pale, stricken expression filled my mind. I heard again her disjointed words. "We all were. She was shaking so badly, I had to help her from the room."

"Thanks for your time, Ms. Harris." Jed gave me a dubious look as he got up somewhat stiffly from the chair. In contrast, Errol popped out of his seat.

My gaze swung to Errol, then back to Jed. "Is there anyone else you want to ask me about, deputies? Members of her writing group, her business partners, or family? They'd known Fiona much better and much longer than Jo."

"No, thank you, ma'am. There's no need." Jed slapped his hat against his right thigh as he prepared to leave.

I stood behind my desk. "Isn't it too early to be so focused on one person?"

Jed rubbed his upper lip. "You have a lot of experience with homicide investigations now, do you, ma'am?"

I inclined my head, conceding the deputy's point. I couldn't allow my concern for Jo to make me lose sight of my limitations. "No, Deputy Whatley. I don't have law enforcement experience. But I can't sit quietly when I know my friend didn't commit this crime you appear ready to charge her with. Have you found the murder weapon?"

Jed sighed. I thought I saw a brief flash of understanding in his eyes. Really brief. "We're searching the store and the surrounding area again, ma'am. I'm sure it'll turn up."

I struggled to contain my frustration. "If Jo had stabbed Fiona multiple times, she would've been covered in blood. How do you explain that she wasn't?"

Jed threw up his arms. "She's the only one with the opportunity, ma'am."

"Apparently not." So this was what it looked like when an innocent person was being railroaded. "The killer had opportunity—and motive. What's Jo's motive?"

Errol frowned. "We don't have one yet, ma'am."

"That's because she didn't have a reason to kill Fiona." I spread my hands. "Jo's innocent. You're wasting your time pursuing the wrong person."

Jed grunted. "Now, why don't you just let us do our job, ma'am? Do we come in here and tell y'all how to arrange your books?"

I arched an eyebrow. "If I'd scattered our books all over the parking lot, I'd hope you'd speak up. That's what I'm doing for you."

"You have a nice day, Ms. Harris." Jed smiled without humor. "Come on now, Errol."

The deputies left my office, taking with them any lingering doubts that Jo was panicking for nothing. It was clear the deputies were fixated on her for Fiona's murder, and they were determined to make the crime fit the suspect.

"You didn't have to come, but I'm glad you're here." Spence welcomed me into his home Monday evening.

"I want to help, and our dinner guests will arrive soon." I smiled at his backward red University of Georgia baseball cap and crimson apron. In white block letters, the apron read, *I Cook, Therefore, I Am.*

Spence returned my smile. "A gift from my mama."

"I like it." I'd briefly stopped at my house after work to check on Phoenix, but I hadn't taken the time to change my clothes. Spence didn't appear to be put out by this.

He closed his front door, then beckoned me with his arm. "Follow me." He led me through his spacious living room.

I thought I could see my reflection in his wood flooring. "You have a beautiful home."

"You say that every time you visit." Spence tossed the comment and a smile over his shoulder, never breaking stride toward his destination.

"And I mean it every time."

"Thank you."

We entered his equally spacious dining room. It had a warm, inviting feel with dark wood furnishings and gold-and-crimson accents. The dining set looked expensive. Its rectangular table was long enough to accommodate eight people. I idly wondered where Spence had hidden the two spare seats. The remaining six chairs featured polished veneers and ladder backs.

"You've already set the table. It's lovely." I moved my gaze over the gold porcelain plates and matching napkins. I was somewhat disappointed. That was a task I could've handled. I wasn't certain about the cooking.

What I saw of his home, both inside and out, reinforced my impression of him as Peach Coast's Bruce Wayne. The classic A-line brick structure was the anti-bachelor pad.

His kitchen was awesome. Standing at the threshold, I marveled again at the high ceiling and the black, white, and silver surroundings. The modern appliances were arranged for the chef's comfort and convenience. The endless counter space offered more than enough room for food preparation.

"You know, for a hobby, you certainly take your cooking seriously."

He gestured toward my *Devil in a Blue Dress* pendant. "As seriously as you take your hobby."

Warm accents kept the contemporary space from crossing the line into cold and sterile. Crimson dish towels hung from hooks, garnet-and-emerald potholders rested beside the black stovetop, and gold curtains covered the window above the sink.

A quick survey of the tidy kitchen revealed how busy Spence had been even before I'd arrived. He'd mixed the ingredients for the chicken and cut the green beans. The oven was warming, and a pot of water was heating on the stove.

"What can I do to help?"

Spence turned toward his center island, on which he'd arranged the ingredients he'd need for the menu, baked chicken and peaches served with Georgia green beans. We'd bought most of the ingredients, including the chicken, yesterday. "I have everything under control. Just keep me company."

I swallowed a sigh of relief but felt compelled to push the issue. "That doesn't seem fair. You're doing all of this because I asked you to."

"*We're* doing all of this to help Jo." He gave me a half smile. "Besides, I don't like help in my kitchen. Too many chefs..." He left unspoken the rest of the well-known maxim about culinary conflicts.

"Well, in that case, let me get out of your way."

CHAPTER 9

I SETTLED ONTO ONE OF THE matching white bar-
stools near the island. "The deputies questioned me
again today."

Spence gave me a sharp look as he placed peach
slices on top of the boneless chicken breasts. "Whatley
and Cole? They questioned me too. I'd thought Jo had
been exaggerating about the deputies' interest in her,
but now I see why she's so concerned. They *have* focused on her as their top suspect."

"Just because the murder happened in her store.
That reasoning is weak at best." I glanced again at the
ingredients as I pondered the gravity of Jo's situation.
Would my librarian coworkers be able to give us insight
that would help clear her name? Did I know the right
questions to ask? I unclenched my fists and rubbed my
damp palms against my slacks.

Spence sprinkled brown sugar, ginger, cloves, and
lemon juice over the chicken and peach slices. I'd read
about the entrée on the internet. Peaches and chicken
sounded like a weird combination to my New York City
sensibilities. But since Spence was doing me the enor-

mous favor of hosting this event, I planned to smile and clean my plate.

A wave of warm air wrapped me as he opened the nearby oven to insert the chicken. "The only motive they have for Jo seems to be a disagreement she and Fiona had over the bookstore event."

I set the alarm on my cell phone for half an hour, the cooking time for the chicken dish. It was the least intrusive way I could think of to help. "What disagreement?"

Spence straightened away from the oven. "Something to do with the placement of Fiona's books in Jo's store."

"Oh, come on." I thought my eyes would roll right out of my head. "As a motive for killing someone, that theory sounds like a nonstarter. What are you hearing about the murder?"

Spence gave me a somber look from over his shoulder as he added salt and the green beans to the boiling water. "People are concerned about a killer being in Peach Coast. They're asking questions about Jo and Fiona, but I don't have the sense that anyone believes Jo's the killer."

"They're looking for a fast arrest." I remembered Floyd's observation. Grumpy Santa was wise. "I just hope their fear doesn't compromise their objectivity."

"I hope so too." Spence returned to the kitchen island to chop the garlic.

I eyed the onion. "May I chop the onion for you?"

He gave me a kind smile. "I've got it."

"You really are controlling in the kitchen, aren't you?" His only response was another smile. I changed the subject rather than push my luck. Creating fancy dinners was out of my comfort zone, but sitting idly while others did all the work made me feel worse. "I've heard you've hosted other dinners for the librarians. I imagine you know them well."

"I went to high school with Corrinne's younger brother. He was a couple of years ahead of me." He set aside the garlic and started slicing the onion. "I haven't had a dinner party since Viv joined the library, though."

"I admire you for knowing so many people in town."

"It helps that I was born and raised here." There was humor in Spence's answer. He put a modest amount of butter into a skillet and sautéed the chopped garlic and onions. "And running the newspaper keeps me connected to the community."

I'd never asked, but I estimated Spence's age to be in his early- to mid-thirties, a few years younger than Corrinne. Peach Coast was a beautiful and charming town. The people were friendly. But Spence was a young man. Did this town have enough to offer him? "Have you ever wanted to live anywhere else?"

"I've lived in other places."

My curiosity roared to life. "Oh? Where?"

He turned off the pot and drained the green beans. "I completed my undergraduate studies at Stanford. And got my master's at NYU."

New York University? "That's *my* alma mater." My eyes widened in shock. "We could have passed each other on campus."

Spence chuckled as he dried the green beans. "I'd have noticed."

"Not in that crowd."

"I would've noticed." His voice was low, but insistent. "I worked for newspapers in Chicago and D.C., but

Peach Coast has always been home. I knew I'd come back."

He put additional butter in the skillet with the sautéed garlic and onions. Then he added the cooked green beans, red wine vinegar, chicken broth, cilantro, and salt and pepper. He turned the burner on low and covered the pan.

He caught me setting my cell phone's alarm for the fifteen minutes the green beans needed to cook. This was according to my previous research on the Georgia green beans side dish. He raised an eyebrow. I shrugged. It went against my nature to not help.

I put down my phone. "A strong sense of community seems to be in your family's DNA."

"It could be."

"I think that's why all your holdings are named after the town rather than your family." I studied Spence's broad back as I expounded on my theory. "It's *The Peach Coast Crier*, not *The Holt Daily News*. The Peach Coast Inn, not the Holt Hotel. And it's the Peach Coast Community Bank, not the Holt Benjamins or something like that."

Spence smiled at me from over his shoulder again. "We've never discussed it, but you do make a good point."

Yes, I had, and I was sticking to it. "Is that also the reason you started hosting these dinners, to keep in touch with the community?"

"And because I enjoy cooking." He turned from the oven. "It seems like a waste to make these meals for just one person."

"It's very generous of you. The library team is excited."

"It's my pleasure. And for dessert, we're having peach cobbler."

My jaw dropped. "You bake too?"

Spence laughed. "I picked up the cobbler from On A Roll. I know my limitations."

There was something about watching a man taking over the cooking in the kitchen. It was almost exotic. Granted, my father and brother had cooked meals for our family. But with them, the vibe in the kitchen had more of a sense of cooking-for-survival. With Spence, the kitchen was a joyful place.

The sweet scents of the chicken and peaches, and the spicy aroma of the Georgia green beans, filled the room. I inhaled deeply as my appetite woke up. "Are these recipes your favorite?"

Spence shrugged his broad shoulders. "They're easy to make and familiar to me, but I don't really have a favorite. I enjoy cooking regional meals. They keep my Southern roots alive."

"If they taste as wonderful as they smell, you may have converted me."

His warm chuckle rolled across the room. "I guarantee this meal will convert you."

"How long have you been cooking?"

"According to my parents, all my life. All of the men in my family were amateur chefs."

My eyes widened with amazement. "The women in your family must've loved that."

Spence's smile didn't come as easily this time. He'd mentioned his father had died several years ago. At times, I could tell he was still grieving. "My mama loves to cook too. My parents were pretty competitive in the kitchen. They were always trying to outdo each other with complicated dishes, which was great for me. It inspired me to try new recipes. And I never missed a meal. I struggled with my weight for years."

"That's hard to believe." Although I hadn't meant to say that out loud, I was sincere. Spence looked quite fit in his onyx shirt and steel-gray slacks. He was about the same height as my brother. It was hard to picture him with excess weight. "Do your siblings cook too?"

"I'm an only child. What about you?"

"I have an older brother, DeAndre. He's married to one of my favorite people, Kaylee. Their four-year-old son, Clayton, is one of the great loves of my life."

"You're very close to your family. Moving away from them must've been hard." Spence filled a cup halfway with cold water, then added a tablespoon of cornstarch to it.

An image of my parents came to mind. They were in their early sixties, but their smooth brown features and still-dark hair helped them look at least fifteen years younger. Regular exercise kept them fit. I shook off my sudden homesickness.

"It was." I didn't recall the cornstarch ingredient for either the chicken or the green bean dish. "What's that for?"

"I'm going to add this to the cooking juices from the chicken to make a sauce."

My stomach growled its approval. My face heated with embarrassment. "I guess that soup I had for lunch wasn't quite enough."

"It won't be much longer." He appeared to check the time on the silver wall clock behind me. "Luckily, there are only six of us for dinner. It's easier—and faster—to cook for smaller groups."

"And you thought the dinner party would be impossible to pull off in such a short time. I wish I could've helped, though."

"I appreciate your company—and your restraint."

"You're welcome for the company. Don't get used to the restraint." Although, recalling his obstinacy when I'd attempted to pay for the supplies for the dinner I'd volunteered him for, restraint seemed to be the better part of valor. That experience had taught me to pick and choose my battles with the bossy amateur chef.

Spence leaned back against his kitchen counter and folded his arms. "Marvey, what makes you think we can solve a murder? Don't get me wrong, I'm happy to help with this investigation, but I don't know how."

"I'm not trying to solve a murder." I met his solemn midnight eyes. "I want to gather enough information to clear Jo as a suspect. Candidly, I don't know if I can do that, either. But I know I need to try."

"And you're certain she's innocent?"

"Aren't you?" The question shocked me, especially coming from him. My faith in Jo was rock solid. I needed Spence to feel the same; otherwise, we couldn't work together on this.

"Of course." His response was fast and firm, much to my relief. "But Whatley and Cole have put her at the top of their suspects list. Are we missing something we need to identify in order to clear her name?"

"No, but I'm pretty sure the deputies are. How much experience do they have? Despite recent evidence to the contrary, everyone keeps saying murders don't happen in Peach Coast."

"Well, there aren't a lot, but—"

I ignored his interruption as my frustration broke free. "As you know, my brief internet search uncovered *one* murder. It happened *two years* ago, but it's still unsolved."

"That's true, but—"

"Is Deputy Cole even old enough to shave?"

Spence raised his eyebrows. "Feel better?"

"Not really." And I was suddenly craving chocolate.

"We'll get to the bottom of this. I just want to make sure we're not missing anything." He pushed away from the counter. "Have you ever heard the saying, 'Don't ask a question you may not want the answer to?'"

"I'm not afraid of *this* question, because I already know the answer: Jo's innocent." I frowned. "If you believe the same, then what are you afraid of?"

Spence paced across the kitchen with restless movements. "I grew up in this town with most of these people. I don't want to think of any of them as a killer."

That gave me chills. I hadn't grown up in Peach Coast, but I'd been a resident for more than four months. What if the killer was someone I knew? A regular at On A Roll. A member of the Peach Coast Library Book Club. A library patron.

I understood why he found the idea so unsettling. "Is that the reason some people are focused on Jo?" His silence was answer enough. "Wouldn't it be more concerning if your law enforcement was ruled by those same feelings? Do you want a killer to go unpunished because you grew up with him? Would you rather an innocent person was convicted instead?"

Spence dragged a hand over his close-cropped hair. His agitation crackled in the air between us. "You're right."

"Let's help clear Jo. Then we'll work on a way to help the community recover from this murder. I know a couple of books that might help."

CHAPTER 10

THE SOUTHERN DEFINITION OF "CASUAL dress" appeared to be "something one would wear to a gala at the Metropolitan Museum of Art."

The other librarians must've driven together, because they arrived at the same time. Their nervous excitement preceded them into Spence's home. Assessing their formalwear, I felt like the poor relation. The memory of our conversation about the dress code for Spence's dinner party played on a loop in my mind. Since when were gowns and tuxedos considered "business casual?"

And why didn't anyone tell me?

Corrinne was almost Spence's height in those silver five-inch stilettos. "Your home is even lovelier than I remembered."

Spence smiled. "Thanks, Corrinne."

Viv, in her amethyst gown, looked like an ad for expensive perfume. "Thank you so much for inviting us."

Spence nodded. "Thank you for coming."

Adrian stepped forward. Where had he gotten that tailored three-piece suit? "I've heard about your dinner parties, but I never imagined I'd be invited to one. Thanks, Mr. Holt."

"Call me Spence. This dinner party is overdue. We haven't had one for the librarians since you joined the staff. Now Marvey's here too, so it's time."

Adrian was blushing as he walked away.

Floyd looked like a character from *The Great Gatsby* in his black tuxedo and bow tie. He inclined his head toward Spence. "I brought my appetite."

Spence chuckled. "You won't be disappointed."

Floyd grunted. "I wasn't last time." High praise indeed.

I couldn't stay silent any longer. "Excuse me, but I thought we'd agreed on *business casual.*" I gestured toward the sapphire blouse, black pants, and matching pumps I'd worn to work. "Floyd, did you rent that tux?"

Corrinne rushed to reassure me. "Marvey, you always look so wonderful."

Viv nodded her agreement. "You'd look perfect in everything, even in sweats."

Spence turned to me, his expression solemn. "Marvey, you look absolutely lovely."

That was spreading it a bit thick, but I allowed their Southern charm to mollify me.

Our host led us into the dining room. The spontaneous gasps and interjections of admiration must've been gratifying. I know I was grateful, and I literally hadn't lifted a finger to help.

Conversation flowed easily from the Southern pecan and apple salad course straight through to the entrée. From his seat at the head of the table, Spence asked a ton of questions about the library and each of us, and seemed genuinely interested in our responses. Since

Adrian and I were the newest librarians, he asked about our previous career experiences.

"This is my first job out of college." Adrian was on Spence's left. He nodded as he finished his second helping of green beans.

Seated across the table from the library assistant, I'd noticed his initial reaction to the side dish. Vegetables didn't appear to be his favorite food group. Spence's Georgia green beans seemed to have changed his perspective. I'd had a similar reaction to the baked chicken and peaches. It was both sweet and savory, like a combination of a main course and a decadent dessert.

Spence sipped his white Zinfandel. "Why did you choose to become a librarian?"

Adrian nodded again. "When I was fixin' to pick a major, my advisor asked me what I wanted to do. Told him I wanted to be a student for the rest of my life. I love learning. He said I should try library science. Working in a place filled to the rafters with books and magazines, well, I reckoned that would suit me just fine."

From her chair at the foot of the table, Corrinne set down her fork. "That's one of the greatest joys of being a librarian: being around books and introducing others to the joys of reading."

Everyone's plate was clean, and there weren't any leftovers. It was a silent round of applause for a meal well served. Floyd had even loosened his belt.

After declining our help, Spence made quick work of clearing the table, then returned with a tray of peach cobbler and vanilla ice cream. He offered each of us a bowl before returning to his seat.

Adrian gave a greedy grin. "I'm already feeling fat as a tick."

In context, that was a Southernism even I could understand.

I slipped Spence a look meant to warn him I was going to start our investigative questioning. "Thank you again for hosting this dinner for us, Spence. It's a nice way to wind down an unsettling day. People around town have been talking about Fiona Lyle-Hayes's murder. We even discussed it at the library."

Floyd waved his dessert spoon. "Didn't the deputies speak to you at the crime scene? Why'd they need to speak with you again today at the library?"

Adrian leaned toward me. "Is it because you're friends with Ms. Jo? Are you like a key witness or somethin'?"

Viv shook her head vehemently. A lock of hair slipped from the bun she'd gathered on the crown of her head. "Jo Gomez is not a murderer. Besides, why would she kill one of the featured authors at a scheduled book signing right before her event?"

Floyd made a disparaging noise. "And then to leave the body in the store? It's one of the stupidest things I've ever heard."

"I agree that doesn't make sense," Corrinne said. "Ever since she opened that bookstore, Jo's whole world has revolved around it. She'd never do anything to jeopardize her business."

"Murder would jeopardize it, all right." Floyd inclined his head in agreement without lifting his eyes from his dessert. "Having dead bodies popping up all over your store will chase your customers away."

Spence and I exchanged a look of relief. Unprompted, the librarians had agreed with us about Jo's innocence.

"Who would you consider to be a more viable suspect for the murder?" I asked the question as casually as I could, but Floyd wasn't fooled.

The older man gave me a suspicious look before directing his question to Spence. "What's this dinner really about?"

I hurried to reclaim Floyd's attention before Spence could respond. "What do you mean?"

"Come now, Marvey." Corrinne's gracious smile softened her chastening tone. "We noticed you arrived here separately."

I tried to shrug that away. "I wanted to check on Phoenix first, since we'd probably be out late."

Viv cocked her head. "You checked on your cat, but you still made it here before us."

"And we were on time, which means you were early," Adrian added.

Caught. But my associates seemed more amused than accusing. Well, I couldn't see Floyd's reaction. He was busy trying to scrape the painted design from the porcelain dessert bowl.

I held up both hands. "I didn't lie about checking on Phoenix."

Floyd made a rude noise. "Never said you did."

I ignored him. "And Spence really had planned to host a dinner for us."

Spence gestured around the table. "As you know, I'm a huge fan of the library. And I have to say I'm impressed with the deductive reasoning skills you used to assess this dinner."

Corrinne inclined her head at the compliment. "Librarians tend to be underrated. We have inquisitive minds and suspected something else might be going on in addition to the dinner."

I cleared my throat. "I apologize for misleading you. That was my idea, not Spence's."

Spence touched the back of my hand. "I was in on this from the beginning. I'll take my share of the blame."

"We can argue that later." I squeezed his forearm before turning back to the librarians. "I'm glad you also believe Jo's innocent. Spence and I are determined to clear her. We're trying to get compelling information to bring to the deputies to show there are much stronger suspects than Jo for Fiona's murder."

Floyd set aside his dessert bowl. "We can help you with that. Fiona didn't have a shortage of frenemies. Got a pen?"

CHAPTER 11

"WHEN BUDDY HAYES DIVORCED MS. Betty to marry Ms. Fiona, Ms. Betty pitched a hissy fit with a tail on it." Adrian's nod added emphasis to his statement.

"Ms. Betty was furious." Viv's dark eyes twinkled as she translated Adrian's Southern phrases for me. "Popular opinion is she was the one spreading gossip about Fiona. Those rumors were pretty vicious. And whenever they crossed paths, Betty would get really stiff and totally ignore Fiona. I'm interested in body language. It expresses a lot that people don't always say with words."

Interesting. "How would Fiona react?"

"She wouldn't." Viv shrugged a shoulder. "She was just normal."

"Granted, Betty was over the top, but I can understand her anger." Corrinne slid aside her empty dessert dish and folded her hands on the table in front of her. "She and Buddy had been married for more than twenty years. Their divorce was such a cliché: husband leaves wife for a *much* younger woman."

"Betty still loved Buddy despite his betrayal." Viv

sighed. Her expression was almost dreamy. "Whenever he was near her, she only had eyes for him. And she was always touching him."

Spence sat back on his chair. "Buddy's death hit Betty really hard."

Hearing this made me feel sorry for Betty and blame Fiona. "Did Betty and Fiona have any public disagreements?"

Corrinne's brow creased. "Not that I can recall." My other companions chimed in to agree with Corrinne.

"But things can't be going that well for Betty," Viv added. "She's taken a second job, working at the general store."

I glanced around the table. "If Betty had that much animosity toward Fiona, why would she attend Fiona's signing?"

Adrian seemed to vibrate with excitement. "If I were a bettin' man, I'd say she was after causin' a scene and ruinin' the event for Ms. Fiona. D'y'all know what Ms. Fiona's book is about?"

Viv's brow knitted in concentration. "The protagonist's husband dies of natural causes, but she suspects he was murdered."

"By his ex-wife." Adrian's gaze circled the rectangular table. "Now, I haven't read the book myself yet, but I found a spoiler site on the internet."

"Did you just ruin the ending for us?" Floyd glared across the table at Adrian.

Adrian rolled his eyes. "Don't go pitching a hissy fit, now. I didn't give away the endin'. I don't think."

A horrified silence hung over the table as the five of us considered Adrian may indeed have ruined Fiona's book for us.

I pulled myself together first. "That motive sounds plausible." I made a note of his theory. "But could you see Betty actually killing someone?"

The room felt heavy with their collective hesitation. Floyd's booming voice broke the silence. "I could see Betty offing Fiona, if she was angry enough."

"And Betty's heartache is still fresh." Viv sighed. "Her divorce from Buddy had been finalized only two years ago. Buddy and Fiona had been married for a year before Buddy died almost a year ago."

Adrian blew out a breath. "Now, that would explain why Ms. Betty's always madder than a puffed toad."

"Betty's definitely on our list of potential suspects to investigate. She has a plausible reason for murder: revenge." I wrote her name in the notebook, along with her motive. "Who else?" I asked the room in general.

"No one in the writing group liked Fiona." Floyd seemed to relish that point. "That gives you twelve suspects right there."

"Let's put that into context." Corrinne raised both of her hands, palms out. "I had the impression it wasn't that the other writers didn't like her. They didn't know her. Fiona was a difficult person to get close to."

"I agree with Corrinne." Viv leaned into the table. "Fiona used to come in for help with research for her novel. Her manner was cool, as though she was deliberately keeping me at a distance."

Viv's observation corroborated my initial impression of Fiona as secretive. "She kept you at a distance. She kept her writing group members at a distance. Her social media pages are sparse and impersonal. It's as though she was trying to hide something."

Spence balanced his elbows on the table. "Like what?"

A quick look at our dinner companions revealed a variety of baffled expressions. I set aside the idea of Fiona keeping secrets to pursue at a later date. "What brought Fiona to Peach Coast?"

"Fiona was from South Carolina. Beaufort," Floyd said. "Her uncle had property here. When he died, he left that property to Fiona, and she hired Buddy to sell it."

"Buddy was a really successful real estate agent." Viv got a wistful look in her eyes. "They never sold the property, though. Instead, they got married."

Floyd grunted. "I would've sold the property. Less of a headache."

"What's Bobby's story?" My pen sped across my mini-notepad as I recorded their information.

Adrian's blue eyes gleamed with intrigue. "The scuttlebutt is Mr. Buddy left Bobby's inheritance in a trust to be managed by Ms. Fiona until his twenty-fifth birthday."

My eyebrows rose. "How old is he now?"

"He just turned twenty-three." Spence spoke with confidence. It amazed me what he recalled about the people in his town. *His town.* It fit. But whereas Spence seemed to know only the good things, Floyd appeared to dig up all the dirt.

"Fiona was supposed to oversee Bobby's trust for two more years?" I remembered Betty mentioning Bobby worked at a repair shop/hardware store. Was that by choice? How big was his trust fund? "Does Bobby have a problem managing money?"

Corrinne shook her head. Her blond hair swung

above her shoulders. "I've never heard any talk of Bobby having trouble with money."

"This dinner is really eye-opening." Spence sounded amused. "I never thought librarians would be in the center of the town's rumor mill."

Corrinne laughed. "People think of us as quiet and circumspect. We tend to fade into the décor, and the people around us feel free to say *anything*."

Spence arched an eyebrow. "I'm going to have to be more careful of what I say around you."

"A *very* wise decision," I said dryly. "I wonder how Bobby felt about Fiona being in charge of his inheritance."

Floyd crossed his arms and scowled. "Betty wasn't shy about telling anyone with ears she wasn't happy about the arrangement."

"She told me twice," Corrinne said. "And she claimed Bobby was angry about it too."

Spence shook his head. "And she wanted me to report on it for the *Crier*."

Floyd tapped my mini-notebook. "Money's a powerful motive for murder."

I added Bobby's name and possible motive to the short list. "So far, it appears to me that Betty and Bobby have much stronger motives than the deputies have ascribed to Jo."

Floyd grunted. "I'd have to agree with you there. Jealousy and money both outweigh a temper tantrum."

"I went to school with Errol Cole." Adrian sighed. "He's good people, just new to the force. But Deputy Whatley..." He sighed again. "I've heard that once he's made his mind up, he's as stubborn as a mule."

I totally agreed with that Southernism as it applied

to Jed. "We have Betty and Bobby. Can you think of anyone else?"

"Zelda Taylor, president of the Coastal Fiction Writers." Floyd offered the name without inflection.

That caught my attention. "Tell me more."

"The tension between those two was thick enough to cut with a knife."

Viv folded her arms on the table and leaned forward. "More than once, Ms. Zelda would be in the library. If she saw Ms. Fiona come in, she'd leave. Same thing would happen in On A Roll. I saw it myself. Ms. Zelda would be waiting in line at On A Roll. If Ms. Fiona came into the shop, Ms. Zelda'd get out of the line and walk out of the café—before she even placed her order."

That seemed extreme. If I was already in line, I would've placed my order and asked for it to go. "What caused the tension between them?"

Floyd jumped in. "No one knows for sure, but it was around the time Fiona's firm, Lyle and Duggan CPA Group, was auditing the books for the bank where Zelda worked. Right after the audit, Zelda upped and started her own business."

"I thought that was odd as well." Corrinne straightened on her chair. "Zelda had been very proud of her position with Malcovich Savings and Loan. She'd hinted she'd expected another promotion."

I looked from Corrinne to Floyd. "Do you think her leaving was connected to the audit?"

Floyd shrugged. "It would explain why she suddenly soured on Fiona."

Spence spoke after sitting in silence through most of the discussion. "You all have been talking as though the murderer had been at the bookstore's signing: Ms. Zelda, Ms. Betty, and Bobby."

"That's true." I glanced at my notes.

"Remember what you said, Marvey." Spence turned to me. "If one of the people who attended the signing is the killer, what had they done with the murder weapon, and their bloody clothes?"

I shuddered to think of the alternative. "What if the killer hadn't attended the signing?"

Floyd grunted. "Then a whole lot more names would be added to your list. Don't think the deputies would take kindly to that."

By the time Spence and I had wished the other librarians good night and cleaned up after the dinner party, it was after nine o'clock. Spence had declined my help preparing for the dinner, but he hadn't hesitated to accept my help tidying up at the end of the evening. Perhaps that wasn't so odd.

Once the dining room and kitchen were returned to their original pristine condition, we called Jo.

The sweet and savory aroma of the baked chicken and peaches entrée lingered over the dining room, bringing back fond memories of good food and interesting company. Spence took the chair at the head of the table. I returned to my seat on his right. He rested his cell phone on the table between us and pressed Jo's pre-programmed number.

She answered on the first ring. "How was dinner?"

"I think it was very productive." I looked to Spence for confirmation.

He nodded. "I agree."

"What?" She sounded confused. "I'm talking about the food. How was it? What did people say?"

I cupped my left hand over my eyes and shook my head. *Unbelievable.* "The food was wonderful. Spence is an amazing cook. But, Jo, we need you to focus right now."

"You're right." Jo's sigh was long and deep. "I guess I'm still in denial that I'm a *suspect* in a *murder.*"

My heart broke for my friend. "You're not going through this alone."

"Marvey's right." Spence focused intently on his cell phone, as though Jo could see him. "The librarians agree with us that you're innocent, and we're doing everything we can to prove it."

"Thank you." Jo's voice wobbled in the middle, squeezing my heart a little more.

I took a moment to gather my thoughts. "All right, then. We were right to ask Spence to host this dinner for the librarians. They shared a wealth of information." With his assistance, I recapped our initial three suspects and the possible motives for each of them.

"I'd never thought about it before, but I've seen Zelda abruptly leave the bookstore after spotting Fiona too." Jo's disembodied voice rose in amazement.

"Do you have any idea why?" I glanced between Jo— or rather the phone—and Spence.

"No, but now I wish I'd asked." Her tone was heavy with regret. "Whatever it was, it must've been pretty bad."

I mulled over the observations Viv and Jo had

shared, playing them like movie scenes in my mind. "In each scenario, Zelda was the one who left. She could've been exhibiting classic avoidance behavior, as though she was the one who'd done something wrong."

Spence cocked his head. "You sound like a psychologist."

"I'm a librarian. I know a little about a lot." I switched my attention back to Jo on the phone. "I think we have solid leads to start with."

"I agree." She sounded much more enthusiastic. "When do we confront them?"

"Confront them?" I shifted my puzzled gaze to Spence. He looked baffled as well. "We can't just walk up to them and ask if they killed Fiona."

"Why not?" Jo's question was sulky.

I stared at the phone in amazement. "For one thing, even if one of them *was* the killer, they would deny it. Meanwhile, we would've tipped our hand, letting them know we were suspicious of them. If it turns out one of them is the killer, they'd destroy any evidence against them that they may have kept, like the bloody clothes and the murder weapon."

"If they haven't destroyed those things already." Spence spread his hands.

"All right." An edge of grumpiness entered Jo's voice. I couldn't blame her. "You have a point. So what's our next step?"

"We should share our notes with the deputies." Spence had rolled his shirt sleeves up just past his elbows while he'd washed the pots and pans. Now he was unrolling them and buttoning the cuffs.

"The deputies? That won't do any good." Jo's response was near to tears of frustration. "You might as well ball up that list and pitch it into the trash."

Spence gave his phone a fond look I was certain he'd meant for Jo. "We need to show them Ms. Zelda is worth questioning, and Ms. Betty and Bobby have stronger motives to kill Fiona in comparison to your disagreement with her."

Jo groused. "My very *minor* disagreement with her."

"Spence might be onto something." I studied him. "He has quite a bit of clout in this town. The deputies might listen to him."

"I don't know." Her stubbornness lingered. "No offense to Spence."

"None taken." His lips curved with wry humor.

"Suppose they try to stop us?" Jo asked. "Didn't you tell me they'd warned you off the investigation when they came to your office this morning?"

Had it only been this morning? It already felt as though that exchange had happened days ago. But Fiona's murder had happened two days ago, and the deputies had questioned Jo at her home on Sunday.

"Exactly." I folded my arms on the table and pictured Jo. "They warned *me* off the case, but Spence could approach them in his role as editor of the town's paper, checking on the status of the case."

He nodded. "It's something I or one of the reporters would do anyway, regardless of whether we were trying to clear your name."

Jo was doubtful. "I just don't want the deputies barring us from looking into Fiona's murder on our own."

I shared her concerns. "We'll address that if and when it happens. In the meantime, I think this tactic is worth the effort."

"So do I." Spence stared at his phone as we waited for Jo's verdict.

"All right." She sighed. "I really appreciate everything

you're doing. You're both the best friends that someone law enforcement suspects of murder could have."

Before ending our call, the three of us arranged to meet the next day—Tuesday—for lunch. Spence assured us that would give him enough time to speak with the deputies in person before joining us with an update on the case. I slid my notes from our dinner/criminal investigation to him.

I followed him to his coat closet to collect my purse. "Thanks again so much for all of your trouble. Tonight was a lot of fun. You're an amazing chef and an even better host."

"Thank you." Was Spence blushing? The idea made me smile.

I accepted my purse from him, then turned toward the door. "Good night."

"Marvey." He paused as I turned back to him. "Have you considered what we'll do if the deputies don't pursue these other suspects?"

"I'd rather leave crime fighting to the professionals, but if the deputies don't pursue these leads, we'll have to. Or at least I will. I'd understand if you'd rather not."

He swept his hand aside. "I wouldn't leave you to do it on your own, but Marvey, we'd be investigating a *murder*."

I frowned my confusion. "We're not trying to solve the murder. We're only trying to convince the deputies there are other far better suspects with much more concerning motives than Jo's."

"I know, but will the killer understand the difference?"

CHAPTER 12

S OMETHING WAS WRONG. I GOT a strange vibe as I strode into On A Roll Tuesday morning, the fourth day of May. Fiona's murder had occurred three days earlier. The atmosphere in the little neighborhood café was...tense. The early morning customers kept sending furtive looks toward the front of the dining area. They may have thought they were being subtle, but they weren't.

Following the path of their gazes, mine landed on the apparent source of their interest: Willy Pelt, Fiona's friend from Beaufort. He sat alone at a corner table for two.

"Your usual, Marvey?" Anna May's customary—albeit delayed—greeting distracted me from my discovery.

The scents of warm rolls, sweet pastries, and hot coffee carried me up to the counter. Along the way, responses to my greetings to the other regulars were either delayed or distracted. People seemed more interested in Willy Pelt's next breath. I made a mental note to pay my respects to him on my way out.

"Good morning, Anna May. Yes, please." I stopped

at the cash register and dug into my purse for the exact change. "And some of your delicious peach cobbler as well."

"Of course." She drew her attention from Willy to give me her seal of approval: cherubic smile and twinkling eyes.

"Anna May." I leaned forward, lowering my voice as she gave me her attention. "Why is everyone staring at Willy Pelt?"

Her eyes sharpened with interest. "What do you know about him?"

"Just that he's known Fiona's family for years." I struggled not to glance over my shoulder to look at him again. "I had the impression he and Fiona were friends. He was at her signing."

Anna May lifted her chin as though I'd confirmed her previous intel. "Folks didn't know much about Fiona. When word spread that one of her friends was in town, people's natural curiosity came out."

"Has anyone spoken with him?"

"Why would someone do that?" She cocked her head as if I'd just asked the most unexpected question.

I blinked. "To offer condolences or just to say hi." Anything seemed better than treating him like a book display.

"Hmm. That's something to consider." Anna May turned away. Her period of consideration was very brief.

Soon the music of her grinder and the aroma of freshly ground coffee beans wrapped me in a morning embrace. I inhaled deeply and tried to keep my attention from straying back to Willy.

The usual array of customers congregated within the café—business professionals, college students, and retirees. Many seemed oblivious to everything but Willy. Did he realize he was the center of attention? How could he not?

A male voice called behind me. "How's Jo holding up?"

I turned to see Dabney McCoy sitting with Etta Cole at their customary table closest to the counter with their bowls of peach cobbler.

A weight settled on my shoulders as I remembered how stressed and desperate Jo had sounded when Spence and I had spoken with her last night. "She's concerned the deputies seem to be focusing on her."

Dabney took the final bite of his cobbler and nudged aside the empty dish. "Nobody 'round here thinks Jo Gomez killed Fiona Lyle-Hayes."

"The deputies do." I stepped closer to the older couple to hear them over the sound of the espresso machine.

"I can't speak about Errol. He's a young man and still new to the department." Etta shrugged her thin shoulders. "But I taught Jedidiah Whatley high school English, and I can tell you he didn't become a sheriff's deputy to solve murders."

I'd known Etta had been a high school teacher, but it hadn't occurred to me that she'd been *Jed's* teacher. Could she help explain why he wasn't interested in the library? "Why did he go into law enforcement?"

Etta switched her attention from Willy to me. "Well, sweetie, I suppose he thought that was the best way he could help people."

Dabney snorted. "The best way he could be a town nuisance, you mean."

Etta scooped up more peach cobbler. "If you didn't speed—"

Dabney ignored Etta's interruption. "All he ever does—"

"—or park illegally—"

"—is hand out tickets."

"—then you wouldn't get traffic tickets."

Dabney snorted again. "Maybe if Jed Whatley spent less time handing out tickets and more time protecting residents, we wouldn't have had such a gruesome murder in our town."

Etta dropped her spoon into her dessert bowl. Her face drained of blood at the reference to Fiona's crime scene.

Dabney's gaze dropped to her half-eaten cobbler. "Are you done with that?" Without waiting for her response, he tugged the bowl to him and shoveled his spoon into the pastry.

I didn't agree with Dabney's depiction of Jed's responsibility for Fiona's murder, but I was amazed he'd yet again managed to claim Etta's dessert. "Neither of you believes Jo's guilty. Have you given any more thought to who would have such animosity against Fiona?"

"Nope, not a one." Dabney spoke around a mouthful of cobber.

Etta glared at him before shifting her attention to me. "I wouldn't have a clue. But you might want to ask Jo who'd want to frame her for murder."

That was a very good question.

After collecting my café mocha and peach cobbler from Anna May, I went in search of Willy, mentally practicing my speech as I strode through the café. I hoped he hadn't left while I'd been engaged with Etta and Dabney.

To my relief, he was still alone at his table for two. "Excuse me, Mr. Pelt."

Willy rose from his chair, his brown eyes cautious as he looked down at me. He was nearly as tall as Spence. "I met you Saturday over at the bookstore, didn't I?" His Southern roots were exposed in his voice. "Marvey Harris, isn't that right? Please call me Willy."

"Thank you." I swept my arm to encompass our surroundings. "You've found the most popular place in town."

He returned my smile. "This coffee shop was spoken of very highly over at the Peach Coast Inn, where I'm staying. After the breakfast they served me, I can understand why."

"Mr. Pelt—Willy—I didn't get an opportunity to offer my condolences to you Saturday. I heard you and Fiona were friends."

"Thank you, Ms. Marvey. Your words are a great kindness. Do you have time to join me?" He gestured toward the extra seat at his wood laminate table.

I consulted my Apple Watch. There were still a few minutes until I had to be at work, and the library was less than a block away. Glancing over my left shoulder, I found several sets of eyes watching us with open curiosity or blatant surprise. This included Anna May, Etta, and Dabney. I suppressed a smile as I turned my back to them and settled onto the chair. "Thank you, and you can just call me Marvey."

"Thank you." Willy folded his long, lanky body onto

the little chair. "You're the only person who's acknowledged that Fiona and I were friends." His gaze swept the area. I sensed his resentment. "It seems like she didn't have many of those here."

Searching for a comforting response, I recalled a comment Viv had shared during our coffee break yesterday. "People didn't know Fiona well. I heard she was a very private person."

"That's true." A sad smile hovered over the man's thin lips. He was perhaps fifteen years older than my twenty-eight. His rich auburn hair made his skin appear even paler. "I'd wanted to organize a small memorial service for her once the deputies release her body, but I'm afraid the effort would be wasted. I'm not convinced anyone would come."

I felt sorry for the poor man. He needed to share his grief with others who'd cared, but he'd come to the wrong town for that. "I'd come. And I'm sure there would be others."

"No, it'd be a wasted effort." A trace of anger tightened his voice.

I sought to change the subject—and slip in some investigating. "How long did you know Fiona?"

"Almost ten years."

"Wow. That's a long time. How did you two meet?" I sipped my mocha and felt the jolt of the extra espresso. My gaze dipped to the few crumbs on the white porcelain dessert plate in front of Willy. He seemed to have enjoyed Anna May's peach cobbler.

"I was her uncle's lawyer." The happier memories chased the shadows from Willy's broad features. "I own a law firm in Beaufort. That's in South Carolina. Fiona's uncle, Leroy Lyle, was one of my biggest clients. Fiona was very close to him. Lung cancer took his life almost three years ago."

"I'm so sorry." Her uncle had died three years ago, her husband last year, and now Fiona was dead. It was like death had been stalking her. A chilling thought.

"Thank you, Ms.—Marvey. Leroy wasn't just a client. He was also a good friend. Now they're both gone."

My heart ached for him, losing two friends so close together. I couldn't imagine the grief. "It was nice of you to come to Fiona's first author event."

"I wanted to surprise her." His eyes clouded again. "Now, I'm sorry I hadn't gotten into town early enough to see her before the signing. I would've liked to have talked with her one last time, told her how proud I was of her. She had so much talent."

"What time did you arrive?" *Note to self: Check the distance between Beaufort and Peach Coast, and the time it would take to travel between the two.* Willy's grief seemed genuine, but I needed to cross all the T's and dot all the I's.

Willy paused. "I drove straight to the bookstore and pulled into the parking lot. I didn't have time to stop at the hotel. It was after four o'clock, and the signing had started. I met Betty Hayes and her son, and Nolan Duggan on my way into the store."

That sounded plausible. Nolan had entered the bookstore alone, but Betty and Bobby had arrived just minutes after him. Willy had been with them. "How long of a drive is that? I find the time and distances between places fascinating."

Willy flashed a co-conspiratorial smile. "Well now, it's not much of a drive, only about a couple of hours.

I didn't even rent a car. Stopped for brunch and still made it in less than two hours."

"But you were highly motivated to attend Fiona's signing." My smile faded. "We didn't know much about her. Now that she's gone, I regret not taking time to get to know her better." I felt guilty for lying to him, but consoled myself that my misrepresentations were in an effort to get justice for Jo—and Fiona.

Willy looked around the café again. "I know Ms. Betty and her son have unjustly maligned Fiona's character to everyone in this town who'd listen. I have a feeling that would be pretty much everyone. Buddy Hayes should've put a stop to it. A gentleman would have. I...I would have."

"Maybe Buddy tried."

"He should've tried harder." Willy's piercing gray eyes burned with anger and outrage for his friend. "Hayes was her husband and, according to Fiona, a prominent member of this community. He should've done more to protect her from Ms. Betty's slander."

Willy's temper was like a thick wall between us. I was reluctant to push him while he was grieving, but the clock was ticking, and I needed answers. "Did Fiona ever say anything that led you to believe Betty's gossip was putting her life in danger?"

"All I'm saying is that if he *truly* loved Fiona, Hayes wouldn't have allowed his ex-wife and son to spread malicious lies about her." A scathing expression settled on his face as he looked at the other customers. "Other people will believe what they want to believe about Fiona. I choose to remember only the good things about her."

"But Fiona never actually said she felt threatened by Betty and Bobby?"

"People were often jealous of her success, but she worked hard for everything she had. I told that to the deputies."

"Do you think Fiona was killed by someone who was jealous of her?" I searched Willy's eyes, trying to gain insight into Fiona's impassioned friend. He wasn't giving me much.

His lips thinned. "Jealousy's an ugly emotion."

On that, Willy and I agreed. The librarians also had identified jealousy as a motive for Fiona's killer. So far, the only person to whom we could attribute that motive was Betty. Now didn't seem to be the time to share that information with Willy, though.

"Did Fiona confide in you any problems she was having in town?"

Willy gave me a sarcastic look. "Besides with Ms. Betty and Bobby? Fiona wasn't much of a talker. She didn't like to complain, but I had the feeling her marriage wasn't happy."

This was new intel. "What gave you that idea?"

Willy paused as though he wasn't certain he should confide in me. I did my best to look trustworthy. "Before Hayes died, Fiona called me. She wanted legal advice about getting a divorce. Hayes had a lot of cash flow problems, and she was tired of him treating her like the First National Bank of Buddy."

"Why would Buddy need Fiona's money? I thought he was a wealthy and successful real estate agent who'd left a trust fund for his son?"

"That's what Hayes wanted everybody to believe, but the truth was something very different."

Perhaps Corrinne had been right. Could Buddy have been in financial distress toward the end of his life? Would Fiona have wanted a divorce if he had been?

"And then Buddy died." I prompted Willy to keep the conversation moving.

Willy drank more coffee. "His death was unexpected. I believe it was a heart attack. But Fiona told me Ms. Betty and Bobby were going around town, claiming he didn't have any of the risks associated with heart attacks."

"Do Betty and Bobby think Fiona killed Buddy?" My team of intrepid librarians hadn't told me that.

Willy nodded. "That's what they were implying. And now someone has killed Fiona."

In his eyes, I read the same question that flashed in big neon lights across my mind: were the two deaths related?

CHAPTER 13

"THE DEPUTIES WEREN'T INTERESTED IN our leads for other suspects in Fiona's murder." Spence joined Jo and me for lunch on Tuesday as we'd arranged. We'd found a cozy table for four in a quiet corner of On A Roll, separate from most of the other diners.

Several people already had made a detour toward us to offer Jo words of encouragement and support. Contrary to her fears, these University of Georgia Bulldog fans had accepted their University of Florida Gator neighbor.

It was a well-known secret the deputies were focusing their investigation on Jo. Despite that, the small town was rallying around my new friend. Their reactions touched my heart. It showed how much she meant to the community that meant so much to her. I was relieved, for Jo and for myself. I hadn't wanted to accept that my neighbors could believe my friend was capable of killing someone. Their show of support bolstered my confidence that I could make a home here—tennis shoes, coke, peach cobbler, and all.

Now if I could just convince Phoenix...

"Did you speak with both deputies Whatley *and* Cole?" Jo's voice cracked as she seemed to struggle under this setback. "What did they say?"

Spence's dark eyes softened with sympathy. "They said they'd questioned Ms. Betty, Bobby, and Ms. Zelda the afternoon of the signing, and their alibis had all checked out."

My disappointment was almost overwhelming. "*We're* Jo's alibis. We checked out too. So could they tell you why she's still under suspicion?"

"The deputies think Jo's a stronger suspect than the other three." Spence gave her an apologetic look. "You were the last person to see Fiona alive. They also think you could've disposed of the bloody clothes and the murder weapon more easily than our suspects. Because of that, they said you're their primary suspect."

Color drained from Jo's face.

I fisted my hands beside my blackened chicken salad. "Will they at least add the others to their list?"

Spence sighed his regret. "They didn't say no, but they didn't appear inclined to."

Jo stared down at her chicken noodle soup. "And in the meantime, I have a murder charge hanging over my head, and foot traffic at the store has dropped off."

The sensation of being watched made my skin itch. My attention drifted from Jo to an older woman sitting alone at a small table diagonally in front of us. Delores Polly was the administrative assistant at St. Michael Catholic Church. She also accompanied the choir on the piano sometimes during the Saturday evening Mass.

Delores was dressed quietly and conservatively in a plain peach dress with a modest neckline and tight sleeves. Her thick, round glasses masked half of her face and magnified her serious gray eyes. I smiled at her in greeting. Delores narrowed her gaze at me.

I returned my attention to Jo. The homicide investigation must be affecting my friend's sleep. Her makeup did little to mask the circles under her eyes. And she'd been biting her fingernails again. I drew a deep breath, exhaling on a sigh. The scents of savory soups and seasoned meats had joined the aromas of fresh breads and strong coffee.

Reaching over, I squeezed Jo's left forearm as she sat across the table from me. "This is only the first day the store has been open since Fiona's murder. The decline in shoppers isn't a reflection of whether people think you're innocent or guilty."

"Marvey's right." Spence allowed his gaze to circle the coffee shop. "Just a few minutes ago, several people came by to give you their support. Everyone's still in shock, Jo. Give them time to recover."

Jo spooned up her soup. "Maybe you're right."

"There's something else you need to know." Spence's tone was reluctant. He gave Jo and me a cautious look.

Jo seemed apprehensive. Her tone was stiff. "What is it now?"

"The deputies asked me to stop interfering in their investigation." Spence shifted his gaze from Jo to me. "Well, they specifically asked that *Marvey* and I stay out of their way. They said when they have something to report, they'll contact the *Crier*."

"We'll do our best to stay out of their way as we gather information to prove Jo's innocence." I shrugged my shoulders, then adjusted the collar of my powder-blue blouse.

Jo continued to play with her soup. Spence barely touched his grilled chicken and cheddar sandwich on whole grain bread. I ignored my salad. Lunch would've been a celebratory meal if the deputies had at least agreed to spend as much energy focusing on Betty, Bobby, and Zelda as they were spending on Jo. But since they'd rejected our request—and had gone the extra step of warning us not to interfere in the case—the atmosphere was much more maudlin.

My gaze was drawn once again to Delores's table. She scowled as she returned my stare. Had I done something to offend the church's pianist? I combed through my memories.

"Marvey, do you think it's a good idea to ignore the deputies?" Spence's question interrupted my thoughts. He gave me a look of such grave concern I almost doubted myself.

Almost.

I took a deep drink of my iced tea, which the locals referred to as "sweet tea." Who'd have thought there'd be so many cultural differences within the nine hundred seven miles separating Brooklyn, New York, and Peach Coast, Georgia?

"Perhaps ignoring the deputies' orders isn't the brightest idea I've ever had, but how would I feel if I didn't do anything and our worst-case scenario became real?" I trusted them to understand I was referring to Jo's arrest. I didn't want to spell it out.

Spence held Jo's worried gaze as he spoke. "I won't speak for Marvey, but I'd feel horrible."

"So would I." My tone was grim.

Jo dropped her soup spoon. "I can't ask either of you

to risk angering the sheriff's department—or worse—for me."

I reached across the table to grip Jo's forearm again. "This is bigger than you, Jo. There's a murderer in Peach Coast."

"That's what I'm saying." Her voice was dancing on the cusp of hysteria. "It's too dangerous."

"I'll be careful." I released her arm.

Spence corrected me. "*We'll* be careful. I'm not going to leave the two of you to investigate a murder on your own. We're in this together."

"Thank you." The tension in my neck and shoulders eased.

Jo silently assessed Spence and me. I could sense her searching for words to change our minds. Finally, she gave a heavy sigh and tugged two books from her To Be Read tote bag. "All right. If you're both determined to continue this investigation, I'm grateful. Believe me. But I'm also worried." Jo passed Spence and me a copy of *In Death Do We Part*. "As Marvey asked, I've brought you each a copy of Fiona's book."

Although I'd seen Fiona's debut mainstream mystery in the library, I skimmed the back cover description again. "Fiona's writing will give us some insight into her personality. Criminal psychologists say that to identify the killer, it helps to know the victim."

Spence looked at me with a combination of amusement and admiration. "That's good insight."

I rolled my eyes at him. "Scoff if you want—"

"I'm being sincere." He held up his hands, palms out.

"— but whatever we learn about Fiona will help us identify potential suspects in her murder."

Jo swung her gaze between Spence and me. "What's our next step?"

Despite my efforts to ignore her, I was aware of Delores's unceasing surveillance. Why was she staring at me? Or was I being paranoid? I glanced at her again, and again encountered her vexation. No, I wasn't imagining things.

Doubling down on my efforts to block her from my conscience, I sat back against my seat to consider our approach. "Since the deputies won't re-interview Betty, Bobby, or Zelda, we'll need to follow up with them ourselves."

Spence leaned into the table. "The hardware store where Bobby works is on my way home. I'll stop by after work to talk with him."

"Great." I recalled Zelda's business card was still in my purse. "When I get back to my office, I'll give Zelda a call to see if she'll meet with me."

Jo looked from me to Spence and back. "Which one of you is going to talk with Betty?"

I stared at Spence, trying to think of a persuasive argument for him. I came up empty. "I thought you might want to speak with her."

Spence gestured toward me. "I thought she'd be more comfortable speaking with you, woman to woman."

"Oh, no." I waved my hands. "Everyone likes and respects you, Spence. You'd have a much better chance of getting her to open up."

Jo chuckled. It was good to hear her laughing again. "I'm glad you decided I couldn't help with the interviews, since people wouldn't feel comfortable speaking freely in front of me. I wouldn't want to interview Betty about the murder of her ex-husband's wife, either."

"Humph." I crossed my arms in mock irritation. "It's very convenient for you to use that reasoning now, isn't it? You resented the suggestion when it kept you away from Spence's dinner party."

Jo laughed harder, as I'd hoped she would. "If you can't see the difference between missing Spence's dinner party and skipping Betty Rodgers-Hayes's interview, then you're just hopeless."

Spence tossed her a grin before facing me. "Let's talk with Betty together."

I smiled. "Good idea. You can take the lead."

He laughed. How would he react when he discovered I wasn't joking?

A flurry of movement drew my attention to the other side of the aisle. Delores rushed past our table, generating enough wind to flutter my napkin as she sailed past us. I shifted on my seat, tracking her progress toward the front exit.

What was that about?

The voices were moving closer to my office.

"This is a restricted area. You don't have permission to come back here." The flustered warning came from Viv.

"I don't give a flying fig about y'all's restrictions. She doesn't have *permission* to go around town badmouthing my boy!"

Seated behind my desk Tuesday afternoon, I looked

up from my computer. The exchange was loud. And hostile. I suspected the "she" in question was me, and that the angry speaker was Betty Rodgers-Hayes. I circled my desk and hurried to my doorway, hoping to diffuse the situation.

Unfortunately, my timing was off. Betty almost bowled into me. I jumped back to prevent a pileup in my doorway. The older woman's milky complexion was spotted red with temper. Her permed chestnut hair pinwheeled around her face. Her startled brown eyes first widened in surprise, then narrowed in accusation. I'd come face-to-face with an avenging warrior-parent.

Viv was a step behind Betty with Adrian a half step behind her. My colleagues wore identical expressions of horror and dismay.

Confronted with the trio, I said the first thing that popped into my head. "Who's watching circulation?"

We couldn't leave the circulation desk unattended. Suppose a reader needed assistance?

"Danny has everything under control." Viv's reference to one of our more seasoned circulation members reassured me. "I'm so sorry, Marvey—"

"What in *tarnation* do you think you're playing at?" Betty's growl interrupted the circulation supervisor.

I offered Viv and Adrian a confident smile. "It's all right. I'll speak with Betty."

"You're darn right you will." Betty was panting like a waking volcano. I could almost see smoke billowing from her ears.

"Are you sure?" Viv and Adrian spoke over each other. They exchanged dubious looks.

"Yes, but thank you." I smiled again, then gestured for Betty to precede me into my office before closing my door. Something told me this could get loud. "Betty, please take a seat. How can I help you?"

This was as good a time as any to interview one of our suspects, but I wished I felt better prepared. Betty had caught me off guard. I'd have to play it by ear.

Betty remained standing. She settled her silver purse more firmly on her left shoulder and glared at me across the narrow expanse of my desk. "You know darn good and well why I'm here. You're getting ready to spread a rumor around town that my boy and I killed Fiona. That's a darn lie, and you know it."

My back and neck stiffened as my tension grew. How could Betty have known that... The image of Delores rushing out of On A Roll blinked across my mind. "How long have you and Delores Polly known each other?"

Betty gave a smug smile. "Since grade school."

"Can she read lips?"

Her smile grew into a grin. "She sure can."

Since she remained standing, I did too. The muscles of my back and neck tightened. I braced my hands on my desk in front of me, buying a little time to gather my thoughts. Beneath my sweating palms, I felt the cool stack of papers I'd intended to review this afternoon. They'd have to wait. "Betty, there's been a misunderstanding. I don't plan to start any rumor about anyone. I'm just—"

"The good Lord knows that my boy and I, we'd never do anything like that. Never." Betty's voice was on the rise again.

In response to her attack on my investigation, I decided the best defense was a strong offense. "You and Bobby had a history with Fiona. You're the jilted ex-wife. You were shouting to see Fiona during the signing.

Why aren't the deputies questioning you in connection with her murder?"

Betty seemed to be vibrating with rage. Her heavily powdered cheeks flushed a deeper shade of red. "You'd better not be trying to point the finger at my boy for Fiona's murder just to get your friend out of prison. If she's guilty, then the good Lord knows that's where she belongs."

"Jo's innocent." I was proud of my calm, even tone.

Betty arched a dubious eyebrow. "Then y'all don't have anything to worry about, do y'all?" Her voice was suddenly sweetness and light. How did Southerners manage that?

I studied her smug expression. "What about you and Bobby? Do either of you have anything to worry about?"

She gaped at me like a fish out of water. "We surely do not."

"How was your relationship with Fiona?"

"That's none of your darn business." Betty crossed her arms. "I'm here to tell you to stop slandering my boy."

Would Viv consider Betty's body language to be defensive? I would. The helicopter mom wasn't going to say another word. Then why wasn't she leaving? Was there something she wanted to tell me—or something she wanted to hear?

I watched her closely. "People have told me you and Bobby had a lot of animosity toward Fiona."

Betty's eyes narrowed to an angry glare. "What are folks saying about my boy?"

"I've heard Fiona was in charge of the trust fund Buddy left for him. Is that true?" I searched her features closely for even a flicker of reaction.

Her teeth snapped together with an audible click. "That doesn't mean he killed her."

So it was true. "Did Bobby resent her control over his money?"

"He wasn't going to throw a barbecue for her, but that doesn't mean he killed her."

Betty had a lot to say about *Bobby's* innocence, but she didn't say much about her own. "Did *you* resent her control over your son's money? You'd already spread enough malicious gossip to turn the town against her."

Betty looked to her right and left before rallying. "Gossiping about the woman who tore my family apart doesn't make me a killer."

"You're right. It doesn't make you a killer, but your animosity toward her gives you a motive." I wasn't searching for a killer; I was looking for suspects. I wasn't trying to solve Fiona's murder, and maybe that made me a bad person. I'd leave that part to the deputies. I only wanted to clear Jo.

"For the last time, my boy is no killer. And neither am I." Betty spoke slowly as though she thought I was confused. "So don't you lie on my boy. You hear me?" Final warning delivered, she spun on her heel and started toward my door.

"Why did you attend Fiona's book signing?"

Betty stopped and faced me. Her eyes simmered with resentment. "Jo's bookstore is a public place, and I have the right to go anywhere I want. Don't I?"

"Where were you before the signing?"

"I was at home. Alone." Betty clipped the words. "Doing chores. Not that it's any of your darn business."

The deputies had told Spence they'd checked Betty's alibi. Household chores weren't much of an alibi. How had the deputies verified that? Had they given her home a white-glove test?

"What about Bobby?" I searched her defiant features, looking for any shift in her expression. "Do you know where he was?"

She hesitated. A shadow flickered over her features. "My son's not a cold-blooded killer, and you'd darn well better not go around saying anything different."

A chill chased down my spine as I dropped onto the chair behind me. Betty's voice was confident, but her words weren't. I detected the ambiguity in her response. Was it possible Mama Bear had doubts about her Baby Bear's innocence? What had Bobby said or done to put that uncertainty in Betty's mind?

CHAPTER 14

"**B**ETTY *ATTACKED* YOU?" JO SCOOTED forward on the overstuffed sky-blue sofa in my living room, where she sat with Spence later that evening. Her voice squeaked with anger.

"Not physically; verbally." I faced Jo and Spence from the matching armchair across the room. My mind was still spinning from the angry confrontation with Betty. Luckily, Jo and Spence had been able to meet with me on short notice after dinner.

Phoenix didn't care that we had company. He'd snubbed us, choosing to remain alone in the foyer. He gave us his back as he stared out the French doors. Earlier, I'd tried to lure him away from that spot, but nothing I'd said or done had had any effect. In the end, I'd brought him his food and respected his solitude.

He'd once again dragged all his belongings—his bed, food bowl, toys, and favorite blanket—to the living room and stacked them in front of the door. I'd stumbled over them when I'd gotten home earlier. Was his action a sign he was feeling ignored? He'd never done that in New York. After I'd put away his treasures, I'd again called the veterinarian Lonnie Norman, the pet shop owner, had recommended. As Lonnie had predicted, the doctor's calendar was full—which was an encouraging testament to her popularity—but her receptionist had found an opening for Friday evening, three days from today. I think it had helped that Lonnie had called her on my behalf.

"Betty's just moved to the top of my suspects list." Jo's comment tugged me back to our meeting. "Regardless of whether her attack was physical or verbal, she obviously has a temper."

"Which probably was caused by her perceived threat to her child." Spence gestured toward me. "Marvey said Betty seemed focused on protecting Bobby, not defending herself."

Jo switched her frown from me to Spence seated beside her. "Whose side are you on?"

Spence's expression softened. "I'm after the truth, and I know you're innocent."

"I'm sorry." Jo's shoulders relaxed. "I'm still irritated that the deputies are determined to investigate *me* while ignoring Betty and Bobby, and not even looking into Zelda's past with Fiona."

"Betty's a much stronger suspect than you." I rubbed the creases between my eyebrows. "That's all we're trying to convey to the deputies, that there are suspects with equally strong if not stronger motives than yours."

Spence propped his right ankle onto his left knee. "One meeting isn't enough to go on, especially since she was so emotional."

"Spence is probably right." Jo started to bite her nails. She caught my warning look and dropped her hand to her lap. "As much as I'd love to point the finger at someone else, I don't want to implicate an innocent person just to clear my name."

"I checked with my contact at the coroner's office." Spence looked from Jo to me. "Fiona died from blunt force trauma to her head."

Curiosity had me on the edge of my seat. "Who's your contact in the coroner's office?"

"Journalists must protect our sources." He gave me a wry look before continuing. "Fiona was probably pushed backward. Her head hit a corner of the table as she fell. She died almost instantly."

"That explains why no one heard her scream." I experienced a wave of grief almost as strong as the one that had hit me the afternoon we'd discovered Fiona's lifeless body.

Spence nodded somberly. "Based on the angle of the wounds, my contact believes Fiona was stabbed as she lay on the ground. Her body sustained five wounds from a curved, eight-inch blade."

"A curved blade?" There was dread in Jo's voice. "The killer must've used one of our box cutters. There were two in the storage room. One's missing."

Spence and I exchanged a concerned look. That the murder weapon belonged to Jo—or rather, to her store—was another factor against her. First, Jo and Fiona had argued. Second, it was Jo's store. Third, it was Jo's knife. Three strikes.

Ice collected in the pit of my stomach. "If the killer pushed Fiona, doesn't that make it seem as though there had been at least a brief struggle?"

"Perhaps." Spence nodded. "My source agrees this was a crime of passion. The fact the killer kept stabbing Fiona—five times—even after she was on the ground makes it seem like the murder was done in a rage. It wasn't premeditated. The killer didn't bring a weapon. They used one that was at the scene."

"I wonder if the killer was injured." A memory from the book signing surfaced. "Bobby had several scratches on the back of his right hand Saturday. I noticed them when he was showing Jo his snake tattoo."

The news seemed to revive Jo. She shared a look between Spence and me. "Maybe he got those scratches in a struggle with Fiona."

Spence was quiet for a moment, contemplating Jo's response. "Bobby told me that before the signing, he was home alone, eating lunch and watching a movie. He has no opinion on who killed Fiona, but it wasn't him or his mama."

"How did the deputies verify his alibi?" My frustration was showing. "Did they ask him twenty questions about the movie?"

Jo sniffed her disdain. "I'd like an answer to that too."

I leaned back against my armchair. "Betty wouldn't tell me why she'd attended Fiona's book signing. Adrian thinks it was to confront Fiona about her book."

"Now that right there was payback for all the ugly lies Betty spread about Fiona around town. I'm sure of it." Jo crossed her right leg over her left knee and tapped her foot against the air in a silent off-rhythm beat.

Spence balanced his left elbow on the sofa's arm. "Why would Betty risk the exposure of killing her in a public place?"

"Your coroner friend called it a crime of passion. Maybe things got out of hand." Jo crossed her arms and legs. "But if you ask me, Betty's ugly gossip should've landed her on the deputies' radar to start with."

"For now, let's keep her on our list of people of interest." I remembered the woman's hesitation as I asked about Bobby's relationship with Fiona. And the scratches on the back of Bobby's hand. "But if Betty isn't the killer, could she be covering for one?"

"I'm so sorry, Phoenix." After Jo and Spence left Tuesday night, I gathered the cat into my arms and sat on the floor beside the French doors. He didn't resist as he had when I'd first returned home. Instead, his soft, warm body curled into me. Progress. "I know you don't like going to the vet. I don't like going to the doctor, either, but I need to know what's wrong. You're not yourself."

I pushed myself to my legs and carried Phoenix upstairs to my study, also known as the spare bedroom, at the end of the second-floor hallway. "You'll be happy to know this vet comes highly recommended by Lonnie. I hope you like her."

I hope I like her too.

"For now, come help me make a book pendant for Jo. I think that'll cheer her up. Don't you?"

Phoenix willingly joined me in my study, but he withheld his opinion on our Pendant Project. The room was comfortably warm. It smelled of vanilla, courtesy of the plug-in air freshener to the left of the threshold. The feel of the warm wood flooring gave way to the textured sensation of the cream-and-gold Berber area rug in the center of the room.

I'd hung several of my wood-framed book cover sketches on the walls. They shared space with my bookcases. I sat on my desk chair and settled Phoenix onto my lap. Powering my laptop, I launched the internet browser and started searching for book cover images. The spark of curiosity I sensed from Phoenix healed my heart.

"Do any of these covers appeal to you?" I paused for Phoenix's response. Nothing. Not a meow or a purr; not even a yawn. But I'd felt his brief interest, and he seemed relaxed as he remained on my lap. I continued our one-sided conversation. "Jo has a lot of favorite books, which weirdly enough makes it harder for me to pick a cover image for the pendant." I glanced at the top of Phoenix's head. "There are just too many choices."

I did a search for *How the García Girls Lost Their Accents* by Julia Alvarez. Jo loved this novel. There were several beautiful versions of the cover, some illustrations, others photographs. A couple were text treatments.

I opened another web tab and asked for images of *The House on Mango Street* by Sandra Cisneros, another book that I recalled had pride of place on Jo's "keepers" bookshelf. This search also resulted in myriad images—illustrations, photos, and text treatments. But one of the illustrations was a vivid drawing of three women, looking downward. The image used striking colors to convey movement and emotion. The picture drew me in and made me sigh with pleasure.

"We have a winner." I sent the file to the printer.

As the machine clicked and whirred, I stroked Phoenix from the spot just above his nose to the top of his head. He closed his eyes and kneaded my thigh. I smiled, part pleasure and part relief. Maybe he was getting back to his old self.

Still petting Phoenix with my left hand, I stretched to pluck the printout from the machine with my right. I studied it for a while, then showed it to Phoenix. "I can feel the emotion. Can you?"

My cell phone vibrated in the front right pocket of my turquoise denim shorts. I pulled the device free and checked the identification screen. The caller was my mother, Ciara Bennett-Harris. I'd just spoken with my parents Saturday. My smile faded as I realized why my mother was calling.

Oh, boy.

I took a deep breath and answered the phone. "Hi, Mo—"

"Have they caught the killer yet?" My mother's sharp question interrupted my greeting as I answered her call.

"I'm sorry, Mom. This isn't like *Law & Order.* Murder isn't solved within the format of a sixty-minute television show."

"There's no need to get cheeky." My father's admonishment lacked heat as it traveled across the phone line. The echo in the background confirmed my parents were using their speaker phone feature. "Besides, it's been more than sixty minutes. You called to tell us about the murder Saturday. That was three days ago."

A jazz instrumental played faintly in the background, providing a soundtrack to our conversation.

"I'm sorry, Dad. I was—"

"We're your parents." My mother bowled over my words again. "We have the right to worry."

"Of course, Mom. I understand." And I loved them for it, even as I wished they weren't so concerned.

Angry car horns carried through the speaker phone. Had someone double-parked down their street again? "I don't have—"

This time, my dad interrupted me. "We've been following the case through *The Peach Coast Crier.*"

Had I heard them correctly? "You've been reading the *Crier?*"

"We bought an online subscription." My mother sounded like subscribing to the small town's newspaper was completely normal. To her, it probably was.

"Okay, Mom and Dad." I rose from my desk chair to pace my office. "I really appreciate your calling to check on me, but let's take a breath."

I pictured them sitting together in their warm gold and pale brown foyer. The room was in the front of their two-hundred-plus-year-old home. There were windows on two sides of the room, which during the day flooded the space with light.

"How can we take a breath?" Beneath my mother's tense question, a siren blared. Briefly, I wondered whether it was an ambulance. It didn't sound like a police car or a fire truck. "How can we relax when our daughter's in danger? There's a murderer running around loose in your town."

Seriously? "There are murderers running around loose in Brooklyn." My tone was dry.

"The difference is you were minutes away from us when you lived in Brooklyn." Dad sounded defensive. "Now you're several hours and hundreds of miles away. It wouldn't be as easy or quick to jump in the car and go to you if you need us."

I acknowledged his point. "About thirteen hours and

thirty-five minutes. It's a nine-hundred-seven-point-four-mile trip approximately."

"That's our point," Mom said. "We thought you'd be safer in a small town. Maybe we were wrong. The odds may be that you're less safe in a town of fewer than one thousand people versus a borough with more than two-and-a-half-million residents."

How many more times would we have the "personal safety" discussion?

Shaking my head, I scooped up Phoenix and carried him back down to our living room. The wood flooring was warm beneath my bare feet. The sun had set hours ago. I lowered him to the floor and returned my attention to my parents.

"I wish you wouldn't worry. As soon as the deputies know more about the murder and the investigation, I promise to call you." This wouldn't be a good time to tell my parents that I also was working on the case. In fact, there probably would never be a good time to share that with them.

Mom's voice was tight with anxiety. "You have to promise us you'll be very careful."

"I promise." More guilt. "And I do have the home security system with motion-sensing lights outside. Phoenix and I will be fine. Don't worry."

"Has Phoenix gotten used to the new place yet?" Dad asked.

I glanced toward the foyer. My cat had once again settled in front of the French doors. "Not yet. He's being very quiet, almost lethargic. He's just not himself. The first vet said this was normal, but I don't know. I have an appointment in three days with a new vet for a second opinion."

After a few more minutes of chatting with my parents, I wished them both a good night. Collecting Phoenix and his bed from beside the backdoor, I carried both upstairs. "Let's see if it helps you to sleep in my room."

Phoenix looked at me, then looked away. I sensed an eye roll in his response. At least he was responding.

CHAPTER 15

S UDDENLY, I WAS WIDE AWAKE. Why? The clock read two in the morning. What had awakened me? I lay still and scanned my bedroom. Every visible surface. Every shadowed corner. Nothing. I was alone. Well, except for Phoenix who, forsaking his bed, lay snoring softly on the pillow beside me.

What had—

There it was!

The motion sensor flooded my backyard with light. Someone was sneaking around outside my home. My blood turned to ice. My heart sprang into my throat. And stayed there. For a second, I was too afraid to breathe, too afraid to move.

And then I couldn't move fast enough.

I scooped Phoenix from the spare pillow and scrambled out of bed. Startled awake, he drove his claws into my chest. I ignored the pain as I crept to the bedroom's rear windows. I felt bad for scaring him, but I needed to keep him close. I needed to keep him safe.

What if someone was trying to break in?

I peeked through the cream venetian blinds. My

backyard seemed empty. I froze, straining to listen. No unidentifiable movements. Then the lights at the left side yard came on. Through the rear windows, I could see the lights illuminating the lawn.

When the rear lights came back on, I tightened my grip on Phoenix. Was the trespasser circling my house? Why? What did they want? My cat squirmed in my arms. Could he hear my heart racing? I kissed the top of his head and murmured nonsense, trying to calm him. Trying to calm myself.

I crept toward my front windows. Along the way, I grabbed my cell phone. With my right thumb, I dialed emergency services. I pressed Phoenix to my heart with my left.

"Nine one one. What's your emergency?" The dispatcher sounded so loud.

"I think someone's trying to get into my house." I peeked out my front windows. I gasped as the motion-sensor lights blinked on.

Someone was there. Where? In the bushes? Beneath my eaves? On my porch? Why did they keep circling my home?

Moving stealthily through my house, I checked the doors and windows. The dispatcher bombarded me with questions. I answered just as quickly. My motion sensor lights. Started a few minutes ago. Phoenix and I were alone. My address.

My need for them to hurry.

Thankfully, they did.

Patrol cars with their flashing lights pulled up in front of my house before I'd thanked the dispatcher and disconnected the call. I opened the door to the deputies—and found Jed and Errol on my porch.

"Ms. Harris." Jed inclined his head in greeting. "Everything all right in there?"

"Yes." The word emerged on a sigh of relief. Despite my previous tense encounters with the deputy duo, their presence instantly made me feel safer.

Jed's eyes searched mine as though looking for confirmation that the intruders weren't inside, threatening me. He must've found that confirmation. "All right, now. Cole and I are going to search your property. We'll be right back, so y'all stay inside for now."

Phoenix and I remained on the porch, less than an arm's length from the doorway. I held him tightly, murmuring soft words and stroking him, giving as well as receiving comfort. A dusting of stars blanketed the sky. A cool breeze carried the earthy scent of the swamp. And somewhere nearby, an intruder lurked.

Since I remained outside, my motion-detection light stayed on, illuminating the front of my property to the sidewalk. The New Yorker in me remained vigilant in the event the intruder somehow made it past the deputies and into my home. My gaze swept the perimeter from my right side yard, the walkway in front of me, my left side yard, and my—hopefully empty—living room behind me.

The deputies returned. Jed turned off his flashlight as he climbed the three steps to my porch. "Well, now, Ms. Harris, we didn't see anyone loitering around your yard."

Errol stopped beside him. "Are you sure someone was out here?" As he spoke, he looked around as though double checking that we were alone.

"Yes, I'm certain. Their movements activated the motion lights." I was reluctant to let go of Phoenix. It had been a disquieting experience, and my poor cat had been through enough with the move.

"Probably just some teenagers. They tripped your lights, walking past your house." Jed adjusted the waistband of his polyester brown stripe pants.

"Walking past my house at two in the morning? On a school night?" It was only Wednesday. That didn't seem logical. Even in my old neighborhood in Brooklyn, teenagers weren't out that late on a school night. And Peach Coast was a much quieter—and older—community.

"It could happen." The older deputy seemed defensive.

Errol lifted his attention from Phoenix. "Did your cat get out?"

"No, he was asleep." I looked from Phoenix back to Jed. "The noises didn't sound like a group of kids. And whoever it was walked the perimeter more than once. He activated the lights on at least three sides of my house, not just the front. His actions seemed deliberate."

My attention shifted to the sidewalk, searching beyond the light to the shadows on the other side. The trespasser had wanted me to know he'd been out here in the early hours of the morning, casing my home while Phoenix and I had slept. I was sure of it. A chill chased down my spine.

Jed rubbed his upper lip. "Like I said, it was probably a couple of kids, playing a prank."

I arched an eyebrow. "Kids playing pranks at two in the morning? Does that happen a lot in Peach Coast?"

"Well, no, ma'am." Errol gave me a puzzled frown.

"Then why are you so sure it happened this time?" I looked from Errol to Jed. Errol seemed confused, as though he didn't understand why I wasn't buying their explanation. Jed gave me a stony stare. Apparently, that was his story, and he was sticking to it. They were determined to dismiss the incident as the work of adolescent jokers.

I looked over my shoulder and up and down the street. No one was out now. My neighbors were all asleep. Maybe I was making too much of this. Maybe my conversation with my parents had unnerved me more than I'd thought it had. I wanted to believe the deputies because the alternative—my theory—wouldn't allow me to go back to sleep.

I eased my hold on Phoenix. "I appreciate you coming out to investigate."

Jed inclined his head. "You're welcome."

Errol's smile revealed even white teeth. "Our pleasure, ma'am."

"Why were you the ones who answered the call?" I glanced from Jed to Errol and back. "I thought you worked the day shift."

"Our shifts rotate." Jed shrugged. "Nothing changes much in Peach Coast, but no two days are the same for us. Is there anything else we can do for you, ma'am?"

"No, thank you." I shifted closer to my door. "Thanks again for coming out."

Jed turned to leave. "You're welcome. Again."

Errol tipped his hat. "Try to get some sleep, ma'am."

"Thank you. Be safe out there." I carried Phoenix back inside, locking the door securely behind me. "Maybe the deputies are right." I mounted the stairs back to my room. "It seems odd, but maybe it was just kids cutting through our yard. At two in the morning. On a school night." I settled Phoenix back onto the pillow where he'd been sleeping. "Whatever it was, let's keep this incident between us. No need to mention it to your grandparents. Okay?"

Phoenix curled up and went back to sleep. I took his silence as agreement and crawled into bed beside him. I didn't think I'd actually sleep, though. A glance at the alarm clock beside my bed showed that the entire event had taken less than half an hour. It had seemed like half the night.

While Phoenix slept, I stared at the ceiling. In the morning, after my run, I'd survey the perimeter of my house myself. Perhaps the trespasser had left behind marks or evidence that he'd been on my property, footprints or shifted potted plants. The more I thought about it, the more I discredited the theory of the meddlesome kids.

I believed the incident was something much more sinister. I believed someone had been trying to intimidate me by deliberately activating my security lights, knowing they'd wake me.

I believed tonight's visit had been a not-so-subtle threat.

Coming up empty after walking the perimeter of my house Wednesday morning for signs of an intruder hadn't reassured me. I was out of sorts after the early morning scare and the deputies' flippant attitude in response to my emergency.

Anna May's warm welcome as I purchased my usual from On A Roll helped settle my nerves. Hopefully, my doctored café mocha and Floyd's pleased expression—

"pleased" was a relative term for the grumpy old guy—when he saw the peach cobbler would further lift my spirits.

As I neared the exit, I finally registered the oddly familiar reaction of several other early morning customers. Just as on Monday, a handful of them kept shooting furtive and unsubtle glances across the dining area. Following the direction of their interest, I spotted Willy seated at the same front table. He was with Bobby Hayes. The two appeared to be in the middle of a heated exchange. Interesting.

Like the other café regulars, I wanted to listen in on their argument, but I was too far to hear anything over the competing sounds of conversations, laughter, and espresso machines. Anna May's café opened early and filled fast. Most of the tables were occupied. The customers who weren't focused on Willy and Bobby were reading, chatting with friends or family, working on laptops or tablets, or sitting alone people watching.

As I maneuvered closer to Willy and Bobby's table, I noticed a narrow coffee station that offered napkins, stirrers, various packets of sugar, creamers, and other coffee and tea additives. I pounced on it. Standing in profile to the two men, I forced myself to appear casual and aloof. I first pretended to go through my carryout bag, which had only the one small box of peach cobbler. Then I examined my café mocha with extra espresso—which was already sweet enough. I plucked a few napkins from their holder to do I-didn't-know-what with.

Although I strained to tune out other sounds, I still couldn't decipher their dispute. I could only hear their tightly controlled, angry voices as they threw words at each other. Waves of hostility rose from their table.

Their body language was combative. Fingers jabbed the air between them. Arms flew up and out like overly dramatic band conductors.

Seconds after I'd settled into my performance at the coffee station, Bobby surged from his seat and stormed out of On A Roll. He walked right past me. His strides were so quick, they generated a breeze that ruffled the napkins beside me. What had their argument been about? Could it impact the deputies' case against Jo?

Squaring my shoulders, I approached Willy. "Good morning."

He gave me a polite smile as he briefly rose to his feet. Tension shimmered around him. Angry color marred his pale cheekbones. "Good morning, Marvey. How are you?"

"I should be asking you that question." I studied him with concern. His eyes were shadowed and bracketed by dark circles. Like me, he must not have gotten much sleep last night. But whereas nerves had pulled me from bed early, I suspected grief was the reason for his restless night.

Willy gestured toward the spare seat at his table, the one Bobby had just vacated. "Do you have time to join me, or do you have to get to work?"

His change of subject didn't escape me. I decided not to push him. Yet.

I checked my watch before sitting. "I have a few minutes. Is that your breakfast?"

The white porcelain mug he embraced with both hands looked like it contained regular black coffee. Anna May must've been disappointed. She loved making the fancier drinks.

Willy shoved his broad hand through his thick hair. "I'm not very hungry."

I sat back on my chair, aware of the frequent and furtive attention we drew. "How long will you be in Peach Coast? You must be anxious to return home." Back to people who could be supportive as he grieved. Being here couldn't be helping him process Fiona's death, especially if he had to endure scenes like the one I'd witnessed between him and Bobby.

"The sooner, the better." Willy's knuckles turned white as his hands tightened around his mug. "But I want to do whatever I can to help the deputies catch Fiona's killer first."

"Of course. I'm so sorry." I felt bad that I may have upset him, but his response triggered another question in my mind. What had Willy given the deputies as his alibi? Granted, they didn't require much, unless your name was Jo. Betty had been cleaning. Bobby had been watching TV.

Willy claimed he'd driven his own car straight to To Be Read, and hadn't arrived until shortly after four PM. Had the deputies found a way to verify that? *Note to self: Ask Spence to verify the time Willy had checked into the Peach Coast Inn.* The hotel was one of his family's many holdings.

"I don't know how much help I can be to the deputies." Willy looked around the café as he drank his coffee. Did he notice the attention we were getting? "I reckon there's a whole town full of suspects they can pick from. But they don't seem to think their investigation will take long."

Was that because they were only focusing on one suspect, Jo—who, by the way, was innocent?

Frustrated, I turned my attention to the scene outside of the window beside us. The sky was a blinding shade of blue. A few old live oaks, Georgia's state tree, flourished along the sidewalk.

Turning back to Willy, I sipped my mocha. The creamy, sweet, caffeinated drink sent a jolt through my system. A couple more sips, and I just might wake up. "I'd think the deputies would appreciate having you here. It must be helpful to their investigation to have the insights of someone who knew Fiona well and cared about her."

"People who cared about her are definitely in short supply around here. That's one of the reasons I'm making arrangements to have Fiona's body sent back to Beaufort. I think she would've wanted to be laid to rest with family."

I blinked. "Wouldn't Fiona want to be buried beside Buddy? He was her family."

Willy's features tightened. Storm clouds gathered in his piercing gray eyes. "Was he? He surely didn't act like it."

"Because he didn't defend her against Betty's malicious gossip, you mean?"

"That's exactly what I mean." Anger flashed in his eyes like bolts of lightning.

"Then why didn't Fiona leave him?"

"She should have."

"But why didn't she? Didn't it bother her that someone she loved and who claimed to love her wasn't defending her?" It would bother me.

Willy shrugged listlessly. Even from across the table, I could feel his tension. "Fiona didn't know why Hayes wasn't defending her. Maybe he was afraid. Apparently, Betty has a temper."

I'd seen that firsthand. "What about Bobby? Couldn't Buddy get his son to stop gossiping about Fiona?"

Willy spread his hands. "All I know is Fiona was upset about Betty and Bobby lying on her, and Buddy not doing anything to stop them."

I couldn't imagine the husband who wouldn't do anything to defend his wife—or the wife who'd stay with a husband like that. "Did Fiona ever confront Betty or Bobby herself?"

"Yes, and I was proud of her for it. Fiona didn't like confrontations. But whatever she said didn't work, did it? Betty and Bobby continued to lie on her until the day she died."

"It sounds as though you think the deputies should be investigating Betty and Bobby."

"I'm letting the deputies handle their own investigation. I'm sure they'll find her killer—or killers."

I didn't share Willy's confidence. I took another drink from my mocha, inhaling the scent of chocolate and caffeine. The extra espresso helped.

Willy drained his coffee mug. The caffeine didn't seem to have given him any extra energy. "Are you going to ask me about my argument with Bobby? I'm sure you noticed it."

"Now that you mention it, I am curious." My smile was unrepentant.

Willy moved his shoulders restlessly. "Bobby was trying to pressure me into giving him the details of Fiona's will."

I frowned. "How would you know about it? Are you licensed to practice law in Georgia?"

Willy shook his head. "Fiona had asked for my advice when she'd updated her will after her marriage to Buddy. After Buddy died, Bobby had been angling to be her sole beneficiary. He really wanted to get his hands on the property Fiona had inherited from her uncle."

Something else occurred to me. "Since Fiona didn't have any heirs, who are her beneficiaries?"

Willy gave me a regretful look. "I'm not comfortable discussing her personal affairs with a stranger. But I can tell you she said she was leaving her uncle's property to me."

I sat back on my chair. "You must've been a *very* good friend."

This new information added another question to my growing list—did Fiona's generous bequest to Willy give him a motive to commit murder? Or did it give someone else another potential victim?

"You won't get away with it." Delores Polly confronted me as I was leaving On A Roll Wednesday morning.

Had she been waiting for me? I looked over my shoulder. Through the coffee shop's glass façade, I could see Willy seated at the table I'd just left. Delores was a few inches taller than me, which meant she had an even better vantage point. Had she been watching us? That was disconcerting. But then, Delores was the one who'd misrepresented my investigation to Betty.

Bracing myself, I faced the older woman. "Good morning, Delores. What won't I get away with?"

She narrowed her angry gray gaze. "Blaming innocent people for Fiona's murder in order to protect your friend."

I caught my breath. "That's not what I'm doing. And you're not the expert lip reader you claim to be. The information you gave Betty about what I supposedly said was wrong."

Under different circumstances, Delores and I could be friends. She played the church's piano beautifully for the Saturday evening choir. She was a regular library customer, picking up and dropping off books during her lunch hour every other Monday like clockwork. And judging by the tabby hairs on her beige-and-white patterned cap-sleeved blouse, she loved cats. But it was what it was.

"You're going around town saying poor Betty and Bobby killed Fiona. Don't you care that you're tearing this town apart?" Delores spoke in a stage whisper. She was making an effort not to draw the attention of the few pedestrians near us.

Amazing. Today was the start of only the fourth day of our investigation, and already Delores has me destroying the community. "Since we're discussing Fiona's murder and unfounded accusations, what makes you so certain Jo's guilty?"

Delores straightened her shoulders. She tried to look down her nose, but she wasn't that much taller than me. "The deputies are investigating her, aren't they?"

A hot bullet of overprotectiveness shot through me. "The deputies don't have *any* evidence that Jo's done *anything*. She's innocent until *proven* guilty. In fact, you're the one who's smearing the good reputation of an innocent person, not me."

Delores gaped at me like a fish out of water. "You

should let the deputies do their job instead of going around town trying to dig up dirt on people."

"Don't you want justice, Delores?"

She sniffed as though I'd offended her. "That's what the sheriff's department is for. You're not investigating anything. What you're doing is a character assassination."

I searched my mind for the right words to change hers. "I understand a lot of people didn't like Fiona—"

"That's an understatement." Her tone was as dry as dust.

"Perhaps there were valid reasons for that, but Fiona still deserves justice." I paused, searching Delores's stubborn expression. "We need to consider every conceivable possibility, not just narrow our focus to one person or even two people. I didn't know Fiona, but I do know Jo, perhaps better than you do. She cares deeply for this town. She opened her bookstore to share her love of reading with you."

A flicker of doubt crossed her thin, pale features before she scowled it away. "Betty and Bobby love this town too."

Why weren't my words working? I tightened my grip around my tote bag and strained to keep my voice level. "Someone in our community was killed. We're all scared. We want to find the killer and put them behind bars, but we want to arrest the *right* person, don't we?"

She fisted her small hands at her sides. "Are you saying Betty and Bobby are the right people?"

I swallowed a sigh. "No, I'm not."

"You don't have any evidence against them, so you don't have any right to accuse them of anything."

"The deputies don't have any evidence against Jo, either. So why are you suspicious of her?"

Delores did another one of her impressive fish impersonations. Circling her, I continued on my way to work.

To confront me the way she had, Delores must feel as protective of Betty as I felt toward Jo. If Delores believed Betty was innocent, why was she trying to intimidate me into leaving Betty alone? Why wasn't she looking for other suspects the way I was, or ignoring my inquiry? Was she really convinced Betty was innocent— or was she more afraid she was not?

CHAPTER 16

I'D ALREADY BEEN BUSY AT work when Viv, Floyd, and Adrian walked into my office Wednesday morning. Floyd must've made quick work of the cobbler I'd left on his desk. It wasn't much after eight o'clock, and I couldn't imagine him coming to see me before eating it.

"Thanks for the cobbler." Floyd tossed his gratitude toward me as he patted his stomach.

"You're very welcome." Even though I'd brought a cobbler to Floyd every work day for the past almost four months, he sought me out to thank me every time.

"Any new developments in the investigation?" Adrian settled his hips against the small blond wood circular conversation table beside my desk.

I took a moment to consider my answer, and gestured for Viv and Floyd to make themselves comfortable. They took the two gray guest chairs in front of my desk.

I passed over the details about my early morning intruder. There wasn't any evidence linking that event to our case, only a very strong hunch. Besides, I wasn't ready to talk about it. Instead, I filled them in on the information from Spence's contact in the coroner's office.

Viv wrapped her arms around her waist. "That gives us an idea about the killer. It's probably somebody with a bad temper."

The memory of Bobby's argument with Willy this morning crossed my mind. Bobby had been pretty angry. But then, Betty seemed angry all the time. "On another note, who do you think Fiona would've most likely retained as her lawyer to handle her will?"

"There are a couple of well-regarded law firms in Peach Coast." Viv's dark eyes shone with a gleam of interest.

Floyd frowned in consideration. "You should start with Buddy's lawyer, but you aren't going to get anything about Fiona's will out of him."

"I know." I balanced my elbows on my desk. "But maybe I could gain some insights based on nonconfidential information."

Viv gave me a dubious look. "Buddy Hayes retained Gillis & Sweets, Attorneys at Law. They're the highest-profile firm in town."

Floyd made a rude noise. "I don't know how Buddy was able to keep them. I did an internet search and found he hadn't moved any real estate for almost a year before he died. And by my calculation, those commissions had been small."

That was an interesting detail. "Why did his business income drop off?"

Viv played with her ruby earring. "Competition among real estate agents in Peach Coast got tougher. When Buddy first started, he was one of the only agents in town. Now, there's an agent in every neighborhood practically."

This information made me curious again about the size of Bobby's trust fund. "Would you say Buddy was accustomed to a high-profile lifestyle?"

Adrian laughed out loud. "Do dogs hunt?"

I took that as a yes.

"Those high-priced lawyers were just the beginning, though." Floyd used his fingers to count off Buddy's additional expenses. "He was keeping up appearances with Fiona, paying alimony to Betty, and helping Bobby with his bills."

I played with my book pendant. Today's image was the cover of James Baldwin's *If Beale Street Could Talk*. "Why was he helping Bobby with his bills?"

"Probably the same reason my parents are helping me." Adrian shrugged. "My student debt has me so broke between paychecks that I can't even pay attention."

I was intimately acquainted with the strain student loans could be on a person's budget. "How was Buddy able to pay for all of that if his business was struggling?"

"Fiona's accounting firm was doing well." Viv spread her hands, drawing attention to her crimson nail polish, which matched her silk blouse. "But I did wonder why they didn't sell Fiona's vacation cabin. It would've brought in a lot of money."

That was a good point. I had another one. "If Buddy was dependent on Fiona's income, then Fiona didn't marry Buddy for his money. And if I'm right about that, what other rumors about Fiona were false?" A calendar reminder drew my attention to my computer monitor. It was almost time for Floyd, Viv, and I to join Corrinne for our standing Wednesday morning managers meeting. "We'd better get moving. It's almost eight-thirty."

I followed Viv and Floyd to Corrinne's office. Adrian turned toward the circulation desk in the opposite direction.

Corrinne looked up as we arrived. "Ah, our meetings have been starting earlier ever since you joined us, Marvey."

I settled onto my usual seat on one of the cushioned armchairs in Corrinne's spacious office. "To be early is to be on time," I quoted.

The meeting progressed as it usually did. Corrinne invited us to give our department updates. Floyd reviewed the status of various reference resources and renewed his request for additional materials that were in demand by the community. Viv discussed the new books on order. This was an ever-dwindling wish list due to our tight budget. I was excited about our first-ever book swap, another event aimed at increasing engagement and awareness of the library and our resources. The book swap would also serve to help us launch our summer-quarter fundraiser.

"I've been promoting our Summer Solstice Book Swap on our social media pages." I glanced at my notes, highlighting the June twentieth event. "I'm donating some of my gently used books, and of course you're all welcome to do the same."

Viv's expression was dubious. "I'll see if I find any I can bear to part with. I'll let the circulation team members and Adrian know about this as well."

Corrinne gave us an update on her budget proposal meeting with the five-member town council. "The good news is that three of the council members are supportive of our budget requests. For now. The remaining two don't understand why we need a library when there's a perfectly good one in the next town over."

Looking around Corrinne's conversation table, I wasn't the only one left gaping at the lack of understanding of the value of libraries.

"Every community needs access to a well-funded library." I quoted the American Library Association motto: "'The best reading, for the largest number, at the least cost.'"

Corrinne nodded. "I tried to explain that to them."

"And of course, the library is about more than borrowing books." I gestured in the general direction of the circulation area. "There are job search services, educational programs...the list goes on."

Floyd grunted. "Do you think the three rational members will be infected by those two geniuses?"

"That's a possibility." Corrinne stared across her office, seemingly deep in thought.

Viv looked distressed. "What more can we do to persuade them to invest town revenue in the library?"

A glint of determination sharpened Corrinne's gaze. "We need a show of force. It's the squeaky wheel that gets oiled. Instead of monthly reports, let's send the council weekly reports on the number of books borrowed, reference requests, and community engagement events."

Viv tapped her pen against her notepad on the desk in front of her. "For the sixteenth straight week, we've increased our number of library applications. I'll include that in our weekly report."

"Excellent. Thank you." Corrinne looked around the

table. "The council meeting is at seven tonight. Are you all attending with me?"

We all nodded, and Viv volunteered that Adrian planned to join us.

"All of the subscription costs for our reference materials have gone up." Floyd's voice was tense. "If we don't get a bigger budget, we're gonna have to start picking and choosing which ones to keep."

A distressed hush slumped into the office. No one wanted that.

Corrinne broke the brittle silence. "Those are the stakes we're facing. So let's make sure we use those weekly reports to show the council how much this library means to our community and the good we can continue to do."

That was a plan I could support. In addition to the value the library had to the town, it also was my livelihood. If it closed, I'd be away from my family *and* without a job.

"We need to find Fiona's lawyer." My statement was met with a somewhat startled silence from Spence's end of the phone line later Wednesday morning. "Hello? Spence, are you there?"

"Hi, Marvey. Are you having a good morning?"

I threw my head back against my cushioned and battered seat. "Why do you make me go through this *every time* I call you?"

His chuckle was warm and surprisingly playful. "I'm trying to get you accustomed to life in a small town.

You need to slow down and enjoy the moment and the people in it."

I'd gotten this particular lecture from him so often I could've delivered it myself, even in my sleep. Little did he know if I couldn't help Corrinne and the rest of our library team squeeze a bigger budget out of the town council, I could be returning to big-city life.

I glanced at my watch. It wasn't yet noon, but the morning was sprinting by. "How was your morning, Spence?"

"It's been a good morning so far, Marvey. Thank you for asking. I've already fielded a couple of complaints that our article on the Peach Coast Women's Auxiliary's fundraiser for the animal shelter was too short and lacked enthusiasm."

A startled laugh escaped me. "That's what constitutes a good morning for you, reader complaints?"

His voice was rich with humor. "I was able to answer some emails and finish my coffee during those calls."

"Wait a minute." I frowned as I pictured the article on the auxiliary's event. "That article was a full page with photos." As I recalled, the story included several great, full-color photos of the volunteers and animals that benefitted from the fundraiser.

"My mama puts the same couple of ladies up to those complaints every year. One of these years, she's going to realize those calls don't make a bit of difference."

"But this is not that year." I found his predicament entertaining.

"No, it's not." He paused as though listening to my amusement. "Now, wasn't this better than just rushing into a thing?"

"No, actually, it wasn't, but I did enjoy your story."

Spence laughed. "Well, then, we're just going to have to agree to disagree. So what's this about Fiona's lawyer?"

"Do you know who they are?"

"No, I don't."

It had been a long shot, but one worth trying. Spence knew almost everyone in town. "Then we'll need to start with Buddy's lawyer. He retained Gillis & Sweets, Attorneys at Law."

He paused. I imagined him enjoying another sip of coffee as we talked. "Now why do we need to speak with Buddy's lawyer?"

"Buddy's lawyer may also represent Fiona, or at least know who Fiona's lawyer is."

"I assume this is about Fiona's will?"

"That's right."

"Marvey, I can make an appointment for us with the firm, but you do know that no lawyer—Buddy's or Fiona's—is going to tell us about her will, don't you? That'd be a breach of attorney-client privilege."

My stomach growled. It must be noon. I ignored the interruption. "I don't want the details of Fiona's will... Well, I wouldn't mind having the details, but what we need to know is whether she recently changed her will. Willy and Bobby were arguing about it in On A Roll this morning. Willy says Bobby claimed to have been named as the sole beneficiary in Fiona's will."

"What?" Spence's response was satisfyingly similar to my own.

"That was my reaction." My stomach complained again. I took a drink from my now-cold second cup of coffee. "But Willy says he doesn't believe Fiona would've left her uncle's property to Bobby."

"Based on the rumors around town, it's hard to believe she would've left *anything* to Bobby." Spence spoke as though deep in thought.

I nodded, then remembered we were having this conversation over the phone. "I agree. Willy said Fiona left that property to him."

"They must've been really good friends." Spence broke the brief but comfortable silence. "Of course, this gives Bobby *and* Willy a motive to kill Fiona."

"For Bobby, it's *another* motive," I corrected. "We already had him on our list because Fiona had control over his inheritance. With Fiona's death, it's possible he gets his money."

"Things aren't looking good for him." Spence's tone was as grave as I felt.

"If any of this is true, then no, they're not. But things don't look so great for Willy, either."

"Two people with the same motive."

"At least." I leaned into my desk, staring at my piles of reports, proofs, and other paperwork as I shifted my thoughts. "Speaking of Willy, could you check on something for me? Could you ask your Peach Coast Inn manager what time Willy checked into the inn, please?"

"Sure." Spence's voice filled with curiosity. "Why? What's going on?"

"I'm hoping to tie up loose ends." I plucked a pencil from my holder to roll between my fingers. "Willy said he drove straight from his home in Beaufort, South Carolina, to To Be Read. I have no reason to believe he's lying, but I'd feel better if we could verify it."

"I'll ask Isaiah, the manager, to find out." Spence sounded distracted. I wondered if he was creating a reminder note as we spoke. "I'm glad you thought of this.

Check-in is two PM, so he would've had time to check in, then drive—or even walk—to To Be Read before the four PM signing."

"That's a good point." A chill traced my spine.

I wanted to help bring compelling evidence to the deputies, evidence that would at least take the spotlight off of Jo, if not completely clear her name. But every time I reviewed our suspect list, I felt queasy at the thought that I might have come face-to-face with a cold-blooded killer.

Betty shifted her feet and hunched farther into her oversized cream sweatshirt. If that sweatshirt, dark sunglasses, and navy baseball cap were meant to be a disguise, they were epic fails. I hadn't known her long, but I'd recognized her right away.

I'd been on my way back to my office Wednesday afternoon, but after spotting Betty in front of the library's display of new and old books by Georgia authors, I was inspired to make a detour.

En route, I passed the customer line, which was winding its way toward the circulation desk. Employees from nearby businesses were visiting the library on their lunch hour. The Peach Coast Library didn't have money for self-checkout machines, at least not yet. For now, the counter was staffed by two part-time employees serving the dozen or so guests who'd made their selections. It cheered my heart. A busy library was a joyful place.

I stopped within an arm's length of Betty. A couple

of copies of Fiona's book, *In Death Do We Part*, were stocked within reach of us. The book was in high demand, in part because of Fiona's murder, I was certain. But also it was a very good book. I was halfway through it and found it hard to put down.

Connecting Fiona's book with Betty's disguise brought a mischievous smile to my lips. "Good afternoon, Betty. Can I help you find anything in particular?"

The other woman jumped at my greeting. "Marvey! What? No, I'm not... There's nothing in particular I'm looking for. No. Thank you. I'm just browsing. Well, actually, I'm not looking. For anything. I'm just waiting. For someone. Who's not here. Yet."

I scanned the library, noting new faces among the more familiar ones. None of the guests seemed to be waiting or watching for Betty. "Who are you waiting for?"

"That's none of your business." She stood straighter. Beads of sweat were forming on her pale brow and thin upper lip. I couldn't see how she'd be comfortable in that sweatshirt. The library was warm. Betty must feel like she was carrying around her own personal sauna.

"Would you like a glass of water?"

The offer surprised her. It surprised me too. "I'm fine." She used the tips of her fingers to dry her upper lip.

"While you wait for...whoever, I'm happy to make a couple of reading recommendations for you." I glanced at Fiona's book.

The rosy flush to Betty's cheeks suggested she realized I'd guessed her secret mission. "I said I don't need your help. Why don't you go find someone who does?"

I gestured toward her uncomfortable costume.

"Instead of trying to disguise yourself, why didn't you just buy Fiona's book online? It would've been so much more convenient, and no one would've been the wiser."

She straightened her shoulders, looking down her nose at me. "Don't you have work to do?"

The proverbial lightbulb turned on in my mind. "You don't want to actually pay for Fiona's book. Is that it? You resent her so much, you don't want to help her sales."

She glared at me, retaining her stubborn silence.

"All right, I want to talk with you about something else, anyway." I faced her, straining to read her reaction in her eyes. Her dark sunglasses made that difficult. "Please stop telling people Jo killed Fiona. You know that's not true."

Betty's flush deepened to a painful-looking red. "I... didn't... I never actually said she *killed* Fiona."

"But you implied it." I drew a calming breath. "I understand you being upset with *me*. *I'm* the one who's trying to draw the deputies' attention to other suspects for Fiona's murder, including you and Bobby. If you truly need to strike back at someone, strike *me*. But leave Jo out of this. She's *innocent*."

Betty's glare burned through her sunglasses. "So are my boy and I."

I recalled her response during our last exchange when I'd said the same about Jo. "Well, in that case, neither you nor Bobby have anything to worry about, do you?"

She narrowed her eyes. She remembered our exchange too. "Why should I keep quiet about Jo when you're still going around town saying things about Bobby and me?"

"I have never spread rumors about anyone in this

town." Despite my library training, it was a struggle to keep my voice low. "You're trying to turn public opinion against Jo, but this isn't a popularity contest. The person with the most likes doesn't win. This is a *murder* investigation. We're trying to protect Peach Coast and get justice for Fiona."

Betty had the decency to lower her gaze. She removed her sunglasses. "Fiona and I never had a kind word to say about each other."

That was true of Betty. I didn't have evidence Fiona had spoken ill of the other woman—unless you looked closely at the plot of Fiona's story. "Do you think that's why she wrote her book? Was she trying to discredit you?"

Betty's flushed and sweaty cheeks paled. Her eyes grew mean. "What are you talking about?"

"I think you know." I stripped all inflection from my voice. "Fiona's story is about a woman who suspects her husband's first wife killed him and staged it to look like a heart attack. Were you concerned some people might take that to mean *you* had something to do with Buddy's death?"

"*I* didn't have *anything* to do with Buddy's death." Betty lifted eyebrows she'd plucked to within an inch of their lives. "What would *I* have gained from killing him? He'd already *divorced* me. *Fiona* was the one who stood to gain from his death."

"And Bobby. Buddy left him a trust fund."

"Leave my boy out of this." Her words were clipped and angry. She used the pads of her fingers to swipe the sweat from her hairline. She really did look overheated.

"Why did you go to Fiona's signing? It was obvious you were angry with her. Did you intend to confront her about her story?"

"Have you forgotten Fiona was probably dead already by the time I got there?" Betty hooked her hands on her hips. Her voice was a low hiss. "What's supposed to have happened, huh? I killed her, went home, cleaned up, then went *back* to the bookstore?"

"Yes." Okay, it sounded crazy, but that was the only way it could've happened. Jo was innocent.

"That makes *no* sense."

"Why not?"

"For starters, it was *Saturday*." Betty's triumphant shout drew the disapproving attention of several nearby library guests, as well as Danny, who was restocking a bookcase.

"And?" I didn't even attempt to mask my confusion.

Betty gave me a smug smile. "I couldn't have killed Fiona. *Saturday* is my *cleaning* day." She announced this as though it was the eleventh commandment.

Somehow, I didn't think it would hold up in court. Betty would remain on my suspect list.

CHAPTER 17

I SPOTTED BOBBY THROUGH THE LIBRARY'S front picture window. He was leaning against a small dark
sedan parked at the curb. His arms and legs were
crossed in a pose that denoted he expected to be waiting
for a while. I made another detour on my way back to
my office, postponing lunch a few minutes more.

A quick check over my shoulder confirmed Betty
was still contemplating Fiona's book. If she decided to
borrow the mystery, I'd have at least a few minutes with
Bobby. If not...well, I'd figure out some way to smooth
things over with her if she caught me questioning her
son.

I pushed through the double glass doors of the library's main entrance and was hit by a blast of warm
air heavy with moisture from the nearby coast.

I approached Bobby with a smile. "You didn't want
to come in?"

Bobby's smile was full of boyish charm and subtle
humor. His dark blue jeans, ice-blue short-sleeved
shirt, and matching baseball cap looked more like a
uniform than casual wear. "Mama wanted me to wait

out here. Guess she doesn't want me to see her borrowing Fiona's book."

Surprised laughter burst from me. I glanced over my shoulder before turning back to Bobby. "So you know about that."

His only response was a shrug of his broad shoulders.

"I suppose Betty doesn't want anyone—not even you—to know she's curious about Fiona's book. Have you read it?" I studied his tan, blunt features. The brim of his cap shadowed his hazel brown eyes. His thick black hair hung a little long in the back.

It occurred to me I'd never seen a picture of Buddy Hayes. Bobby didn't look much like Betty, so he must favor his father. In that case, I could understand why Fiona would go after the man and why Betty resented the heck out of the woman for luring him away from her. Bobby was a handsome young man.

His smile remained in place as he returned my steady gaze. It felt as though he was determining how best to answer my question. "I have a copy. I'm not much of a reader, though." His shrug managed to convey both apology and humor.

My eyebrows knitted. "Why did you buy the book then?"

Bobby answered with another shrug.

I gave him a considering look. He wasn't much of a talker, either. "Does Betty know you have a copy of Fiona's book?"

"No, ma'am."

I didn't think so. If I were him, I wouldn't have told her, either. She wouldn't be pleased. "Do you know what the book is about?"

Again Bobby took his time answering. He lifted his ball cap and ran the thick, blunt fingers of his right hand through his glossy dark hair. His orange, black, and brown snake tattoo undulated as his fingers flexed. The scratches on the back of his hand were fading.

Bobby pulled his cap back on and crossed his arms before tossing me a half smile. "Doesn't the woman suspect her husband's ex-wife of killing him?"

Bobby's expression was open and friendly, yet I sensed him daring me to ask the obvious question: did he believe Betty may have killed Fiona because of her book?

No one believed Betty had anything to do with Buddy's death. And only Betty suspected Fiona of killing Buddy. The coroner had ruled Buddy died of natural causes. But could the plot of Fiona's book make Betty angry enough to do more than confront Fiona about it? Could it have pushed her to kill the woman?

As difficult as this was, I had to ask the uncomfortable question to clear Betty and Bobby of suspicion—or further pursue them as viable suspects.

I braced myself as best I could. "The plot of Fiona's book turns the tables on your mother. She'd been very vocal about her suspicions that Fiona had something to do with your father's death." When he didn't comment, I continued. "Did your mother attend the signing to confront Fiona?"

"Did she?" Bobby's gaze never flickered. His stance never shifted.

"Was your mother very angry about Fiona's book?"

Bobby removed his hat and dragged his fingers through his hair again. He resettled his cap, refolded his arms. His half smile grew into an engaging grin. "Ms. Marvey, I understand you're concerned about Ms. Jo. I feel really bad that the deputies consider her a suspect. Ms. Jo's a real nice lady. She has great taste in ink. But as nice as Ms. Jo may be and as bad as I may feel about the situation she's in, I'm not going to help you convince the deputies that either my mama or I—or both of us— are killers. That's just not going to happen."

Bobby had made that entire speech without making threats, raising his voice, or losing his smile. Impressive.

I inclined my head in acknowledgement of his message. He was at least as protective of his mother as I was of Jo. "Understood, Bobby. And I want you to understand I'm not going to let my friend be punished for something someone else has done."

Bobby touched the bill of his ball cap. "Understood, ma'am."

"One more question." I gestured toward his right hand. "How did you get those scratches?"

His eyes laughed at me. "Replacing a water heater, ma'am."

We took each other's measure one last time before we said our goodbyes. Well, I said goodbye. Bobby gave me another boyish smile.

He was a man of few words. During our conversation, he'd never volunteered a single detail about himself or his mother. I still didn't know how he felt about Fiona, if he believed she had something to do with his father's death, or whether he planned to read Fiona's book. Before re-entering the library, I glanced over my shoulder. Bobby was studying me with a brooding stare.

I sensed his languid persona masked a killer intellect.

I carried my leftover baked ziti, which I'd reheated for lunch in the staff kitchen, back to my office Wednesday afternoon. After my encounters with Betty and Bobby, I would've preferred chocolate-covered peanuts, though.

As I approached my desk, a warning whispered in the back of my mind. Was something different about my office, or was I imagining things? Laying the plastic container that held my lunch on my desk, I stepped back for a visual sweep of my room. Everything appeared as expected. My cluttered desk was still cluttered. My guest chairs and my conversation table and chairs seemed the same. With a mental shrug, I returned to my pasta. A knock on my door stopped me from crossing to my seat.

Adrian stood in the threshold, looking sheepish. "Sorry to interrupt your lunch, Marvey, but I pulled the information on the library cardholders that you were askin' for."

"No problem. This is a working lunch. Come in." I settled onto my chair. But as Adrian rounded my desk, the ground moved beneath me. I began to fall.

My gasp of surprise morphed into a cry of fear. Large hands gripped my upper arms. My head bounced back against a flat abdomen. My feet scrambled for stability on the plastic mat beneath my desk, even as Adrian pulled me up.

"Thank you." My gratitude was breathless.

What just happened?

"You're welcome." Adrian seemed equally disturbed.

I pressed a hand to my chest. My heart pounded beneath my palm. "Thank God you have such quick reflexes." My voice shook.

"I played basketball all through school. Are you okay?" His blue eyes were dark with concern as he regarded me. His hands still cuffed my arms. I couldn't tell whether it was to steady me or himself.

My muscles trembled as though an electric current cycled through my body. I nodded, and Adrian let his arms drop.

"What happened?" I turned back to my desk and stared at what used to be my chair. "The chair had probably been here when the bus depot opened sixty years ago, but it was sturdy."

The item in question now lay in parts on the gray Berber carpet. Its legs had rolled under my desk and toppled over. The back lay wobbling beside Adrian and me.

"That coulda been a bad fall." Adrian looked over his shoulder toward my window. "Your head would've banged up against the windowsill."

My gaze dropped to the oak wood sill—and its knife-sharp corner. I swallowed. Hard. "I might've knocked myself unconscious."

"Or worse."

An image of Fiona's lifeless body in Jo's storage room settled in my mind. I briefly squeezed my eyes shut, forcing it away, then turned back to Adrian. "Thanks again. I'm really glad you were here."

"I am too." He bent to collect the chair's legs, then crossed to put them beside my office door.

"Oh, I should do that." I followed him, carrying the broken chair back.

Adrian shoved one of the chairs from my little conversation table to my desk. "You can use this until you get a new one." He stepped back.

"I'll leave a note for maintenance." I surreptitiously checked the replacement chair, giving it a rough shake to check its construction. It seemed fine. "I keep thanking you." I chuckled, struggling to feel normal again.

"And I keep sayin' you're welcome." He flashed an unsteady grin. "You're sure you're all right? It was a close call."

"Yes, it was, but I'm fine now. Why would the chair have collapsed now when it's been fine all week?"

"Beats me. I'm just glad you're okay." Adrian headed toward the door. "I'll leave that cardholder report with you, then. Let me know if you have any questions."

I glanced at the report on my desk. "Right. I want to analyze the demographics of our new cardholders to see who we're reaching."

"I'll leave so you can get to it." He looked back over his shoulder. "And to your lunch before it gets any colder."

I returned to my desk. My poor baked ziti. Not even a few wisps of rising steam remained, but I was too hungry to care. I settled onto the sturdier—I hoped—chair and returned to my lunch. I tried to read the report Adrian had printed for me, but my mind kept straying.

The food helped me concentrate. It was hard to think on an empty stomach, and I'd need to remain focused if I was going to help campaign for a bigger library budget as well as work on clearing Jo's name.

"You don't have to call me every day." Jo's voice traveled down the phone line with exaggerated patience Wednesday evening.

"I know I don't have to." I balanced my elbow on my desk and kept one eye on the clock in the lower-right corner of my computer monitor. I needed to check on Phoenix before leaving for tonight's town council meeting. "I want to. How did it go today?"

"The same as yesterday, unfortunately." Jo's sigh was full of frustration. "Customer traffic is still at a snail's pace."

"We're only four days out from the murder. It's probably too early to be worried."

Jo sighed again. "My mind agrees with you, but it's hard not to be anxious. This is my livelihood. My store provides jobs for the community. If my profits take a serious nosedive, I need to fix it fast, or a lot of people will be affected."

My grip tightened on my cell phone as I picked up Jo's tension. Everything she said was right and identified another reason why our inquiry was so important. The longer Jo remained under suspicion and Fiona's murder remained unsolved, the more damage would be done to Jo, personally and professionally.

"Clearing your name so the deputies can actually solve Fiona's murder will go a long way toward restoring normalcy in Peach Coast." I spoke with confidence, hoping to ease some of Jo's anxiety.

"You're right, and I appreciate everything you and Spence are doing to help me."

"That's what friends are for." I imagined Jo sitting in her office—or perhaps she was at her customer counter—smiling.

"For keeping each other out of jail? I appreciate that." Her voice was thick with humor. "Have you had any new developments in the inquiry?"

"Unfortunately, nothing concrete, at least not yet." I filled her in on my strange conversation with Betty and my even stranger conversation with Bobby.

"Well, a lot of people are fixated on certain routines." Jo sounded as confused as I'd felt after speaking with Betty. "I suppose if you're used to cleaning on Saturdays and it had become a habit, you'd assume everyone would feel the same way."

"I'm not buying it, Jo. It sounded a little delusional to me."

She laughed. "It does to me too."

Having brought a smile to her day, my job was done. "Same time tomorrow?"

Jo chuckled. "You don't have to check in with me every day."

"But I want to."

After wrapping up our call, I hurried home. I couldn't be late for the council meeting. We needed everyone to show up in support of the increased budget request. This vote was too important.

I felt like a member of a family of ducklings as Viv,

Floyd, Adrian, and I followed Corrinne across the town hall's lobby after the council meeting Wednesday evening. Corrinne stopped less than an arm's length from Mayor Byron Flowers, who was pontificating in the direction of several town council members.

The council president looked up as we arrived. The expression in the older gentleman's watery brown eyes telegraphed he knew why we were there, even if the mayor didn't. In fact, I had the sense he and the other council members had been expecting us.

Our head librarian straightened her shoulders. Viv, Floyd, Adrian, and I flanked her.

"Excuse the interruption, Mayor Flowers." Corrinne's voice was clipped to military precision. The council members used her interruption to vanish. "We were disappointed by your insistence that the council table tonight's discussion of the library budget. May we ask why you did that?"

Byron was a tall fit man with impeccable—and ostentatious—taste. His double-breasted brown pinstriped suit probably cost as much as the library's annual budget. His toothy grin shouted, "I want to be everybody's friend!"

The mayor's cerulean blue eyes glinted at my boss in barely veiled admiration. "Corrie! Seeing you always brightens my day."

Corrie? Viv, Adrian, and I exchanged quick, questioning glances. Floyd looked like he wanted to pull up a chair and rip open a bag of popcorn.

Corrinne's temper chilled the air around me. "Why did you table our budget discussion, *Mayor Flowers*? That increase is crucial to our goal of expanding our outreach and providing more services to our community."

It was little things like Corrinne's emphasis on the mayor's title and name that made me think she and the town official had a history. I didn't know her well enough to ask. Yet.

"The meeting was running a little long, didn't you think so, Corrie?" Byron folded his hands together in front of his hips.

Virtual steam wafted from Corrinne's ears, seeming to increase the heat in the crowded lobby. It was disconcerting to see someone who was usually so coolly serene on the cusp of erupting in anger. "*Mayor Flowers*, I'd prefer you address me as Corrinne. And no, I didn't think the meeting was running long. Were you late for a hair appointment?"

I caught my breath. Corrinne had asked the question with the feigned sincerity for which Southerners were famous. Now I wanted to pull up an armchair beside Floyd and share his make-believe popcorn.

"Touché, Corrie—Corrinne." The golden-blond hair currently under discussion glinted beneath the bronze lantern chandeliers. The mayor smoothed a hand over its perfection. "I'm sorry you're disappointed—"

"I'm not the only one who's disappointed. My team and I asked our patrons to attend tonight's meeting to show their support for our budget request." She threw both hands out to encompass us. "My team's here tonight because of that agenda item, and yet you insisted the council remove it."

Byron's gaze remained on me. "You must be Marvella Harris from New York City. I'm Mayor Byron Flowers."

I inclined my head in greeting. "Do you support increasing the library funding, Mayor Flowers?"

The mayor seemed taken aback by my directness. In

my peripheral vision, I saw Viv and Adrian send me a quick look. Floyd smiled. Too late, I recollected Spence's numerous lectures on "easing into a discussion." This probably would've been a good time to practice that.

Byron bounced on his toes. "I understand you've been doing some amateur detecting, Ms. Marvella."

Proceed with caution. "What makes you think that, Mayor?"

"Oh, I hear the rumors that get around town." Byron clasped his hands behind his back and puffed his chest forward. "A good mayor keeps one ear to the ground. Now, I don't know how things operate in a big city like New York, but here in Peach Coast, we have plenty of law enforcement types. We don't need any more help." He winked. I could envision him, standing in front of a mirror, practicing the gesture.

I tried to arrange my features to convey clueless innocence. My older brother, DeAndre, insisted I excelled at that. "I don't know what you consider 'amateur detecting,' Mayor. I've only been asking a few questions out of curiosity about my neighbors."

Byron looked skeptical. "There's no need for that, Ms. Marvella. I assure you, our law officers don't need any help." He shifted his attention back to Corrinne. "In fact, I'm surprised you'd let her get involved, *Corrinne.* Why, it gives the impression your staff doesn't have enough to do."

Let me get involved? Byron's words stirred me to introduce him to a side of me he probably wouldn't enjoy meeting. I was aware of Viv and Adrian giving me more distance. Floyd seemed almost gleeful.

I opened my mouth to set Byron straight about my

needing anyone to *let* me do anything, but Corrinne spoke first.

Her gaze continued to blast the mayor. "Are you attempting to tie the budget of the town's library and resources to our individual behavior, *Mayor Flowers?*"

Beside me, Floyd grunted. "Sounds like it."

Viv crossed her arms over her flowing silver blouse. "Voters, especially women, will have a problem with your implication that a woman needs permission to exhibit intellectual curiosity, Mr. Mayor. What do you think, Adrian?"

The librarian assistant seemed surprised to be brought into the conversation, but quickly rallied. He shoved his large hands into the front pockets of his tan Dockers and rocked back on his brown loafers. "Beggin' your pardon, Mr. Mayor, but I think you're outside of your mind with that kind of talk."

Even I could figure out the gist of Adrian's response. I struggled to contain a smile as I turned back to Byron. His face was flushed with embarrassed color. His gaze bounced from Floyd, to Viv, to Adrian, then me before returning to settle on Corrinne.

"That's not what I meant." Byron's voice stalled. He appeared to search for an explanation. The future of five votes depended on it. "I mean, all I meant was that...citizens can't take matters into their own hands. I mean, the deputies are responsible for the investigation, Ms. Marvella."

"I didn't mean to imply otherwise, Mayor." I widened my eyes to emphasize my clueless innocence. "But I'd really like to know whether you support the proposed increased for the library's budget next year."

Byron cleared his throat. "My staff and I are looking

into that. Please excuse me. I have to have a few more words with the town council president. Have a good night." His eyes locked with Corrinne's before he spun away.

I watched him walk off in the opposite direction from the council president. "Why would the mayor be opposed to increasing our funding?"

"It's an election year." Floyd sounded disgusted, as though he'd gotten a dry pastry. "He probably doesn't want to have to defend supporting a bond issue on the ballot."

Adrian nodded. "Or explaining to us why he doesn't support it."

I hid a smile behind my hand. Was he anxious about explaining his lack of support to all of us...or just *Corrie*?

CHAPTER 18

T HEY SAY AUTHORS SHOULD WRITE what they know. If that bit of conventional wisdom held true for Fiona's debut mystery, the novel may have prompted the sheriff's department to open an investigation into Buddy's death. In fact, several people may have recognized themselves in the story and had their feelings hurt. The narcissistic ex-wife whose every conversation was a ballad of self-pity. The stepson who drifted through life without direction or goals. I wondered about the "dangerously attractive" business partner. Was there anything personal between Fiona and Nolan, or was their relationship all about business?

I rolled off the puffy seafoam sofa, where I'd sprawled with a copy of Fiona's *In Death Do We Part* shortly after returning from the town council meeting Wednesday night. Earlier, I'd changed into baggy sapphire cotton shorts and an oversized navy T-shirt. Grabbing my empty glass, I padded barefoot into the kitchen for a refill of water.

Although I'd only been reading the mystery for two days, I already was more than halfway through it. Fiona's story was indeed a page turner. She'd built a world of diverse characters, each creepier than the last. The protagonist was empathetic. The villainous ex-wife was thoroughly unlikeable.

After adding fresh ice and refilling my water glass, I returned to the living room. Phoenix had taken my spot, stretching out on the sofa. He tracked my progress as I re-entered the room. This wasn't the first time he'd displaced me. Without missing a beat, I settled onto the opposite end of the cloth sofa. I could feel him staring at me as I drank my water.

I glanced up and met his glare. "Why are you looking at me as though I've asked you for money?"

He didn't bother to explain himself. Instead he continued to track my movements.

"I understand why Fiona was getting such rave reviews for her book. And she was deserving of every word. Snappy dialogue. Tight pacing. Lots of tension."

I showed Phoenix the cover. The title was set in big, bold silver type at the top. Fiona's name appeared below in similar but smaller type. The image was a cozy cottage home at night. "What do you think? Do the house and scenery remind you of Peach Coast? The fictional town in her book is Peachberry Corners."

As a neighbor, I mourned Fiona's death because of what her murder meant to the community. As a reader, I grieved the loss of all the great stories she could've written for the world.

"The question, Phoenix, is how close is this story to Fiona's own experiences?"

Phoenix rose to his paws. He crossed the width of the sofa, then curled down onto my lap in the space between the book and my torso. I kissed the top of his furry head.

"In this story, the protagonist suspects her husband's first wife of killing her husband and making it look like a heart attack." Not wanting to unduly alarm Phoenix, I kept my voice low and soothing. "In real life, Buddy's death was ruled to have been caused by an acute myocardial infarction. A heart attack. According to the other librarians and Spence, neither Betty nor Fiona was ever accused of killing Buddy, although Betty did her best to cast suspicion on Fiona. Spence should know. His newspaper did several articles on Buddy's death. The deputies never suspected foul play, but Betty did."

I stroked the bridge of Phoenix's nose. His purr was long and low. I slipped my bookmark in between the pages of Fiona's book to mark my place. Continuing to pet Phoenix, I rose to my feet to pace between the living and dining rooms.

"Question—does Fiona really believe Betty could've poisoned Buddy and made it look like a heart attack?" I meandered between the two downstairs rooms. "Or was the book simply a way for Fiona to get even with Betty for the rumors she'd spread?"

Deep in thought, I paced for a while with only Phoenix's purrs breaking the silence. The lingering scent of my after-work lemon-orange herbal tea soothed me. My steps carried me past my two floor-to-ceiling built-in white wood bookcases. A series of framed photographs of my family and friends crowded the mantel above my black-and-white fireplace.

"Betty and Bobby claim they haven't read Fiona's book." I kept walking and talking although I sensed him nodding off in my arms. He was an exceptionally good listener, even on his worst days. "But they wouldn't have to read the whole book. The review in the *Crier* and the book's description on the back cover gives readers enough information to know what the book's about."

I settled carefully back onto the sofa, aware of Phoenix resting drowsily in my arms. "But why did Fiona write this story? Was it payback for Betty smearing her reputation with vicious gossip? Or did she truly suspect Betty of killing Buddy?"

Anna May's hot pink T-shirt this Thursday morning read *Coffee: A Friend for Life.* "Your usual, Marvey?"

"Yes, please, Anna May, with *two* slices of your delicious peach cobbler to go."

The sounds of my low-heeled navy pumps against the hardwood flooring were muted beneath the laughter and chatter of friends meeting for coffees and cakes. My progress to the customer counter was slow as I stopped to return cheerful greetings from the other regulars. The air was redolent with the sweet scents of pastries and flavored coffees.

It was one of the rare mornings in which I'd driven to work. Rather than staying late at the library, tonight I planned to take files home in an effort to get caught up—perhaps even get ahead?—with my projects. Hope springs eternal.

"Marvey, why did you have to go and tell me about that crime fiction series?" The question carried across the room from Ned the bike shop owner. "Now you know I'm hooked, and I'm already busier than a moth in a mitten. I don't have time to be readin'.'"

I gave him my best librarian's smile. "There's always time to read a good book, Ned. And if you're tight on time, watch less baseball."

The café erupted into gales of laughter. Non-sports fans teased the groaning baseball fans. Anna May looked on with near-maternal pleasure.

I stopped at the counter, adjusted my American Library Association canvas tote, and offered exact change for my purchase. "How's your week treating you, Anna May?"

"I can't complain. Thanks, Marvey. And how's yours?" She took my cash and turned it into a receipt.

"About the same. Pretty busy."

"Maybe you wouldn't be so busy if you weren't going around town, saying Betty and her boy killed Fiona." The voice that joined our conversation had not been invited.

The temperature in the café dropped suddenly and drastically as I turned to greet Delores. "I wish you'd stop saying that, Delores, because it's not true."

"What are you talking about, Dee?" Anna May sounded irritated and confused.

I surreptitiously surveyed the dining area to find we'd attracted attention from a number of nearby customers, including Dabney and Etta, who had their usual table near the counter.

"No, she hasn't," Dabney defended me loudly.

Delores gaped at him. "How could you know? You weren't here when she did it." She threw her arm toward the back of the coffee shop. "It was during lunch on Tuesday. And she was at a table all the way in the back."

I opened my mouth to defend myself, but Etta spoke over me.

"That doesn't make any sense." The retired woman snorted. "Tuesday was two days ago. If Marvey had been spreading rumors about Fiona's murder since then, someone here would've heard them."

Anna May tapped my shoulder to gain my attention before serving me my mocha and cobblers. "And Marvey wouldn't have accused Betty or Bobby of murder without evidence. That would be slander, and she could be sued."

Delores's eyes swung from Anna May to Dabney and Etta before landing on mine with a glare. "Well, she may not have said that directly, but that's what she meant."

Dabney scowled. "Well, if she didn't say it directly, then you don't know what she meant."

Anna May took on a more reasonable tone than the septuagenarian. "Listen now, Dee, everyone knows Marvey and Jo are good friends. If Betty were being accused of a crime you know she didn't commit, wouldn't you help clear her name?"

Delores angled her chin. "Yes, I would, but I wouldn't slander an innocent person to do that."

Anna May shrugged. "Neither is Marvey."

I started to defend myself again, but again Etta spoke first.

"Wisdom, justice, and moderation, Dee. Why, surely you recognize our state motto. Marvey's after the truth. We all should be supporting her. It's the only way to keep our community safe."

Anna May planted her hands on her counter. "So if you don't have anything nice to say, Dee, hush it."

Delores's eyes widened with shock. Her right fist tightened around the purse strap on her shoulder before she spun on her heels and marched out of the café.

I swallowed the lump of emotion in my throat as I tracked her exit. "I'm so sorry. I think I just cost you a customer." My voice was husky.

Anna May humphed. "Don't mind that. You have to know Dee. She could start an argument in an empty house."

"That's the truth." Dabney grunted. "That woman craves attention. She'll be back."

I blinked rapidly to force back tears before shifting to face my three champions. I cleared my throat. "Thank you so much for defending me. You didn't have to do that, but it means so much that you did."

"Well, we appreciate you too, sweetie." Etta's smile was warm and caring. "You moved in here from New York City and in just a few short months, you made yourself a part of our Peach Coast family."

Dabney's usual cantankerous lines softened to grandfatherly concern. "But if you really are looking into this murder, you just make sure you're careful."

"I will be. I promise." I turned to find the door before their caring melted me into a puddle.

You made yourself a part of the Peach Coast family.

Leaving my family behind in Brooklyn had torn a gaping hole in my heart. Etta's words had filled that hole with love and kindness. They'd given me confirmation I'd been welcomed into this community. I didn't just have a house and a job here. I had a home and a family. I was almost overwhelmed with emotion.

I stealthily wiped a tear from my eye on the way to the door. A movement in my peripheral vision captured my attention.

As my Southern friends might say, *Well, butter my butt and call me a biscuit.* What was Betty doing with Willy Pelt?

CHAPTER 19

S EATED ALONE AT A BACK table, Willy and Betty were deep in conversation, neither seeming aware of their surroundings. The tables around them were empty. Betty picked daintily from the pecan Danish on the porcelain plate in front of her. Willy ignored his coffee. Whatever he said to Betty made her blush and giggle like a schoolgirl.

Since I was driving today, I could delay my leaving for the library a few minutes longer. I made my way to the condiments counter and found a position that allowed me to keep Willy and Betty in my line of sight while remaining relatively hidden. Just then, Betty rose from their table. A winsome smile curved her lips. She looked ten years younger. Willy stood with her. He took her right hand in both of his. His touch lingered. Curious.

Betty turned to leave. Startled, I spun so my back was to her. I waited a moment or two, then checked the coast was clear to approach Willy. He saw me coming.

"Good morning, Willy." I plastered a guileless smile

to my face. "I see you're still coming to the café. The coffee and pastries are delicious, aren't they?"

Willy stood with a smile. "Yes, indeed they are. It's good to see you again, Marvey."

I gestured toward the exit behind me. "Was that Betty Rodgers-Hayes leaving the café? What did she want with you?" I couldn't afford the luxury of subtlety if I wanted to get to work on time.

Willy rolled his eyes. "Yes. She's a piece of work, isn't she?"

I withheld comment. From his smiles and lingering touch, Willy didn't seem to find Betty to be much of a burden. Why would he claim he did? His credibility had just taken a significant hit. "What did she want?"

Willy stretched his shoulders as though easing the tension building there. "She heard about my argument with her son. She's not happy about it."

"Oh, I'm sure. She's a textbook helicopter mother. I'm not surprised she'd try to fight Bobby's battles for him. Poor Bobby." I considered Willy's brown slacks and tan button-down shirt. They looked new. Understandable. It had been five days since Fiona had been murdered. I doubted he'd expected to be here so long.

"I don't feel sorry for Bobby. They deserve each other." Willy pushed his hands into the front pockets of his pants and sent a glare around the café. "I'm counting the days until I can watch this town disappear in my rearview mirror."

His criticism stirred my protective instincts toward my new home. "Peach Coast is a great town, and the people are warm and friendly. I'm sorry that wasn't Fiona's experience."

Willy huffed a laugh without humor. "I don't know if

I agree with you about this town *or* the people. I haven't felt welcome here since people found out I was Fiona's friend. In fact, someone tried to run me over last night."

My eyes stretched wide. "What?"

"Someone tried to kill me last night." Willy looked to a nearby window and gestured vaguely toward the streets outside. "I was having dinner at a restaurant near the inn. When I left, a car tried to run me over in the parking lot."

"Did it aim at you? I mean, was someone speeding through the parking lot, or were they targeting you?"

"They were targeting me. I'm sure of it." Willy seemed insulted by the question. "One minute, it was parked in a parking space. The next, it was coming straight for me, full speed."

How frightening! "Were you hurt?" I scanned his face and his arms, left bare by his short-sleeved shirt. I didn't notice any scrapes or bruising.

"No, thank goodness." He shook his head. "I was able to jump out of the way, so it sped past me. It never stopped. It never hesitated. It just sped right at me."

"You're lucky you weren't hurt."

Willy shook his head again as though overwhelmed. "Just thinking about it rattles me. I've been trying not to dwell on it."

"Can you describe the car?"

Willy huffed another breath as he stared at the café's floor. "It was a sedan. Small. A small, dark sedan. Perhaps black or dark blue or gray. But it was dark, so I'm not sure of the color."

I held his eyes in a direct stare. "You should file a report."

He shook his head. "No, no. I don't want to do that."

I blinked. "Why not?"

He waved a hand flippantly. "There's no call to make a big deal out of this."

My eyebrows shot up. "Someone's already made it a big deal by trying to kill you."

Willy shook his head again. "If I file a report with the deputies, it'll only prolong my stay here, and I'm not looking to stay any longer than it takes to make arrangements to transport Fiona's body and attend the reading of her will."

I couldn't fathom not wanting to file a police report after someone aimed their car at me and tried to run me over. In fact, if an attempt had been made on my life, I would've gone directly to the sheriff's office to file a report and demand round-the-clock protection. In fact, I would've slept at the desk right next to Deputy Whatley.

I tightened my grip on my handbag. "You have to file a report and get this attack on record."

Willy remained stubborn. "They were probably trying to scare me into leaving town, which is exactly what I'm going to do as soon as possible."

I crossed my arm over my grass-green linen blouse, which I'd paired with my cream cotton pants. "Who'd want you out of town so badly that they'd try to kill you?"

Willy frowned. "I think we both know the answer to that."

Indeed. Didn't Bobby drive a dark sedan?

Someone tried to kill me last night.

Willy's words replayed in my head, but now with an ominously personal meaning. When I entered my office Thursday morning, the sight of the battered blue reception chair I was using until my desk chair could be repaired or replaced stopped me midstride. Was yesterday's accident really an accident?

Crossing to my desk, I stored my chocolate handbag and canvas tote in my bottom drawer. Then I hooked my hands on my hips and turned back to study my ruined chair, which lay in pieces beside my door. That had been a close call. Would someone have deliberately tried to hurt me? I didn't want to believe it, but I needed the truth.

I forced my reluctant limbs back across my office and hunkered in front of the destroyed chair. Yesterday, when Adrian had helped me carry its remnants to the corner, we hadn't taken a close look at it. Maybe we should've. In the light of a new day, I examined the pieces and parts of the furniture and was troubled by what I saw. Three of the four screws intended to attach the chair's seat to its rolling legs were missing. The fourth screw had worked itself loose. None of this could've happened on its own.

Someone had tampered with my chair.

My blood chilled. In my mind, I relived the events from yesterday. The chair collapsing under me. Adrian catching me as I started to fall. My head had been so close to the windowsill. I was glad I'd gotten Adrian that peach-cobbler thank you.

Struck by inspiration, I pushed myself to my knees and crawled over to my desk to study the carpet.

"What are you doing?"

My heart almost stopped at the sudden and unexpected sound of Viv's voice from my doorway. I sat back on my heels and pressed the palm of my right hand to my chest. "You scared me."

"Sorry." She scanned the carpet as she walked toward me. "Did you lose something?"

"No." I pointed toward the pale gray carpet weave in front of my desk. "Do you see this indentation?"

Viv kneeled beside me, pushing the dark brown tresses of her inverted bob away from her heart-shaped face. "Yes."

I measured it with my thumb before crawling to the left side of the desk. "And here?" I measured that section as well.

Viv followed me. "Yes." She sounded confused. "What are you doing?"

We both flinched as we looked up toward my doorway. Adrian and Floyd stood just inside my office, regarding us with concern.

I pushed myself to my feet and offered Viv a hand.

She gave our coworkers an accusatory look. "You scared us."

"That's what was different." I brushed off the knees of my pants. "I knew something was off with the spacing in my office yesterday afternoon, but I couldn't put my finger on it." With my right index finger, I directed Adrian's and Floyd's attention to the carpet. "Based on those indentations, it seems as though someone had shoved my desk back and to the right, which would also have moved my chair from its usual spot."

Adrian's eyes stretched wide. "Closer to the edge of the windowsill."

I nodded. "By at least two and a quarter inches."

He and I shared a look. Was he remembering how

he'd placed himself between me and the windowsill when he'd caught me yesterday? I was.

Adrian's Adam's apple bobbed as he swallowed hard. "Thanks for the cobbler."

I blinked. "Thank *you*."

Floyd glared at the carpet. "Why would someone move your desk?"

"I'm glad you asked." I gestured toward Adrian in silent encouragement for him to bring Viv and Floyd up to speed on the subject of my booby-trapped chair and its missing screws.

Viv sank onto the spare seat at my conversation table. "Who'd do something like that?"

Floyd watched me closely. "Did you tick off one of the staff?"

"Floyd!" Viv admonished him.

"I hate to say it, but he has a point." Adrian gave me an apologetic look. "I like you, Marvey, but visitors aren't allowed back here unless one of us comes with them, so how would a stranger have been able to rig your chair?"

Floyd laughed. "People get back here all the time. That policy may cut back on *how many* get past the desk, but it doesn't eliminate intruders altogether."

I wrapped my arms around my waist. "During the four months I've been here, I've noticed the circulation desk unstaffed at least half a dozen times."

Viv pressed a hand to the base of her throat. Her perfectly manicured nails were polished a shade between frost and pink, complementing her pale rose blouse. "Those rules are in place for a reason. I'm going to start fining people who don't remain at the desk during their entire assigned time."

"Just last week, Ms. Betty got past the desk and into Marvey's office." Adrian jerked a thumb toward Viv. "And we were both at the desk."

I searched my mind for other plausible ideas. "Since I don't think I've offended a coworker, an outsider must've gotten into my office while I was out."

Floyd grunted. "Okay, then this must've happened yesterday. The way they took apart your chair, they intended for it to collapse right away."

"I agree." I looked over my shoulder toward the remnants of my office furniture. "Isn't Bobby Hayes a repair person?"

Adrian frowned. "That's right. He works at the repair shop and hardware store."

I hesitated. "He'd know how to tamper with a chair to make it collapse, and he'd have the tools to do it. I spoke with him in the parking lot Wednesday afternoon while he was waiting for Betty."

He'd been leaning against a dark blue compact sedan.

I shook off the memory of Bobby's car and faced my team of librarians. "Have you started Fiona's book?"

Floyd rocked on his feet. "Finished it last night. It was surprisingly good."

Adrian raised his hand. "I have a couple of chapters left."

Viv nodded. "Me too."

Close enough. "What are your impressions? Do you think the story could've made Betty or Bobby angry enough to kill Fiona?"

Floyd snorted. "I could see it. It sounds like the gossip Betty had been saying about Fiona since Buddy died, but applied to Betty."

I shared my gaze with each of them. "Did the sheriff's office investigate Buddy's death?"

Adrian nodded. "According to the paper's reporting, Mr. Buddy died of a heart attack. Ms. Betty went around claiming he didn't have a bad heart, but the autopsy showed he had coronary artery disease."

I leaned back against my desk and crossed my arms. "How do you know Betty was behind the rumors? Could it have been someone else?"

Floyd shrugged. "Well, I didn't pay *that much* attention to it. But from what I remember, the gossip was contained only to people who were close to Betty, and everyone was saying the same exact thing she'd said. Like a pandemonium of trained parrots. No one else gave Buddy's death a second thought. Buddy didn't have what people call 'healthy habits.'"

I sank onto my temporary chair. "I wish I could make more progress on this investigation. I feel like I'm not getting anywhere. What about the writers group? Do you think we might have some suspects there?"

Floyd grunted. "Tons. No one liked her, especially after she was published."

I raised my eyebrows. "Were a lot of the members jealous?"

Floyd tilted his head in thought. "Yeah, but they didn't care for her much before that, either."

"Why not?" Adrian asked.

Floyd considered his answer. "I think they didn't like her because Zelda, the group's president, didn't like her, and they're all loyal to Zelda. They knew her longer."

I shook my head in amazement. "How do you know all of this?"

He shrugged. "I belonged to the group for a little

while. I left a couple of months after Fiona joined. I wasn't getting as much from their meetings as I'd wanted."

Excitement propelled me forward on my chair. "Floyd, are you writing a book?"

His face darkened with a blush. He looked at us self-consciously. "Yeah."

I clasped my hands in excitement. "Wow! That's wonderful. What are you writing?"

"A children's fairytale," he muttered.

I blinked. There was so much more to the grumpy old man than met the eyes.

CHAPTER 20

"**E**XCUSE ME, MARVEY, BUT THE deputies, they're back." Adrian sounded concerned. Deputies Jed Whatley and Errol Cole circled him to enter my office Thursday morning.

"Thank you, Adrian." I offered my young coworker a reassuring smile. Still appearing anxious, he moved away but left the door open. Did he plan to linger outside my office to eavesdrop on my meeting with the deputies? I directed my guests to the visitors' chairs. "How can I help you, deputies?"

The two men removed their campaign hats and settled onto the seats. Errol's body language was tentative. Something appeared to be troubling him. Jed's movements were tight, as though he was irritated. Irritation seemed to be his default mood.

"Ms. Marvey." Jed's opening was delivered on a long-suffering sigh. "Perhaps you could clear up a misunderstanding for us."

I spread my hands. "I'm happy to help if I can, deputy."

"Alright, then. I appreciate that." Jed glanced at

Errol before continuing. "Ms. Betty came to see us the other day. It seems she thinks you're *still* investigating Ms. Fiona Lyle-Hayes's murder. Now, that just can't be true. Could it, Ms. Marvey? Because Deputy Cole and I, we remember specifically asking you *not* to investigate."

From Jed's line of questioning, I understood Errol's tentative motions. He'd recognized before I had that we were in the company of a gathering storm. "Of course it couldn't be true, Deputy Whatley. How could I investigate anything? I don't have a forensics team. I can't issue warrants. All I can do is ask a few questions. There's nothing wrong with my asking questions, is there, deputy?"

If anything, Jed's frown darkened. I thought I detected a muscle twitching beneath his left eye. "Ms. Marvey, your questions are interfering with our investigation."

"Really?" My attention shifted to Errol. The junior deputy looked uncomfortable. I felt sorry for the guy, but I turned back to Jed. "How?"

Jed sputtered for a moment or two before his thoughts seemed to gain traction. "Leave the investigation to me—us." He jerked his campaign hat toward Errol. "Stick to your role with the library. Don't worry about asking questions. That's *our* job."

Since I didn't like the point he was making, I chose to misunderstand it. "I'm not worried about asking questions. 'The greatest gift is not being afraid to question.' Ruby Dee said that. She was a renaissance woman— civil rights activist, actress, playwright, screenwriter, poet, journalist. Did you know that?"

Errol's eyes widened. "No, I didn't know she did all those things. I knew she was an actress. She was from Cleveland, Ohio, wasn't she?"

"Yes, she was." I nodded approvingly, and smiled when Errol seemed to preen. "I also like Eugene Ionesco's quote, 'It is not the answer that enlightens, but the question.' He was a French playwright of Romanian descent."

Errol's brow creased. "I don't know him."

I leaned toward the deputy and gave him a considering look. "Do you have a library card, Deputy Cole?"

His eyes widened. "Why, yes, ma'am. I haven't borrowed any books in a while, but—"

"Could we get back to the investigation?" Jed's delivery was terse.

I made a mental note to find a time to continue my side discussion with Errol. Something told me with very little encouragement, the young deputy could become a voracious reader and an enthusiastic library champion. "Yes, of course, Deputy Whatley. I'm happy to. Has Willy Pelt spoken with you?"

Jed's expression grew more frustrated. He waved his arms with exasperation. "About what?"

I split my attention between the two men. "This morning, Willy told me someone tried to run him over last night as he returned from a restaurant near his hotel."

Jed exchanged a look with Errol. The younger deputy shook his head as though to confirm Willy hadn't reported this incident to him, either.

Errol turned to me. "Was he hurt?"

"Fortunately, no." I sat back against my chair. "He said he was able to jump out of the way in time, but the event left him badly shaken. He's convinced the driver was intent on harming him. His exact words were, 'Someone tried to kill me last night.'"

Jed scowled. "Then why didn't he report it?"

I spread my hands. "I agree he should file a report with you, but he said he doesn't want to prolong his stay in Peach Coast."

Jed gave me an impatient look. "There's nothing tying Mr. Pelt's event to Ms. Fiona's murder."

I shook my head. "I didn't say there was. I just thought you should know about the incident."

"Thanks." Jed's gratitude was grudging.

I continued. "However, since you haven't spoken with Willy about his encounter, how can you know whether what happened to him is or isn't somehow related to Fiona's murder?"

Jed shrugged. "Why would the person who killed Ms. Fiona want to kill Willy? What's the connection?"

"I don't know. You should ask him," I answered without inflection. "Willy said the car that tried to mow him down in the parking lot was a dark compact sedan. Jo drives a bright orange hatchback. What do Betty and Bobby drive?"

Errol turned to Jed. "Don't they drive dark sedans, J.W.?"

A light shifted in Jed's eyes as though he'd also drawn the link. "Plenty of people in town have dark cars."

I once again seized on his statement. "Not Jo."

Jed scowled. "You keep making leaps like these two events are connected."

"And you refuse to consider they could be." *Note to self: Replenish supply of chocolate-covered peanuts.* "Maybe you could at least ask Betty and Bobby whether they'd been driving their dark sedans around town last night."

"If Pelt didn't think the incident was important enough to report, why should I?" Jed stood as though to leave. Errol and I rose with him.

I braced my hands on my desk. "Because you're a Peach Coast deputy. Long after Willy leaves, you'll still be responsible for protecting this town. That's why you should consider Willy's near-death experience important."

Errol turned to his partner. "She has a point, J.W."

I shifted my gaze to Jed. "Willy's anxious to return to his practice, so you may want to speak with him sooner rather than later."

Jed arched an eyebrow. "I suppose you're expecting us to tell you what he says?"

"No, Deputy Whatley, I'm not expecting that." I smiled. "But it would be nice."

After chocolate-covered peanuts, a hot, strong cup of coffee was my second favorite go-to comfort food. Corrinne was already in the break room when I arrived after my encounter with the deputies late Thursday morning. Our offices were next to each other, but it was the first time I'd seen her that day.

I propped myself against the counter beside her. "How are the phone calls to the council members going?"

"How did you know I'd been on the phone with them?" She held the carafe aloft in a silent offer of coffee service.

I gratefully accepted. "Your office door has been

closed all morning, and we're running out of time to persuade them to support our budget increase."

Corrinne shook her head. Her features were tight with frustration. "I left a message for three of the council members. The other two wouldn't commit either way."

I grabbed a creamer and three sugar packets. "What additional information do they need to make a decision?"

Corrinne replaced the carafe. She was cool and professional in a pale yellow skirt suit and tan stilettos. Her voice was controlled, belying the irritation snapping in her grass-green eyes. "I have no idea, and neither do they. We've given them a list of the events we've hosted in the past fiscal year, as well as the attendance, information on our monthly visitors, and the increase in our library cardholders. What else could they possibly need to know?"

"Maybe *we're* not the ones they need to hear from." I contemplated my coffee as I stirred in the sugar and creamer.

"What do you mean?" She shifted to face me.

"I think it's time they heard from the voters. We need to encourage our patrons to call the council to show their support for the library."

"That's a great idea." Corrinne sighed. "But how do we get them to do that?"

"We ask. I'll put together signage we could post around the library and fliers to distribute to patrons from the circulation desk." My mind raced with additional ideas, including a special-notice e-newsletter and an announcement in the newspaper.

"I'll leave that effort in your capable hands then. Thank you, Marvey." Corrinne gestured toward the library's main area. "How's the investigation progressing?"

"I don't feel as though I'm getting anywhere." I swallowed a sip of coffee and a sigh. "There are several people who seem to have much stronger motives than Jo. They had the same opportunity to attack Fiona that Jo had, but I can't persuade the deputies to even consider them as viable suspects. For some reason, they're just fixated on her."

Corrinne nodded. "She represents the easiest suspect. For that reason, the deputies aren't interested in investing time, effort, or resources looking into anyone else."

"That's what makes this all the more frustrating and frightening." I caught her eyes. "I want to thank you."

Her perfectly shaped eyebrows knitted. "For what?"

"For defending me to Mayor Flowers last night when he asked you to stop me from making inquiries into Fiona's murder. Instead of listening to him, you supported me. That meant a lot. Thank you."

Corrinne waved a hand dismissively. "There are no thanks necessary. Byron can be utterly clueless."

Again I wondered at the apparent shared history between my boss and "Byron." "The mayor's not the only person who objects to my interest in Fiona's murder, though." That was an understatement. "Why are you supporting it?"

Corrinne seemed deep in thought as she drank her coffee. She was silent for several moments before finally giving me an answer. "Since you've been here, the team is reengaged. I don't know whether that's entirely because of the investigation, but it hasn't hurt. In a way, your work to clear Jo's name has also helped strengthen the library's connection with the community."

"I'm glad you think so." I didn't know if that was accurate, but she'd been in Peach Coast since before the library's inception. That would give her a better perspective.

"Not everyone in Peach Coast sees the value of a local library."

"That still amazes me."

"Me too." Corrinne shook her head and went back into her thoughts for a moment. "To convince the naysayers that yes, there is value in Peach Coast having its own library, we have to raise our library's profile. We have to give the library a presence in the community. That's why I hired you."

Getting this opportunity was like a dream come true. "I'm enjoying the work I'm doing."

"It shows. Even though you didn't join our team until February, well into the first quarter, you exceeded my first-quarter expectations. And you're on track to exceed my second-quarter expectations. Perhaps I should set higher expectations."

"Let's not get ahead of ourselves."

She flashed a pearly white grin. "In the four months you've been with us, in addition to the increased foot traffic and cardholders, our team has more energy and enthusiasm. I believe there's more to that than the peach cobbler you've brought Floyd on a daily basis."

My face heated with embarrassment from her praise. "I don't think you can attribute all of that to me. You've put together a dedicated team, and you provide great leadership."

Corrinne was shaking her head even as I spoke. "Before you arrived, I was terrified the mayor and the town council would shut the library."

I gasped. "No."

"Yes." She nodded emphatically. "I've had too many sleepless nights over that to count. The library's closing would've been devastating not just to our team but to our town."

"I know. The nearest library to Peach Coast is twenty point eight miles away."

Her eyes clouded. "Because of you, I have hope our library will continue to thrive. For that reason, *I* should be the one thanking *you*."

"I'm grateful for everything you're doing as well."

"Just be as careful and discreet as possible. Don't lose sight of the fact you're investigating a *murder*. I don't want you to get into danger." Corrinne squeezed my forearm before disappearing beyond the breakroom.

She'd left me speechless. Her kind words and support had overwhelmed me. But thinking back to her warning for my safety, I recalled the person creeping around my home early yesterday morning, and my chair, which had been tampered with yesterday afternoon. She didn't want me to get into danger?

Too late.

"You're early." I greeted Spence with a pleased smile as I hurried to meet him in the library parking lot late Thursday morning. Although I was five minutes early, he'd still been waiting for me.

He returned my smile as he straightened from his

steel-gray hatchback. In his lightweight gray suit, sapphire shirt, and maroon tie, he looked camera ready. "Nolan doesn't like to be kept waiting."

I started to respond to Spence's observation about his friend when he opened the passenger side door for me. That was disconcerting. I was accustomed to opening the door for myself. I glanced at him before getting into his car. Having him close the door for me was even more disarming. I lost my train of thought.

"Thank you for coming with me to speak with Nolan." I buckled my seatbelt as Spence settled behind the wheel and strapped himself in. "You said you've known him for decades."

"We've served on a few community boards and organizations together. That's how we became friends. He's a good guy." Spence pulled out of the parking lot and merged with the virtually nonexistent traffic on Peach Blossom Boulevard.

Through the side window, I gazed at the little stores, restaurants, and service shops that created the colorful scenery. They looked like they could've been transported from a Walt Disney sound stage. Even after four months, this shopping district still charmed me. Each building's pale stone or brick façade was perfectly coordinated to complement the others. The landscaping was meticulously tended to tie the group of storefronts together. The result was a picture-perfect and cohesive small town business district instead of a collection of individual stores and enterprises. I kept waiting for the sense of enchantment to fade—and fervently hoping it never did.

"Nolan had a solo practice for years before he formed

a partnership with Fiona." I studied the clean, spare lines and angles of Spence's profile as I spoke.

"You've done your homework." He tossed me a glance before returning his attention to the road.

"Has he ever spoken with you about Fiona?"

Spence was silent for a beat or two as though searching his memory. "Nolan doesn't talk much about his work. I think it's out of respect for his clients' and Fiona's privacy."

"I hope he's able to give us information we can use to help Jo." I returned my attention to the passenger side window. My gaze lingered on the view of the young sugar maple trees that edged the sleepy red brick sidewalks. "I checked in on her right before meeting you. Customer traffic at her store is still down."

"It's going to take a little while for people to feel comfortable enough going into the bookstore." Spence's voice was troubled. "It's not just that someone died there—it's how she died."

"You're right." But I heard again the tension in Jo's voice. Everything—the drop in business revenue, the police investigation, and the fact someone had been murdered in her store—was taking a toll on her mentally, emotionally, and physically. "I wish there was something I could do to help ease her stress."

"You're doing everything you can to clear her name."

"*We're* doing everything we can." I studied his profile again. "I'm grateful for your company, and not just because I'm pretty sure I wouldn't be able to find Nolan's office on my own."

Spence chuckled as he came to a four-way stop sign. "Is your sense of direction really that bad?"

I met his eyes. "Yes."

Spence waited his turn before moving through the intersection. "How did you get around New York? It's a hundred times the size of Peach Coast."

"Actually, New York City is just a little more than twelve point four times the size of Peach Coast."

He gave me a dry look. "I was exaggerating, Marvey."

"But I'm serious." I turned excitedly on my seat to face him. "I was surprised New York wasn't even fifteen times the size of this town. I think the reason it appears so much bigger is New York City has greater than eight point six million people *more* than Peach Coast."

"I'm sure you're right." His midnight eyes laughed at me.

I gave a mental shrug. I was used to that reaction from people who thought my attention to geographic statistics bordered on the obsessive. "I've always been interested in geography, especially distances and times. I'm fascinated by how far apart people are and what it takes to bring them closer together. I think that's even more important to me now that I'm so far away from my family."

"I can understand." His response was sober. "I know what it's like to be far from home."

"I know you do. Going to school in California and New York. Those years must've been rough."

"It was, although the experiences were worth it. I wouldn't change a thing. But how did you get around New York without any sense of direction?"

I was still getting accustomed to Spence's unsubtle change of topics when conversations drifted toward him. "I rarely drove in Brooklyn. I used public transportation or walked."

I rarely drove in Peach Coast, either. I walked everywhere. Usually, Jo or Spence drove if we were going somewhere far or needed to get somewhere fast. Like this trip to Nolan's office. I suspected we could've walked it, but since we were meeting Nolan during an early lunch break, time was of the essence.

Spence returned to my geographical challenges. "You definitely need to have a sense of direction when you're walking. And I'm sure you need it to use public transportation too."

"I suppose." I divided my attention between our conversation and the scenery outside of Spence's car. He'd turned off Main Street and into a neighborhood that was more residential than commercial. The trees were older here. "But it wasn't a matter of whether I was traveling east or west. The directions were more like, 'two blocks over or three blocks up or turn around you've gone too far.' Anyway, I can assure you I got lost plenty of times in New York too."

Spence slowed his car for a left-hand turn into what appeared to be either a very narrow, unnamed road or one of the best-maintained alleys I'd ever seen. "We're going to have to do something to improve your sense of direction. We can't have you wandering around town not knowing where you are."

"Don't worry. I never stay lost for long."

He entered a little asphalt parking lot behind what appeared to be a gingerbread house, relocated from a Hans Christian Andersen fairytale. It was surrounded by lush leafy plants and flowers, only some of which I recognized: chicory, Japanese maples, hostas and, of course, black-eyed Susans. They lured me out of his vehicle in search of fairies and talking birds.

"What are you doing?" His voice came from close behind me. He sounded startled.

Confused, I turned back to him. "Isn't this Nolan's office?"

"Yes, it is." He glanced at it, then back at me. If I didn't know better, I'd think he was at a loss for words.

Now I was even more confused. "Shouldn't we go in, then?"

"Well, yes, but..." Spence gestured toward his car. "You're supposed to wait for me to open the door for you."

I looked at his parked car, then back to him. "Why?"

He seemed momentarily thrown by my question. "It's customary. Men open doors for women."

He wasn't joking. In fact, he seemed very earnest. I bit my lips to restrain a smile. "If only that was figurative as well as literal." I turned toward the gingerbread house. "Come on, Mr. Spence. You said Nolan doesn't like to be kept waiting."

"I know you're laughing at me." Spence caught up with me. "I can see it in your eyes."

Not for the first time, I regretted that my eyes were so transparent. My father always said I had my mother's eyes. He called them "wide molasses pools of your every thought and emotion." It was a poetic yet frustrating truth.

"I'll tell you what." I strode with Spence to the front of the building up the walkway to the entrance. "I'll take the door situation under advisement, but I can't really see myself waiting for other people to hold doors open for me."

He reached around me to open the door to Nolan's office building. "When in Rome, Marvey. When in Rome..."

CHAPTER 21

THE ADMINISTRATIVE ASSISTANT FOR DUGGAN & Lyle CPA was an older woman whose cherubic peaches-and-cream complexion spoke of expensive moisturizers. She'd accessorized her warm gold blouse with a green-and-white patterned scarf. Pearl stud earrings decorated her ears. Her shock of golden-red hair was salon styled into a perfectly sculpted flip that sat on her slim shoulders. Her periwinkle eyes reminded me of Anna May Weekley, the owner and operator of On A Roll. Her nameplate read Lisa May DuVeaux. Surely her name and features weren't a coincidence.

"Well, Mr. Spencer Holt! As I live and breathe. Aren't you a sight for sore eyes?" Lisa May's gruff voice boomed a greeting as Spence and I approached her desk late Thursday morning. "How're you doin'? How's your mama?"

Spence flashed his celebrity smile and added a wink. "My mama and I are fine. Thank you for asking, Ms. Lisa May. How are you and your family?"

"Glad to hear it." Lisa May clapped her hands. "And me and my family are doing just fine and dandy. Thank you, Spencer. Although me and the mister aren't ready to retire just yet. I'm fixin' to work till the day I die, and then Nolan can just prop me up behind this desk and carry on." Her laughter rolled around the room, full and infectious.

The brownstone was just as warm and charming on the inside as it was outside. Lisa May's area must've been the home's great room. Area rugs were positioned under her desk and the coffee table, which stood in front of the overstuffed armchairs in the waiting area. Their matching brown-and-gold patterns were echoed in the furniture upholstery, wallpaper, and doilies.

The peaches-and-vanilla scent that perfumed the air came from the bowl of potpourri on the coffee table. A selection of current magazines, including the University of Georgia Bulldog alumni magazine, was arranged alongside the bowl.

Spence gestured toward me. "Ms. Lisa May, this is my friend, Marvella Harris. She's the new director of community engagement for the Peach Coast Library. Marvey, this is Lisa May DuVeaux. And in case you're wondering, yes, she is Anna May Weekley's sister."

I smiled with pleasure. "I *had* been wondering. I really enjoy your sister's coffee shop. I stop in every morning on my way to work."

Lisa May blushed. "That's mighty kind of you to say, Ms. Marvella. Thank you."

"Please call me Marvey."

Lisa May's periwinkle eyes sparkled. "Thank you."

Spence slipped his hands into the front pockets of his gray suit pants. "Is Nolan available? I'd called him earlier to ask if Marvey and I could stop by."

"Oh, I'm sure he would just love to see you. He'd love

it. It'll help to lift his spirits after the tragedy with Fiona. Let me just double check." Lisa May raised her left index finger. She used her other hand to claim her telephone receiver and tap in Nolan's extension. "Hi, there. Nolan?" Her voice was low and empathetic. "Spencer and Marvella are here to see you. Do you have time to meet with them?" She paused. "Oh, good. Good. Then I'll just send them through, then. Uh-huh. Bye now." Lisa May cradled her receiver. "Y'all can go on up now to Nolan's office. You remember where it is, don't ya, Spencer?"

"Yes, ma'am, I do." Spence nodded.

Her warm smile fanned out laugh lines from her eyes. "I just know he'll be real happy to see you. He was just devastated by Fiona's murder. We both were."

"Were he and Fiona close?" I asked.

Lisa May looked to Spence as though expecting him to clarify my question.

Spence rested his right palm against the small of my back. "Marvey's from New York City."

Her confusion cleared as though those five words had unlocked the key to her understanding me. "Well, Nolan and Fiona weren't exactly friends, but I could tell they just liked and respected each other as professionals, you understand?"

"I understand," I said.

"Yes, well, they were real professional toward each other." Lisa May folded her hands on her desk. "There was never a cross word between them, at least not in front of me."

"Thank you, Lisa May." I met her eyes with somber sincerity. "I'm very sorry for your loss."

Her eyes clouded over. "Thank you, Marvella. I appreciate the kindness."

Spence gestured for me to precede him up the dark hardwood staircase. It creaked comfortably under our weight. The wood bannister was smooth beneath my palm.

Lisa May had stated Fiona and Nolan had never exchanged a cross word in front of her. That didn't mean they hadn't had cross words when she wasn't around. Everyone argued, though. It was human nature. No two people agreed all the time. That didn't mean everyone was a killer. Besides, Spence vouched for Nolan's character. I shot a glance at Spence behind me. I had a hard time believing anyone he'd consider a friend could be a killer.

I crested the staircase and found Nolan waiting for us outside one of the offices near the end of the hall.

"Spence!" A grin split his warm brown face. His close-cropped dark brown hair shone under the hallway's florescent lighting. His conservative white dress shirt, blue-and-red striped tie, and navy pants were a far cry from the jeans and jersey he'd worn to the signing.

"Nolan!"

I stood back while the two men exchanged man-hugs and preliminary greetings. There was no denying the affection between the two.

Nolan turned to me. His brown eyes were warm but tired. "Marvey, it's nice to see you again."

I returned his smile. "Thank you very much for agreeing to meet with us, Nolan. You must be very busy. I appreciate your time."

"It's not a problem." He stepped back, gesturing us into his office.

The contrast between the interior decorating down-stairs and Nolan's office was so stark I almost stumbled across the doorway. The furniture in Nolan's room was shockingly modern and impersonal, considering the homey décor in the firm's reception area. Downstairs, everything was warm woods, patterned fabrics, and cushioning. In here, there was only silver metal, clear glass, and black vinyl. In a past life, the space must've been a bedroom. The office supply closet to the right probably had been a walk-in closet. The windows across the room offered a view of the front of the house. They were bare, flooding the space with natural light.

Spence waited for me to settle onto one of the two metal and vinyl guest chairs in front of Nolan's tan modular desk before taking the one closest to the door.

Nolan claimed his black padded executive chair and rolled it under his desk. "How're y'all getting along?" He directed his question to Spence and me.

Here we go. I suppressed a sigh. "We're fine. Thank you, Nolan."

"Everything's fine." Spence braced his right ankle on his left knee. "But more importantly, how're you?"

Nolan settled back against his chair with a sigh. "Busy. There's a lot involved in transitioning Fiona's accounts. Thankfully, her clients want to remain with the firm, but I'm going to have to bring in another CPA to help with the workload."

"Of course." Quick glimpses around his office didn't reveal any personal insights about Nolan the man. His office was all business, from the publications and binders packed into his black metal bookcase to the community plaques and commendations displayed on his stark white walls. "Did the two of you have a survivorship agreement?"

Nolan gave me a cautious look. "Yes, it's simply a

sound business practice. That way, the surviving partner can take over the business without having to negotiate with the other partner's family or with the courts."

"I'm very sorry for your loss." I looked at Spence before continuing. "I understand you and Fiona worked well together. I hate to intrude on this very sad and stressful time, but the deputies suspect a dear friend, Jo Gomez, of Fiona's murder. I know Jo couldn't have killed her."

Nolan frowned. "I'd heard the deputies were investigating Jo in connection with Fiona's murder. That doesn't make any sense to me. I'm pretty sure Fiona didn't know her. I'd never heard Fiona mention her until she started planning her book event, so I can't imagine Jo killing her, either."

I took a quick breath in relief and thought I'd inhaled a trace of peppermint. My gaze dropped to the brown porcelain mug on Nolan's desk. Was he drinking peppermint tea? "Did you mention that to Deputy Whatley or Deputy Cole?"

"As a matter of fact, I did." Nolan nodded. "They came to my office the other day with some follow-up questions for their investigation. They asked if I knew whether there were any tensions between Fiona and Jo. I told them what I just told you—Fiona barely knew Jo."

I gave him a grateful smile. At least the deputies were asking questions about their theory of Jo as the killer. How long would it take them to accept they didn't have any evidence to support it? "Was Fiona having problems with anyone?"

Nolan shook his head. He dropped his gaze to his desk and the stacks of papers piled neatly across its surface. "I can't think of anyone who'd want to kill her.

I'm sure you've heard about the troubles she'd had with Betty Rodgers-Hayes and Bobby Hayes. But they'd been causing Fiona problems for years. Why would they suddenly up and kill her?"

The point could be made that was exactly what a crime of passion was. It wasn't a planned event. It was sudden, unexpected, and emotional.

Spence gestured toward the other man. "We were hoping you could give us some insights into Fiona so we could understand her better."

"Fiona and I weren't friends, but I liked her." Nolan shifted on his chair. "She was a considerate person and a good business partner."

He was holding back. I didn't want to think that. Nolan was Spence's good friend and he seemed like a nice person, but he was definitely sending out I-have-a-secret signals. Why? What didn't he want us to know? More importantly, how could I get him to open up? "What made you decide to go into business with Fiona? Weren't you concerned the vicious gossip that followed her around town would hurt your firm?"

Nolan shifted on his seat. Again. It was a signal he was uncomfortable about something—and it wasn't the chair. Did Spence also have the impression his friend was being evasive? At a glance, I couldn't tell what Spence was thinking, though he seemed to be watching the other man closely.

Propping his elbows on the arms of his chair, Nolan linked his fingers together over his flat abdomen. "I'm not comfortable speaking ill of Fiona. We may not have been friends, but I did care about her."

Spence spread his hands. "We understand. We don't want to put you in an uncomfortable position, but you worked closely with Fiona for almost two years. You could give us insights that could help shed some light on her murder and perhaps help identify her killer."

Nolan cocked his head. "Are you doing a follow-up story on her murder?"

Say yes! Say yes! I fisted my hands, willing Spence to read my mind.

He nodded. "We're gathering information in preparation for a series of articles. Murders don't happen often in Peach Coast, fortunately. This is a big story."

Knowing Spence, that was the truth. He had too much integrity to lie to a friend.

Nolan switched his attention to me. I sensed him wondering why Spence had brought a librarian along to the interview, rather than one of his newspaper's reporters. For whatever reason, he didn't ask the question.

He turned his attention back to Spence. "I've told the deputies everything I know about Fiona, which unfortunately isn't much. Have you spoken with them?"

Mention of the deputies and their handling of this case triggered a rush of frustration. "Their investigation seems to be stalled on Jo. Please, anything you can tell us at all about Fiona could help us persuade the deputies they're focusing on the wrong person. We're after justice for Fiona, for Jo, and for the community."

Nolan's reluctance to speak was almost like another presence in his office, seated on the table between us. If I didn't know better, I'd think he'd taken a vow of silence. When he finally spoke, the words seemed to be dragged from him. "All right. Fiona had a secret. I think Buddy and I were the only ones in town who knew about it. Buddy didn't find out until after they were married. Fiona was rich."

I blinked. "How rich?"

Nolan smiled. "Very."

I frowned, jabbing a thumb toward Spence seated beside me. "Like, Holt rich?"

Nolan shook his head. "Close, but not quite. The reason she didn't want people to know is she's had a lot of bad experiences with personal relationships in the past. Friends who wanted her to invest in phony businesses. Boyfriends who tried to pressure her into marriage, thinking they'd have access to her accounts. Moving to Peach Coast allowed her to get away from those mistakes and start over."

"I can understand that." Spence's voice was low, as though he was wading through memories as he spoke. "People pretending to like you so they can use you. It takes time to learn the signs that let you know who you can trust."

Reading his eyes, I saw the hurts from Spence's past. "That's a lot of pressure to grow up with."

He forced a smile. "It's a different kind of pressure. Everyone has something they're struggling with."

I nodded my agreement before returning my attention to Nolan. "That's why Fiona was so distant. Well, that and I'm sure she resented the gossip Betty was spreading. But you're saying Buddy didn't know Fiona was rich until *after* they were married?"

"That's what Fiona told me." Nolan seemed much more relaxed now that he'd shared his insights. With both Fiona and Buddy dead, neither would be hurt by his revelations. "And she only revealed it to him because his business was failing. She wanted to help him save it."

"When did you find out?" Spence asked.

Nolan spread his arms. "When Fiona approached me about forming a partnership." He switched his attention to me. His voice was somber. "Fiona didn't *have* to work. She *wanted* to work. She knew who was spreading the lies about her, and knew she could've stopped it. She chose not to because she didn't want to hurt someone she loved. You asked what made me agree to go into business with someone who had so much baggage. It's because her actions showed me who she was. Our actions always do."

Wise words. No wonder Spence and Nolan were such good friends. They were good people. I was beginning to suspect Fiona had been as well, in spite of what Betty had put her through.

Shaking off a sense of sorrow and regret for what Fiona had dealt with, I hurried to ask a few remaining questions before leaving. "How bad off was Buddy's company?"

Nolan's expression implied it was pretty bad. "If it wasn't for Fiona, Buddy wouldn't have been able to keep his company open."

Spence's brow furrowed. "How can you be so certain?"

"I saw his books." Nolan leaned into his desk, dividing his attention between Spence and me. "Fiona was very, very smart. She was great with finances. At first, Buddy didn't want her help to save his company. He was too proud. So she asked me to consult with her on strategies to restructure his company."

Spence arched an eyebrow. "Did you have any suggestions?"

Nolan's sigh was heavy. "Buddy had two choices. He could either close his business or accept Fiona's help.

He didn't like either choice, but Fiona finally persuaded him to accept her offer."

I took a moment to absorb this new information. Spence seemed to be doing the same. "Thank you. You've given us a lot to think about." I glanced at my watch. "We should get going. We've taken so much of your time already." I raised the strap of my chocolate handbag to my shoulder and stood in preparation of leaving. The two friends rose with me. "If I could ask one more question, though. Do you know who Fiona's lawyer was?"

Nolan shook his head. "I'm afraid I don't. Lisa May might have that information. I think Fiona met with her lawyer recently. Perhaps she set up the appointment for her."

Intrigued, I paused. "Why had Fiona met with her lawyer?"

Nolan chuckled. "Are you sure you're a librarian and not a reporter?"

Undaunted, I grinned. "Librarians are naturally curious as well."

"I'm not sure, but I think she wanted to discuss the property her uncle had left her." He frowned. "Now that I think about it, she'd said Willy Pelt had wanted to buy the property from her. In fact, he'd made a bid, but he was lowballing her, so she refused to sell."

I froze. Willy had told me Fiona had willed the property to him. I made an effort to appear nonchalant. "This conversation, was it recent?"

"I think so." Nolan circled his desk. "Within a couple of weeks or so."

Spence stepped aside from his chair, clearing a path

for me to the door. "How did Willy react to Fiona not selling her property to him?"

Nolan arched an eyebrow. "Fiona implied he was *not* happy. I had the impression they'd exchanged some rather heated words."

I doubted that after those heated words, Fiona had willed her property to him. Willy had lied to me. Why?

CHAPTER 22

"**A**REN'T THOSE WOMEN MEMBERS OF Fiona's writers group?" I pointed through the windshield of Spence's hatchback toward the two middle-aged women walking across the library parking lot Thursday afternoon.

"Yes, they are." Spence had driven me back to the library after our very informative meeting with Nolan.

I'd declined his invitation to lunch, requesting a rain check instead. I needed to work through lunch if I had a prayer of getting caught up on my projects. With myriad distractions from this investigation, I hadn't gotten as much work done as I'd planned.

"I need to talk with them." I searched my memory for their names. "I've been meaning to ask them about Fiona's writing style."

"Her writing style?" Spence pulled up at the curb a few yards away from the library's entrance. "I thought you'd finished her book."

"Yes, and that was helpful." I tracked the women's progress across the parking lot toward the library. "But it's just one story. I'm hoping they can tell me about some of her unpublished work. I can't remember their names, though." I'd been so focused on trying to recall the writers' names that I hadn't noticed Spence getting out of the car. When he pulled open the passenger door, I jumped. "Smooth move, Mr. Holt." I laughed as he handed me out of the car.

"You're welcome, Ms. Harris." Spence closed the passenger side door. "Dolly Byrd is the blonde. Tammy Hawkins is the brunette."

"You're the best. Thank you." I drew my hand from his.

He shoved his hands into his pants' front pockets. "Do you want me to talk with Ms. Dolly and Ms. Tammy with you?"

"No, thank you. I want this to be an informal chat. If you're there, they might curtsy." I gave him a teasing grin.

"Very funny." His tone was dry, but I detected a blush stealing up his neck.

"Thanks again for coming with me to speak with Nolan. You were a great help."

"We're partners in this investigation. Remember?" He glanced at his wristwatch. "I'd better get back to the paper. Let me know if you get any good information from Ms. Dolly and Ms. Tammy."

"I will. Drive safely." I watched him climb back into his car and pull away from the curb before I entered the library.

It didn't take long to find Dolly and Tammy. The building wasn't that big. The two women were in the romance section. That's what Zelda had told me they wrote.

"Dolly. Tammy. It's good to see you again." I strode

up to them as casually as I could manage. "I don't know if you remember meeting me Saturday. I'm Marvey Harris, the library's new director of community engagement."

Dolly turned to me with huge blue eyes that dominated her round, porcelain face. "I remember meeting you, Ms. Marvey. And it's so good to see you again too."

Tammy adjusted her black-rimmed glasses. "Yes, how are you, Ms. Marvey?"

"Please, call me Marvey." I folded my hands in front of my hips. "A better question is how are you ladies holding up? I'm so sorry for your loss."

"Thank you." Dolly had a habit of ending her sentences as though she was asking a question. I had to resist the urge to answer.

Tammy clutched her library books to her chest with both arms. "We weren't especially close to Fiona. Still, it's a shock that something like this can happen to someone you know, especially in a town as quiet as Peach Coast."

"I agree. It's just a shock." Dolly's head bob sent her pale blond hair swinging above her slim shoulders. "We were her critique partners but, like Tammy said, we didn't spend much time with her. We just got together to discuss our writing."

I glanced at the shelves of romance novels surrounding us. "You both critiqued manuscripts with Fiona? But Fiona wrote mysteries. I thought you wrote romance."

"Well, at first Fiona wrote romances too. Contemporary romance." Dolly sounded like she was asking me rather than telling me. I was tempted to respond, *I don't know.*

Tammy released her books long enough to tuck her hair behind her right ear. "They were really good. Fiona was a big believer in writing what you know, and you could tell by the stories she wrote."

"That's right." Dolly waved her hands. Her sparkly pale pink nail polish caught my attention. "All her stories were set in small towns. And she wrote a couple of stories about women who'd moved to a new town and fallen in love with one of its wealthy residents."

Tammy tightened her hold on her books. "Well, you can see how that's like her and Buddy Hayes."

"Yes, I see the similarity." And it made sense. Successful novelists often advised aspiring authors to write stories about what they know.

"But then she suddenly stopped attending our critique sessions." Dolly looked to Tammy as though seeking confirmation.

I frowned. "Do you know why?"

Dolly flipped her hands. "When we asked her about it, she said things had gotten really busy at work. She had an accounting firm with Nolan Duggan."

"But we thought maybe she had writer's block." Tammy used her books to gesture between her and Dolly. "So we tried to talk with her about it and encourage her writing. You can see how talented she is."

"Yes, her book is hard to put down." I nodded, hoping Tammy and Dolly would keep their confidences coming.

Dolly tapped the other woman's forearm. "But remember, we did notice Fiona stopped coming to our critique group right around the time Zelda started attending again."

I heard again Floyd's suspicion over the timing of

Fiona's audit and Zelda leaving her job. Had that happened before or after the women had found themselves attending the same critique meetings? Awkward. I made a mental note to follow up with Zelda.

"That's right." Tammy's eyes widened. "We'd wondered if it was a coincidence or if it was deliberate."

Dolly shrugged. "We thought Fiona may have stopped coming because she and Zelda couldn't stand each other, although they're both on the board."

A cloud passed over their faces at almost the same moment. It seemed they were both remembering Fiona wasn't on the board anymore. Perhaps Fiona's death had affected them more than they'd thought. I gave them a moment to gather themselves.

Dolly looked around as though confirming we were alone. Still, she lowered her voice. "Zelda isn't nearly as talented as Fiona."

Tammy nodded in silent agreement, then adjusted her glasses. "Fiona was a natural writer. Zelda...she has to work a bit harder. Just look—Fiona was published less than two years after joining our group. Zelda has been trying to get published for almost a decade."

I took a moment to digest that. What made Fiona switch from writing contemporary love stories to mainstream mysteries? "How long had Fiona been writing mysteries?"

Tammy shrugged, exchanging a look with Dolly, who also seemed at a loss. "She must've switched after she left the critique group. We had no idea she was even thinking of switching genres."

"But it was right around the time Buddy Hayes died." Dolly's sigh was long and sad. "Well, I can understand how you might not be in the mood to write romance if you lose the love of your life."

Tammy hugged her books a little tighter. "And considering Fiona was always preaching about writing what you know, it seemed fitting she'd switch genres."

Dolly scanned our surroundings. "That's right. She turned around and wrote a story so similar to the rumors Ms. Betty started, implying Fiona was somehow responsible for Buddy Hayes's death." She rolled her eyes. "As though anybody believed that."

Tammy brushed her hair from her forehead again as she hummed her agreement. "Nobody believed those rumors but Betty and her clique. But it sure does make for a good story."

Dolly giggled. "And it's a great way to get back at Ms. Betty for planting those rumors all over town."

"Did Zelda or Fiona ever confide why they didn't like each other?" I didn't bring up Floyd's suspicions. I didn't want to share what *I* thought; I wanted to know what *they* thought.

The two women exchanged a look and a shrug before Dolly turned back to me. "Jealousy, maybe? Fiona was a much better writer than Zelda."

"But the tension didn't really start until after Zelda quit her job," Tammy offered. "She and Fiona were both accountants. Maybe Zelda was jealous of Fiona's success with her firm."

"Other than that, we really don't have any ideas."

Tammy nodded in silent agreement, dislodging the swatch of hair she'd tucked behind her ear. Her eyes stretched wide at the scandal. "If the deputies weren't looking into Jo Gomez for Fiona's murder, my money would be on *Zelda* being the one who killed Fiona."

"Mine too." Dolly lifted her pale thin eyebrows. "Zelda couldn't *stand* Fiona."

I glanced at my watch. "I should get back to work. Ladies, I'm very sorry for your loss." I turned to make my way back to my office.

Tammy had said Zelda might've been jealous of Fiona's accounting practice. That didn't seem like a strong enough motive for murder. On the other hand, Floyd might be onto something with his theory of a connection between Fiona's audit and Zelda leaving her job with the bank.

Question: How do you ask a person if they killed someone for getting them fired?

There was a snake. On the driver's seat of my car.

And it was moving.

My heart stopped. My mind blanked. My muscles froze, cementing me to the asphalt parking lot outside of the library Thursday evening. The box of files I'd carried from my office and had intended to deposit on the backseat of my blue compact sedan dropped from my numbed fingers. It created a loud splatting noise that snapped me out of a terrified trance.

My heart galloped. My mind rushed to recall everything I'd read about snakes in coastal Georgia. No sudden or threatening movements. If you didn't bother the snake, the snake wouldn't bother you.

What if the snake was in your car? I think that counted as "bothering you."

How had it gotten into my car?

And how was I going to get it out?

With three slow and unsteady steps, I backed away. I was in an agony of fear with each step. Determining I was out of the snake's line of sight, I spun and sprinted back to the library. My tote bag slid down my arm to hook at my right elbow. My handbag bounced against my left hip. My pulse and pumps pounded in my ears.

At the entrance, I rocked back on my heels. Our patrons couldn't see me so frazzled and afraid. I might cause a panic. I stepped to the side of the door and drew several deep breaths. The evening air was warm and salty from the nearby wetlands as it filled my lungs. Marginally more in control, I straightened my back, squared my shoulders, and reached for the door handle with fingers that trembled. My legs were stiff but my knees shook. Stepping forward, I felt like one of the robots from Isaac Asimov's *The Robot Series*.

Adrian and Floyd were deep in conversation as they strode toward the door behind me. Their shift was over, and their replacements were on duty. But they hadn't yet noticed me.

I blocked their passage and raised my hands to stop them. "There's a snake in my car. On my driver's seat. I think it's a cottonmouth." I spoke in a stage whisper.

Floyd's cool gray eyes darkened with worry as he scanned me. "Did it bite you?" His concern created a comforting space in the center of my panic.

"No." A hysterical sob caught in my throat. It was just after five o'clock. How long had the snake been in my car? I continued speaking in a stage whisper. "I don't like snakes."

The librarians sprang into action.

"I'll get the broom from the storage room." Floyd turned and strode toward the employee offices.

"I'll grab a trash can." Adrian went to the circulation desk, then rejoined me in seconds.

My attention dropped to the large shipping box in his left hand and the trash can hanging from his right. He'd removed the garbage bag. "What are we going to do?"

He lifted the container. "We're gonna sweep the snake into this here bin."

Oh, no, no, no. No. The thought of getting close to that monstrously large and certainly venomous creature made me lightheaded. I closed my eyes briefly. "I... don't know if I can do that."

"Can't do what?" Floyd had returned in time to hear my confession.

I gestured toward Adrian's supplies. "Transfer the snake into the trash can."

"We'll handle it." Floyd held the door open for Adrian and me.

It struck me that my rescuers behaved as though they'd done this before. Finding a snake in a car didn't seem unusual to them. I couldn't think about that now.

My still-shaky legs carried me across the threshold and back into the parking lot. I pointed out my powder blue compact to the two men. My finger shook as though I was conducting the world's smallest orchestra. At about a yard from the sedan's hood, I muted my keyless entry before pressing the button to release the locks. I didn't want to risk startling the snake with the car alarm's high-pitched pinging sound. The muted snick was loud enough.

Floyd stilled beside me. "Your car was locked?"

"Yes." I read confusion in his eyes.

"Then how'd the snake get in?" Adrian sounded as puzzled as Floyd looked.

I spread my arms. "I've been asking myself the same question."

Adrian looked through the side window. "Yep. That's a cottonmouth."

I swallowed to dislodge the lump of fear in my throat. I briefly closed my eyes, still seeing the serpent's orange, black, and brown patterned skin. "Aren't those poisonous?"

"They sure are." The young librarian assistant sounded almost gleeful.

I suppressed a shiver. There were four types of poisonous snakes in North America: cottonmouth moccasins, rattlesnakes, copperheads, and coral snakes. How had I been lucky enough to discover one in my car?

Gathering my courage, I nudged the file box aside with my right foot, then opened my driver's side door. I pulled it wide to give Floyd and Adrian room to maneuver, and to give myself distance from the snake. I watched in fascinated horror as my companions closed in on the enormous, venomous reptile. It was actually sunning on my seat. How was I going to sit there to drive home? My palms were sweating.

Adrian squatted beside the chair, extending the trash can out in front of him. He was more than an arm's length away, but he still seemed so close. Too close. I held my breath, pressing a palm against my chest to keep my heart from bounding out of my body. Floyd extended the broom into the car. I bit my lower lip to keep from screaming. Floyd used the broom to guide the snake into the trash bin Adrian held with his bare hands. The two men worked together to efficiently and effortlessly contain the snake. The entire operation was over in minutes. As I watched, Adrian put the box lid on the trash can and straightened from his crouched position. I knew one thing with absolute certainty— there was no way I could ever do that.

I secured my car. "Thank you both so very much. What should we do now?" But Adrian was already striding away, carrying the now-contained snake toward a trail that led to the park behind the library. "But... if Adrian releases the snake into the park, couldn't it make its way back here?"

"It might." Floyd's shrug was philosophical. "You should get snake repellant. You can buy it over at the general store. Apply it to your car seat where the snake was and spread it around your car."

For a brief moment, I reconsidered this whole small-town librarian situation. Then I remembered how much I loved my job, and that I was falling in love with the town and my neighbors. Well, with the possible exception of Delores.

"I don't understand how the snake could've gotten into my car." I scanned my vehicle, looking for a way the reptile could've slithered in.

Especially because of my concern for Phoenix's safety, before I moved into my house, I took steps to make sure snakes couldn't get in. I'd watched videos I'd found on the internet to learn how to snake-proof my home. I'd followed each step in detail. I'd inspected the house from the attic to the basement to the attached garage. I'd even checked the creepy, cobweb-infested crawl spaces. I'd checked for openings, gaps, and spaces larger than a quarter of an inch, and had sealed them all—every single one—with spray foam and weather stripping. But it had never entered my mind to snake-proof my car, perhaps because Phoenix was rarely in it.

"Are you sure you locked your car?" Floyd held my gaze. "Because I don't think your snake got into your car by itself. I think it had help."

"I know I locked my car." I faced Floyd again. "It's a habit."

Adrian returned at a brisk jog. "The person could've used a car key jammer." The trash container was now thankfully empty. "It's a device that blocks the radio signal from your car remote and prevents your car from locking. I read about it in one of my true crime novels."

My mind was almost overwhelmed by the implications of what Floyd and Adrian were saying. Someone had deliberately put a snake in my car and had planned how to do it. A foggy memory settled over my mind and struggled to take shape. Bobby was fascinated by snakes. He liked them enough to have them tattooed on his forearm in brilliant colors that almost matched the one I'd found on my car seat. Could he be behind this?

"I don't usually drive to work. How could he have known I drove today—and which car was mine?" I spread my arms, indicating the crowded parking lot. The after-work patrons were arriving.

"It's obvious." Floyd sighed, crossing his arms over his chest. "Someone's been watching you, Marvey. And we all know why. Are you sure you want to continue this investigation?"

CHAPTER 23

MY FIRST FOUR MONTHS IN Peach Coast had been quiet. Now, in less than a week—we'd only been investigating Fiona's murder for five days—the stuff had hit the fan: a snake in my car, my sabotaged office chair, and the intruder who'd been sneaking around my home in the wee hours of Wednesday morning.

I'd thanked Floyd and Adrian for their help again—they really had gone above and beyond to help me—before making a beeline to the general store for the snake repellant. I was anxious to get home, check on Phoenix, and then…think.

The general store was huge with lots of aisles and even more people. It seemed to be another town hot spot, like On A Roll. In fact, a few of the café regulars were in the store. They hailed me as I hurried past, slowing just enough to exchange a wave and well wishes before speeding on. I didn't want to spend too much time in the store. I couldn't risk that another snake would turn up in the parking lot and somehow or another work its way into my car. Random, frightening thoughts like that would probably stalk me for days if not weeks until the fright from my snake encounter dissipated.

A helpful clerk pointed me in the direction of the camping section for the snake repellent. After a quick trip through the checkout lane, I was back outside. The shadows had started to lengthen. The weather had cooled, but it was still warm enough to be comfortable without a jacket. The slight breeze carried the scent of the nearby coast.

I spotted my little sedan across the parking lot. From this distance, it seemed snake-free. Still, I prepared myself to enter the vehicle with caution. I glanced to my left before stepping off the sidewalk.

"Watch out!" a female voice screamed from behind me.

At the same time, a flash of movement in my peripheral vision claimed my attention. My head spun to the right. My brain rushed to verify what my eyes couldn't believe. A dark mid-sized sedan was zooming straight toward me. There was no way the driver couldn't see me. It wasn't that dark. They never swerved, never blew the horn. Never. Stopped.

Were they targeting me?

I jumped back up to the sidewalk. As the sedan sped past, a gust of wind slammed into my back. I went cold. The car had been so close. Too close. It could've run me down. My legs quivered like Jell-O before giving out altogether. I crumbled onto the sidewalk. Disjointed thoughts spun around my head: Phoenix, a dark sedan, and an out-of-state license plate.

"Are you all right?" A petite older woman rushed to my side. She pressed both of her hands onto my shoulders as though offering support.

I tilted my head to meet her eyes. She looked almost as panic-stricken as I felt. "You saved my life. Thank you." My voice wobbled in the middle and at both ends.

My guardian angel's brown eyes widened. Her thin black eyebrows flew up her forehead. "Oh, honey, don't think like that. Are you hurt?"

I tried to shake my head, but my whole body was still trembling. "I don't think so."

"That was crazy." Anger pulsed in her voice. "Some people are so selfish. They think they're the only ones allowed to move in the parking lot." She glared in the direction the car had flown. It had disappeared without a trace.

"'Selfish' is one way to describe it." Homicidal was another. I struggled to push myself to my feet.

"Careful. Don't move too fast." My rescuer braced my left arm to support me.

"Thank you." More than anything, I appreciated her just being there after my scare, the second one in less than two hours. "I'm Marvey Harris."

"Sharon Hirose." She looked up at me, cradling my arm as though afraid to let me go. "Do you want me to take you to the hospital?"

"Oh, no. I'm fine." My teeth still chattered, though. "Thank you again so much for calling out to me and for checking on me. You're truly a good Samaritan."

Sharon's pale cheeks pinkened. "Anyone would've done the same."

Being a New Yorker, I wasn't sure about that. "I'm grateful you were nearby."

She accompanied me to my car. We checked the parking lot twice to make certain it was clear before we proceeded. "Be careful on your drive home. Do you live far?"

"No, but I'll be careful. And, please, you do the same." I smiled down at her before deactivating my car alarm. "Thanks again."

"You're welcome. Good night." She turned to leave.

"Sharon?" I waited until she turned back to me. "Did you happen to notice the car's license plate number?"

She gave me an apologetic shrug. "I'm sorry. I didn't, but if you report it to the deputies, I'll be your witness. The license plate looked like a rental." She gave me her email address and home phone number.

"I work at the Peach Coast Library." I fished a business card from my wallet. "Do you have a library card?"

Once back in my car, I found a music radio station and pumped up the volume on a favorite 1980s dance song to help settle my nerves. During the drive home, I stopped feeling shaken and started getting angry. By the time I parked the car in my attached garage, I was once again shaking, but this time with temper, not fear.

Phoenix stretched out at his usual station in front of the French doors, surveying the backyard. I sat cross-legged beside him and scooped him onto my lap. I cuddled and petted him while I filled him in on my day—only the happy parts. He seemed fine. After a few moments, I rose to check on his water bowl and food dish. Phoenix's water bowl was empty, but I wished he'd show a little more interest in the food. Fortunately, our appointment with the veterinarian was scheduled for tomorrow after work, less than twenty-four hours away.

Turning back to the dining table, I fished my phone from my handbag and sent a text to Jo and Spence. *Can you come to my house tonight? Sorry for late notice, but would really like your thoughts on developments I think are related to case.* I proofed the text before sending it to make sure it had the proper punctuation.

Within two minutes, they'd both agreed to join me in half an hour. Perfect! That gave me enough time to apply the snake repellant before it got dark and to call the sheriff's office to report my near-fatal hit-and-run in the general store parking lot. I also might be able to re-search out-of-state-license plates. I was almost certain the car that had tried to strike me was the same dark sedan that had threatened Willy Wednesday night. Why would someone use a rental car to try to harm me? To remain anonymous, of course.

These weren't coincidences. Someone was out to get me.

"Someone's trying to scare me off from investigating Fiona's murder." I looked at Jo and Spence.

My friends had arrived within minutes of each other Thursday evening. We were meeting in my living room. I'd made us my favorite orange herbal tea. They'd both declined additional refreshments, since they'd just fin-ished dinner.

Jo cradled the rose porcelain mug. "Do you mean other than the deputies and Delores?"

I gave her a dry look. "Yes. This is more than some-one who's irritated by my meddling or angry that I've cast aspersions against their friends. This is someone who wants to scare me, if not hurt me."

"What makes you think that?" Spence went still. There was tension in his tone.

I hesitated, still loathe to worry them. "I'm not great at math, but even I know the probabilities are off. I've had four dangerous incidents over two consecutive days. That's more than a coincidence."

Jo's eyes flared wide. "What's happened?"

"What incidents?" Spence spoke at the same time. He set his mug on its coaster on the coffee table and sat forward on the sofa he shared with Jo.

I hated the anxiety growing in their eyes. No one wanted to worry friends, but this information was important to the case. And, well, they were my friends. *I* would want to know if *they* were in trouble. "The first suspicious event happened yesterday, about two in the morning." I stood to pace my living room. The hardwood flooring was smooth under my fuzzy lavender slipper socks. My chocolate shorts and purple T-shirt were loose around me. "The motion-detecting lights above my deck came on and woke me."

Jo looked toward my French doors. "Maybe someone walked past your house." Even she sounded uncertain about that theory.

I shook my head. "They only come on when people come within ten yards of my house."

Spence's eyes darkened with concern. "Ten yards? At that distance, they're practically on your doorstep."

I gave them a humorless half smile. "That distance was a compromise between my parents and I. They wanted the lights to come on if someone was across the street."

Jo and Spence didn't look amused. If anything, their concern deepened.

Spence stared at the living room ceiling as though imagining the layout of my bedroom. "Your windows face north and south."

I blinked. Spence knew I didn't deal in north, south, east, and west. It was left, right, and turnaround. "At one end of my room, the windows face the front and the windows in the back face...the back."

Jo frowned. "Someone was circling your house."

Based on the increasing anxiety in their voices, I decided to give them the abridged version of the events: contacting emergency services, Jed and Errol responding to my call, and the deputies' assertion that the disturbance was a group of kids, playing a prank.

"That's ridiculous," Jo muttered.

"I agree," Spence said.

I shrugged restlessly. "So do I, and I told them as much, but they're certain of their theory."

Spence rose and crossed to the other side of the room. "You said there'd been 'incidences.' What else has happened?" He propped his shoulder against the curve of the archway between my living room and dining room. He didn't look pleased. Neither did Jo.

They were already upset about the lights. Should I tell them the rest? I didn't think I had a choice. We were in this together. My recap went in chronological order— the tampered chair in my office, the venomous visitor in my car, and the psycho driver in the parking lot. My report to the sheriff's office hadn't gone well since I could barely describe the car and I hadn't recorded the license plate.

Jo and Spence stared at me as though they'd been turned to stone. Spence regained his voice first.

"That's it." He crossed his arms over his chest, which

was covered by a ruby cotton polo shirt. "We're ending this investigation. Now. I'm sorry, Jo, but this is way too dangerous."

"I agree." She collapsed back against the sofa. She looked up at me with wounded coffee eyes. "Marvey, I'm so sorry I ever involved you in this."

I held her gaze. "I *chose* to get involved. It was *my* decision then, and it's *my* decision now." I shifted my gaze to Spence. "I appreciate your concern. I really do, but I *can't* stop now. Don't you see? These incidents—the chair, the snake, the car—they must mean we're on the right track."

Spence straightened from the wall, dropping his arms. "These aren't *incidents*, Marvey. They're *attacks*. Whether they're from someone who's afraid you're getting too close to identifying them is irrelevant."

"I disagree." I faced him from the other side of the sofa. Jo sat between us. "It's not irrelevant. In fact, it's very pertinent. The killer knows it's just a matter of time before we identify them."

Spence looked at me as though he was baffled. "This person is trying to hurt you. Tonight, they came too darn close to succeeding. What would've happened if Ms. Sharon hadn't been there? We may not be so lucky next time."

"And there will be a next time, Marvey." Jo's voice was heavy with pain. "You've got to stop. I couldn't bear it if anything happened to you."

Her dark eyes implored me to listen to them. As much as I wanted to give her what she asked for, something inside me couldn't give in, wouldn't give in. I didn't know what it was—our friendship, my quest for justice, my pigheadedness. All of the above. I knew I couldn't walk away from this, knowing I must be just a thought away from identifying Fiona's killer. My eyes were drawn to the kitchen as I pictured the bag of chocolate-covered peanuts stashed in the cabinet closest to the door.

I brought my attention back to my friends and steeled myself to disappoint them. "I promise to be careful." It was the best I could do.

"Think about your family, Marvey." Spence searched my eyes as though trying to read my mind. "What would they want you to do?"

Oh, unfair, particularly since none of them knew about my investigation. The motion-detecting lights had been my parents' idea. Dre had gifted me with the Apple Watch. I suspected he'd programmed it to do more than exchange our activity updates. He may also be able to track my movements.

I sent Spence a look that I hoped expressed my displeasure. "My family knows I wouldn't desert a friend in need. Neither would they."

He threw up his hands. "Then give the deputies the information you have. That wouldn't be deserting Jo, but it would be protecting yourself."

Folding my arms, I wandered away from the sofa. "I've given them updates and they've discounted everything I've said."

"All right." Jo spread her hands. "I appreciate everything you've done and are doing to help me, Marvey. You're a good friend, probably better than I deserve."

I scowled over my shoulder. "Don't be ridiculous."

She continued. "But the situation has gotten way out of control."

"I can't—"

Jo interrupted me. "If you're not going to listen to

reason and stop putting yourself in danger, then I insist on helping you. I'm going everywhere you go. I'm doing everything you do. If that puts me in danger too, then so be it."

She appeared determined to win her argument to get involved this time. But Spence looked as though he expected her ultimatum to convince me to stand down. He was wrong.

"All right. Here's my plan for tomorrow morning." I ignored Jo's satisfied expression and Spence's visible disappointment. "While I was waiting for you, I looked up the trash collection schedule for Bobby Hayes's neighborhood."

Spence frowned again. It seemed that was the expression he'd chosen to wear for the rest of our meeting. "How did you know where he lives?"

I shrugged. "Floyd told me. He really is a Peach Coast goldmine." My description made Spence smile. I was glad he was regaining his good humor. "Okay, so tomorrow's Bobby's trash day."

Jo brought us back to our plans. "Why is that significant?"

I gestured toward her. "Early tomorrow morning, you and I are going to jog to his house and steal his garbage."

She looked from me to Spence and back. "And why would we do that?"

I shrugged a shoulder. "Think about it. If Bobby killed Fiona, he would still have the murder weapon and his bloody clothes. Tomorrow would be the first chance he'd have to dispose of them."

"But wouldn't you be tampering with evidence?" Spence leaned back against the archway again. "If you take Bobby's trash, you can't then give it to the deputies. It wouldn't be admissible in a trial, would it?"

"Actually, it would." I was relieved to be able to answer this very relevant question. "I researched this in *The Comprehensive Private Investigations Guidebook*. In the state of Georgia, as long as the trash is on public property, it's legal for us to examine it, and anything we find would be admissible in court."

"Is that so?" Jo appeared impressed.

So did Spence, but he had more questions. "All right, assuming he's the killer, he may already have disposed of the weapon and bloody clothes. He might've driven to the dumpster outside of town or even stuffed it into someone else's trash can, someone who had an earlier trash collection."

"I'd thought of that." I pursed my lips. "Either one of those scenarios is possible, but the nearest dumpster outside of town has security cameras. I checked. And it would've been risky to put his trash in someone else's bin. Suppose someone had seen him? He'd want to keep a low profile."

Jo spread her arms. "Bobby or someone who's helping him may have a fireplace. They could've burned his clothes as well as the evidence."

Nodding, I gestured toward my friends. "That's also possible. I also considered the killer could've packed everything into a bag and thrown it in the swamp. But they may not have. I want to exhaust every possible avenue. I think it's worth a search of Bobby's trash."

"So do I." Jo slid an apologetic glance toward Spence before shifting forward on the sofa. "What time should I meet you?"

I felt Spence's gaze burning the side of my face. "The

quickest route to Bobby's house is past yours, so I'll meet you at your house by four."

"In the morning? Wow. That's early." Jo started to raise the fingernails of her right hand toward her teeth.

I shook my head to stop her. "The earlier we get there, the less of a chance someone will see us."

"Good point." Spence straightened, bracing his feet beneath him. "I'll meet you there."

"Oh, no you won't." I waved both of my hands, palms out. "You're too well-known in the community to come dumpster diving with us. If Jo and I are seen, no one will think twice. If you come with us, everyone will want to ask about your mother."

Jo chuckled. "That's true. But don't worry, Spence, we'll call you to let you know what's going on."

I grinned as I realized she'd used his words on him.

Spence shook his head. "All right. But if I don't hear from you by six, I'm going to check on you."

Great, another deadline.

CHAPTER 24

W HEN MY BROTHER'S NAME POPPED onto my cell phone's caller identification screen Thursday night, I wondered if he'd somehow known we'd been talking about him.

"Hi, Dre. How're you?" I swung my legs off the sofa, where I'd curled up to re-read parts of Fiona's book. Phoenix was grooming himself on the other end.

"I'm great. How're things in Coconut Coast?" My brother had delusions of comedic genius.

I refused to humor him. "You know that's not what it's called. Have you and Kay figured out how to video-conference me in to Mom and Dad's anniversary party?"

Dre had been married to Kaylee Jones-Harris for almost six years, and she was still laughing at all his jokes. It must be love.

Thankfully, Dre dropped his standup routine and focused on the matter at hand. "We're going to bring my Smart Tablet to their house Sunday afternoon. There's no way we can sneak the software program onto either of their computers without them getting suspicious."

"Good point. Mom and Dad may not be that technologically savvy, but they're not clueless. They'd notice new software on their computers. Bringing your tablet is the best solution." I sighed as another pang of longing hit me.

My parents were celebrating their fortieth wedding anniversary two days from now, Saturday. This would be their first anniversary that I wouldn't be physically with them. Each day, the realization became harder to accept. I knew I'd miss my family when I'd left New York. I hadn't realized how much.

"What time do you want Kay and me to conference you in?" There was a hesitation in Dre's voice. He'd always been attuned to my moods.

I tried to inject more joy into my voice. There was no sense in bringing him down with me. "Whatever time works for you."

"We should be able to get to their house by seven, after the Saturday evening Mass."

"Great! Then you can conference me in at five minutes after seven." The pang of regret was even stronger this time. In the past, we'd attend Mass as a family on my parents' anniversary. It was an unofficial Holy Day of Obligation.

"We'll get as close to that as we can." Dre didn't even chuckle at my joke. "Now that we've settled the time for Mom and Dad's anniversary surprise, tell me what's bothering you."

"What's bothering me is I'm going to miss our parents' *fortieth* anniversary." For the second time tonight, I stood to pace my living room. "I'm not married, but I realize what a big accomplishment forty years of marriage is."

"You won't be here physically, but thanks to technology, you'll still be able to see them and, even more importantly, *they'll* be able to see *you.*"

"I'm sorry to keep repeating this conversation. I just wish I could use my vacation time."

"But you can't, because you've started this job. We understand that."

"Videoconferencing is great, but it's not the same." I stopped in front of my bookcase and absently took in some of the titles, many of which my parents had bought for my birthday or Christmas gifts. I loved getting books for Christmas.

"I know it's not the same, and I'm sorry about that, Marvey." Dre's voice was subdued. The change wasn't easy for him, either. We'd been friends and co-conspirators our entire lives. Age and his marriage hadn't changed that. Distance was trying to.

I made another effort to sound happy. "I appreciate all the extra effort you and Kay are making to include me."

"Of course. Now tell me what else's on your mind."

I hesitated. I should've realized my big brother wouldn't be so easily duped. After all, he'd known me for twenty-eight years. Still, I tried to Bogart it out. "I'm fine, Dre."

"No, you're not. Tell me what's wrong, or I'll tell Mom you're homesick, and she'll be on the next plane to Pineapple Coast."

I sighed. "You know that's not its name." A cold sensation traveled down my spine. "Do you think a horrible sense of humor is hereditary? Is Clay in danger?"

"Have you considered maybe *you're* the one with the bad sense of humor, and that's why you don't get my jokes?"

I ignored his premise as improbable. "Mom and Dad each have a wonderful sense of humor, so maybe the condition skips a generation and Clay will be spared."

"Tell me what's bothering you." Dre's gusty sigh was meant to end the discussion.

"All right." I braced myself for his reaction. Spence's warning wasn't far off the mark. "I'm helping a friend prove her innocence in a murder investigation."

"You're what, now?" Dre's response held a wealth of shock and disbelief, and a pinch of temper.

I filled him in on Fiona's murder, starting with her body being found in To Be Read's storage room. I included everything, even this evening's runaway car in the general store's parking lot. My words sped up as the silence on his end of the line built to a crescendo.

"My God, Marvey. That's dangerous!"

I hadn't heard that particular tone from my older brother since my thirteen-year-old self had shared with him my plans to travel to New Orleans for Mardi Gras and still make it back in time for the Ash Wednesday Mass in Brooklyn.

I prepared my best defense. "Mom and Dad know about Fiona's murder."

"But do they know you're playing Nancy Drew?" Dre's response was an indication that my best defense had fallen short.

I paced away from the bookcase and wandered toward the fireplace. The pale wood mantel was crowded with photos of family and friends, old and new. The current trend was to store photos in electronic albums, but I preferred to surround myself with images of the people who mattered most to me.

Toward the center of the group of photos was a

framed image of Dre after our last run in Marine Park, one of our favorite workout locations. He was dripping with sweat and smiling into my phone camera.

I smiled at the photo. "It's more like Brenda Starr, reporter."

"Are you laughing?" His incredulity was choking him. "This isn't funny. You can't investigate a *murder*."

"I'm not investigating a murder. I'm collecting proof that there are other—better—suspects than my friend."

"And how are you doing that?" His restrained tone was the first sign he was laying a verbal trap for me.

"By asking people who knew the victim if they know who might have a motive to hurt her."

"That's *investigating*, Marvey." His "duh" was left unspoken but still clearly heard.

I turned away from the fireplace mantel. The photo of Dre after our run wasn't a fond memory right now. "What would you have me do, then? For some unfathomable reason, the deputies are solely focused on my friend for this murder. She's innocent. What would you have me do?"

"Peach Coast may be safer than Brooklyn, but that obviously doesn't mean it doesn't have *any* crime. We're talking about a murder."

This didn't seem the right time to point out that he knew the name of the town to which I'd moved. "If you were me, what would you do? Would you walk away from your friend?"

This time his silence was longer. I sensed his turmoil and understood it. I was his family. He wanted me to be safe, but we both knew he'd be lying if he said he'd turn his back on a friend in need. We weren't raised that way.

His weary, frustrated sigh ended the heavy silence. "Just be careful."

"I promise." It was a promise I intended to keep.

"And if there's even the suspicion of another suspicious incident, I won't tell Mom or Dad. I'll come down there myself."

"I understand." I nodded, although Dre couldn't see me. "I love you."

He grunted. "I love you too." He ended the call without another word.

This "discussion" was far from over. Dre was just pausing to regroup and compile additional, more effective ammunition. I'd probably hear from him again in the morning.

Family. We were uniquely qualified to drive each other crazy.

I'd stepped out of the living room for ten minutes, fifteen tops, to get my pendant-making materials. I wanted to work on Jo's gift. When I returned, I almost dropped my plastic tub of supplies. Phoenix had once again stacked all his worldly possessions against my front door—his food bowl, bed, toys, and blankets. He stood beside his belongings, returning my gaze in defiance.

I was tempted to tell him to clean up his mess himself, but I sensed extreme empathy was needed. This moment was an emotional one for both of us.

Swallowing a sigh, I set the tub with my supplies on the coffee table and faced him. "Phoenix, I sense your frustration. I'm frustrated too."

I scooped him up from the entranceway and carried him to my oversized, overstuffed, faux brown leather armchair. Phoenix turned his back to me in a feline snub. I wasn't going to win him over so easily.

I petted him with long, slow strokes from the crown of his head to his tail. "I'm very concerned that you're unhappy. I don't like seeing you this way. You haven't been yourself since our move." He deigned to send me a look over his shoulder before turning away from me again. "Hopefully, our visit to the vet tomorrow will help me to understand what's causing your unhappiness."

Phoenix shifted to lay across my lap. A good sign.

I continued petting him, now in silence. He was getting tired. I glanced over my shoulder toward the door and Phoenix's belongings. In a little while, I'd get up and put his treasures away. For now, I was going to focus on my cat. Jo wasn't my only friend in need of help.

"One block to go." Jo's pronouncement was weak. She wiped the sweat from her eyes as she kept pace beside me on my right.

Early morning dew mingled with the sweat on my cheeks as we jogged toward Bobby's house shortly before dawn Friday morning. Each breath drew in the musky, grassy scent of the wetlands that were always nearby.

"That's right." My wrist muffled my response as I dabbed at the sweat above my lip.

I wasn't sure why we were whispering. Maybe that's what people did when they were on their way to steal another person's trash. Technically, it wasn't stealing to take trash that someone had set out on the curb, though. Police didn't even need a warrant to search it. I'd researched that yesterday.

"Since we're jogging together this morning, do we still need to jog together tomorrow morning?" Jo puffed the question between breaths.

I shot her a wide-eyed look. "Yes, we do. Our Saturday-morning jogs were your idea."

Shortly after Jo and I had met, we'd started jogging together every Saturday. Our arrangement gave her a partner to help motivate her to work out more. She'd gotten out of the habit when she'd been launching her bookstore. In exchange, I had a guide to show me around Peach Coast. Each week, she took me to different neighborhoods, parks, and beaches.

Jo groaned. "But I don't usually jog this far—or this fast—when I exercise alone. I might not be able to keep up this pace two days in a row."

I mulled that over for a few steps while monitoring the vehicle creeping toward us down the center of the two-way street. Maybe I was being paranoid. Maybe not. The evidence that someone was out to get me was pretty overwhelming. It seemed rational to err on the side of self-preservation. The pre-dawn shadows and the vehicle's headlights combined to mask its identifying features. But I could confirm that this SUV wasn't the sedan that had tried to kill Willy and me.

Somewhat reassured, I glanced at Jo. "If you're not up to it, then—"

The sudden scream of the SUV's horn as it stopped beside us smashed the quiet morning and snatched several years from my life. From Jo's panicked expression, it seemed she had the same reaction. I glared past her at the offending vehicle, which had stopped under one of the rare streetlamps. The tinted windows kept me from seeing the driver.

The passenger side window slid down, and a voice called from inside the car. "Jo? Marvey? What y'all doing out this time of night?"

Jo squinted toward the car. "Stella? Is that you?"

The voice did sound like Stella Lowry, one of our Peach Coast Library Book Club members. I winced as I looked around at the still-dark windows in the condos and homes around us. If Stella hadn't woken the residents with her car horn, she'd surely woken the dead with her powerful lungs.

"It's not nighttime, Stella." I called back in a stage whisper. I followed Jo into the street, checking carefully to make sure there weren't any mysterious speed demons lying in wait for us. "It's the AM."

In the dim light from the streetlamp, I read the other woman's skeptical expression. It was also in her voice. "Is it dark?"

"Yes." Knowing where this was going, I smiled.

"Then it's night." Stella nodded to emphasize her conclusion. Her glossy chestnut tresses swept over her shoulder.

Jo considered the direction from which Stella had arrived. "Where are you going at this hour?"

Stella sighed. Her pleased expression dimmed. "I have a friend over in Tampa who's feeling pretty poorly. I thought I'd make a surprise visit to try to cheer her up."

"Who are you going to see—"

"Jo." I sent a pointed look to my partner-in-what-wasn't-a-crime. "I'm sorry, but we should let Stella get moving. Besides, we need to finish our jog so we can get to work on time."

We had no way of knowing what time the refuse trucks would pick up Bobby's trash. That was the reason we'd agreed to err on the side of coming out at the armpit of dawn. If we chatted with Stella much longer, we risked getting to Bobby's house after the trucks.

Her confusion cleared. "Oh, that's right. Sorry. Drive safely, Stella, and have a nice visit."

As we stepped away from her car, Stella tapped the vehicle's horn twice. "Bye, ladies!" Her farewell could challenge an operatic crescendo.

"Oh my God." I scanned the windows around us, looking for shifting curtains. "I'd be surprised if at least a dozen people aren't watching us right now."

Jo looked up and over her shoulders. She gave an awkward wave. "Sorry!" she called in a hushed tone.

"Let's keep going. Just half a block more." I turned to lead us to Bobby's house. "How long will it take Stella to get to Tampa?"

Jo spread her arms in a shrug. "About four hours, give or take. She's probably leaving extra early to beat rush-hour traffic."

"I think it's sweet of her to make the trip. I hope her friend appreciates it."

"I'm sure she will."

The mini-break we had talking with Stella must've revived Jo. She ran with much more energy as we started the final block. The house numbers on this side of the street were even digits. They increased as we jogged up the block. I'd estimated we were within three houses of Bobby's when I noticed an older woman standing her trash can in front of the home next to our target. Light from nearby porches cast a glow around her, making her seem like a character from a young adult paranormal novel.

She watched us as we drew nearer. A cherubic smile softened her rosy-cheeked features. Her pale lavender track suit was roomy around her petite frame. "Ooh, you girls are out early this mornin'."

Jo stopped and returned her smile. "So are you, ma'am."

"I prefer to bring my trash out in the mornin's." A gentle breeze ruffled her wavy white hair as she glanced back at her trash can. Her gaze strayed up toward the still-dark sky, where the stars winked down at us. "I love this time of day. Don't you?"

"Yes, it's so peaceful." Oh, no. I could see Bobby's trash can. It was steps away at the curb in front of his house. I scanned the streets—no sign of the garbage truck, but I could hear it. The sound was faint, but it must be nearby. We were running out of time.

"It's my favorite time of day too." Jo's smile was tense around the edges. She must be anxious also.

Tick-tock. Tick-tock.

Our new friend shifted her stance, bringing my attention to her purple sneakers. "It's so still. One of the rare times you can hear yourself think. I imagine that's why you run this early."

"Yes, ma'am. You're right." I caught Jo's attention and hoped she could read my stare language: *we need a distraction.*

Jo nodded. Was she signaling me, or agreeing with what I'd said? "We usually jog this early."

The older woman's blue eyes examined our features. "Oh? I haven't seen you before, and I'm out most mornin's."

I checked the time on my black-banned watch. We needed to move. Maybe if we continued jogging, we could circle back for Bobby's trash. But the truck was on its way. "We usually jog through different neighborhoods. Excuse—"

Jo interrupted me. "Ma'am, I wonder if I could trouble you for a glass of water? I'm afraid I didn't drink enough before my friend and I met for our run, and my throat's awfully dry."

"Yes, of course, dear." Our companion looked concerned as she turned to me. "Would you like some water too?"

I inclined my head, sending Jo an approving look. "I'm not thirsty, ma'am, but thank you. I should keep going. I want to get my miles in before work."

Bobby's neighbor made certain I wasn't thirsty before she led Jo into her home. I turned to jog past Bobby's house, biding my time until Jo and her hostess were behind closed doors. Jo's ability to read my silent message impressed me. She was a good friend.

As I jogged away, Jo's voice carried across to me. "Ma'am, do you have a library card?"

Correction: Jo was a great friend.

CHAPTER 25

"WE DIDN'T FIND THE BLOODY clothes or knife in Bobby's trash." Speaking with Spence almost an hour later, I was still weighed down by disappointment. "There was nothing incriminating in any of the bags."

I'd texted him earlier to let him know Jo and I had accomplished our mission, but that I'd have to fill him in later. I'd been anxious to go through the two bags before getting ready for work. I hadn't wanted to be late.

"Nothing at all?" Spence's concern worked its way through the cell connection.

"Just a bunch of trash. Bobby recently changed the oil in his car. I found an oil filter, a couple of containers of five-W-thirty, and a lot of oily rags."

Spence paused before continuing. "What did you do with his trash?"

"I put the bags in my trash can." I rolled my chair closer to my desk. Maintenance had repaired it—and gotten rid of the squeak. "The sanitation engineers will probably think I'd hosted a party over the weekend with all the bags of barbecue potato chips and soda."

"You mean Coke."

I heard the humor in Spence's voice. I chuckled. "No, I mean *soda*."

"When in Rome..." He sobered. "How's Jo?"

The disappointment in her eyes would stay with me the rest of the day. "She's pretty upset, but working hard not to show it." I massaged the knot tightening at the nape of my neck. "Until this morning, I don't think either of us realized how much we were hoping we'd find something in Bobby's trash, irrefutable proof of Jo's innocence that would finally—finally—convince the deputies to take her off their suspect list."

Spence paused again. I imagined him seated behind his faux ash wood modular desk in his spacious, bright newspaper office. "If Bobby's the killer, it's possible he got rid of the evidence earlier or some other way."

I remembered him raising that possibility last night. "I can't think of anywhere else to look. For all we know, he's burned his bloody clothes and buried the knife."

Silence settled over the phone as I tried to puzzle out our next steps. Who to investigate? What questions to ask? How best to convince the deputies their stubborn refusal to look at any other suspect was enabling a murderer to walk free? It had been almost a week since Fiona's murder; six days since Jo, Spence, and I began our inquiry.

"It's also possible Bobby isn't the killer." Spence voiced the suggestion I didn't want to hear.

"But his motive is stronger than Jo's, and I'm sure he's behind the threats I've received." I waved my hand toward my office door. "He was here at the library the day my chair collapsed. He's a repair person, which means tampering with my chair would've been quick and easy for him. He drives a dark sedan like the one that tried to kill me and Willy. And he likes snakes, especially those similar to the one that tried to drive away in my car."

"Those are great points, and I'm not discounting them." His calm response had a relaxing effect on me.

"I know you're not." I glanced at my lower left-hand desk drawer. I once again reminded myself to bring in a stash of chocolate-covered peanuts. "But I'm not ready to give up on the idea of Bobby as our prime suspect."

"Remember his motive only works *if* Fiona spent his inheritance."

I closed my eyes briefly. Spence had another good point. "You're right. How can we verify that?"

"Change of plans." Disappointment and frustration mingled in my brother's voice when he called Friday morning.

"What's up?" I saved my computer file and gave him my full attention.

"We need to move up the time for Operation Anniversary Surprise. Can you do a morning call?" Dre's voice was almost overpowered by the cacophony of conversations in the background.

A glance at the clock in the lower-right corner of my computer screen revealed it was almost ten minutes before nine AM, class change at John Jay College of Criminal Justice where Dre taught Forensic Accounting. "Of course. I'm free tomorrow morning. Why? What's going on?"

"Mom and Dad are going to see a play with the Carlisles." The voices were getting closer to Dre. His classroom must be filling up.

Steve and Ruby Carlisle had been my parents' best friends since college. The two couples had met at the University of Syracuse and had been double dating ever since. The Carlisles had just celebrated their fortieth wedding anniversary.

"Oh, that sounds like fun." I smiled, leaning back on my chair.

Dre chuckled. "It's a musical. Dad and Steve are putting a brave face on it. They're going into the city. They have tickets to an afternoon show, so instead of dinner, we're doing breakfast. Do you think we can connect at nine?"

"Nine would be perfect." I had no other plans. "I'll decorate my dining room tonight. Consider it the satellite celebration location. It'll make me feel more like I'm there with you."

Dre laughed. "They'll get a kick out of that."

I laughed too, knowing Dre was right. My parents would love that. "Their grandcat isn't in much of a partying mood, but I'm taking him to the vet after work tonight."

"I hope the vet can help him. Keep me posted." His concern was a comfort. He was more of a dog person, but he and Phoenix had always gotten along well.

"I will. Thanks." I straightened on my seat. "Has my gift arrived yet?"

"I'm sure it'll come today."

"That's cutting it really close." I rubbed the frown lines from my forehead.

"It'll get here. Don't worry. Worst-case scenario, it'll be a day or two late. That's not the end of the world."

"No, I suppose not." But it would feel that way. Their anniversary gifts included a framed photograph of Phoenix and me in front of our new home. Jo had taken the picture for us. I'd also bought them matching University of Georgia Bulldog sweatshirts, my nod to my new home. But I was and always would be a New York University alumna.

"You like Peach Coast, don't you?" His voice was hesitant and concerned.

"I really do," I assured him. "It's a pretty town, and the people are great. I just get homesick now and then. I'm looking forward to you, Kay, and Clay coming to visit."

"So are we." He was beginning to sound distracted. It was almost time for his class to start. "And what about that other thing? Have you put it behind you?"

I sighed. "Dre, you said you wouldn't walk away from a friend in need, either."

"That's different."

"Why? Because you're the oldest? It doesn't work that way anymore, pal."

"If anything happened to you, Mom and Dad would never forgive themselves—or me."

I caught my breath. "Please don't tell them."

"Marvey, I don't like keeping things from them."

I laughed with incredulity. "Since when? I've been protecting plenty of your secrets, and they aren't all from our childhood, Mr. My-Car-Was-Towed-And-I-Had-To-Borrow-Money-From-My-Sister-To-Get-It-Back."

Dre blew out a breath. "Are you really comparing my borrowing money from you because my car was towed to your running around like some comic book superhero?"

I frowned at my cell phone. I wasn't doing any such thing. Was I? "Please, Dre. There's no need to worry them. I promise to be careful."

He grunted his displeasure. Did he know how much he sounded like Dad when he did that? "I won't tell them. Yet. Listen, I've got to go. Class is starting. Stay out of trouble."

"I will." *...do the very best I can.*

A weight settled on my shoulders as we ended our call. It was from more than missing my family and more than my worry over Phoenix. It also was from the worry I was causing my brother and the secret I'd just sworn him to.

Cecelia Jean Holt surprised me with a visit late Friday morning. Rule of thumb: it wasn't a good sign when a member of the library's Board of Directors bypassed your boss and found her way into your office. Even though I was Spence's friend, something told me Cecelia wasn't here to invite me to a surprise birthday party for her son.

Adrian had escorted the board member to my office. From his wide-eyed look, he didn't believe there was a birthday party invitation in my future, either. His retreat was understandably hasty.

I circled my desk and offered her my hand. "Good morning, Ms. Holt. Please have a seat." A whiff of her perfume reminded me of magnolias. The soft fragrance followed her to one of the guest chairs in front of my desk.

"Thank you, Marvey. I apologize for interrupting your morning." In her slim, pale peach skirt suit, Cecelia brought to mind a young Diahann Carroll in appearance as well as style. She was several inches—perhaps half a foot—taller than my five-foot-three-inch height and fashion-model slim.

"Not at all. It's nice to see you again." I settled onto my chair, rolling it with me under my desk. I was so glad it no longer squeaked. That wouldn't have made a good impression on the board member. "How may I help you?"

"My son warned me you had that New York style of getting right to the point." Cecelia's smile was warm and disarming, so like her son's, revealing perfect, white teeth. There was a twinkle in her midnight eyes.

During my more than four months in Peach Coast, I'd learned to be cautious around those charming Southern smiles. "Please excuse me. Poor Spence has told me—on more than one occasion—people in Peach Coast like to ease into a conversation."

"Conversation is an art." Her voice was modest, almost apologetic. She placed her black purse on the empty armchair beside her. "How are you getting on, settling into Peach Coast?"

As my new neighbors would say, I may have been born at night, but it wasn't last night. Cecelia Holt hadn't come to my office for small talk. Whether in New York or Peach Coast, board members didn't have time for that. I coaxed myself to relax and wait, but the New Yorker in me kept my guard up. "I'm settling in very well. Thank you, Ms. Holt. I was just telling my brother how charming the town is, and how friendly and wel-coming everyone has been." With the possible exception of Delores Polly.

Cecelia looked pleased. "I'm glad to hear that. I've heard a lot of wonderful things about you too."

"That's nice to know." I struggled to come up with something else to say. I was from Brooklyn; small talk wasn't my forté. I needn't have worried.

In her slow, Southern style, Cecelia asked about my favorite places so far, where I've been and where I might want to visit next, regional foods I've tried, and restaurants she'd recommend. She finished off with endorsements for upcoming events I wouldn't want to miss.

"I understand you and Spence are running the Cobbler Crawl next Saturday."

Even the thought of eating a pie while racing made me queasy. "Yes, I'm looking forward to it."

"I'm sure you are." Cecelia sounded amused. Had Spence told her about my digestive concerns? She took a visual tour of my office. What did my belongings reveal to my astute guest?

The narrow, three-shelf faux oak bookcase beside the conversation table to my right held marketing and fundraising reference books, and project binders. The bookends cast as Patience and Fortitude, the marble lions that flanked the entrance to the New York Public Library, had been a going-away gift from my former coworkers.

On my desk within easy reach, in addition to my nearly empty inbox, were a dictionary, thesaurus, and *The Chicago Manual of Style*. Several photos of my family lined the shelf above my computer monitor.

Cecelia's attention returned to me. "What a lovely pendant. I've heard about them."

"Thank you." I touched the pendant, reminding myself that today's image was *The Joy Luck Club* by Amy Tan. Like most books, the classic novel had a different cover for each reprint. I'd chosen the one with the illustration of a young woman and an older woman, standing with their backs to the reader, their arms around each other's waist. "Spence suggested I teach people how to make these pendants. I think that workshop would be a nice fundraiser for the library."

Cecelia folded her hands on her lap and squared her shoulders. "The library is very important to me."

Those words warmed my heart, especially coming from a board member. "To me as well."

She flashed a quick smile. "My position on the board allows me to ensure we have diverse stories written by diverse authors, featuring diverse characters. I can make sure the library shows its value to *all* the demographics in our community—young, old, men, women, well-off, and struggling."

"Those things are important to me as well."

Cecelia gave me a level look. "Then you'll understand when I ask that, for the good of the library, stick to promoting it and its services. Let the deputies investigate poor Fiona Lyle-Hayes's murder."

I probably should've seen that coming. But despite my own words of caution, Cecelia had caught me off guard. How should I respond to the board member? Then I remembered what Corrinne had said when I'd asked why she'd defended me to the mayor. Her words gave me the encouragement I needed to oppose the board member.

"Ms. Holt, I'm not working against the deputies." I stacked my hands before me on the cool surface of my desk. "In fact, the deputies and I are working toward the same thing: serving the community. I'm also helping a friend in need."

"Don't you think your investigation is sending the community the wrong message?" Cecelia swept her right arm as though encompassing the library. "I think it's distracting from the library's mission to support literacy and literature."

Her question made me smile. "The library's a place that promotes intellectual curiosity. Books inspire people to learn, to seek the truth, to verify information instead of simply accepting what we're told. I want to be an example of that."

I remained still, giving Cecelia time to digest my words. It seemed she started to argue the point before settling back to consider it.

The silence stretched for a slow minute, and then understanding brightened her dark eyes. "All right, Marvey. You raise a good point." The other woman nodded as her gaze once again swept my office. "I hadn't thought of the library in quite that way."

I breathed a sigh of relief. Another challenge won. I hoped to clear Jo's name before other board members decided to pay me a visit.

CHAPTER 26

To Be Read was hopping. The bookstore had always seemed busy, especially Friday afternoons. It wasn't quite that busy this Friday afternoon, but it was close. During the six days since Fiona's murder, it was understandable customer traffic would've dropped drastically. But people were slowly coming back. Slowly.

Following the aroma of flavored coffee and fresh pastries, I turned toward the little café to the left of the store's entrance. The café was usually standing-room only for lunch in the modest seating area. Today, there were only a few readers/diners and plenty of empty chairs.

I found Jo and Spence near the customer service desk. The concern on Jo's face drove a knife through my heart.

"People are still coming to terms with Ms. Fiona's death." Spence was talking as I joined them. "It hasn't even been a week yet."

"It'll be a week tomorrow." Jo waved a hand in an agitated gesture. "In the meantime, this is a disaster. A right disaster. My poor store has become a paranormal attraction. People have actually asked me if I've seen Fiona's ghost 'yet,' as though they expect it to turn up sooner or later. Can you believe that?"

I winced. "That's a little creepy."

Jo shook her head, setting her thick ponytail spinning behind her shoulders. "Sales are way down because people who *don't* want to see a ghost are staying home, and they far outnumber those who do. Some of those people may never come back."

I exchanged a concerned look with Spence, who stood on her other side. "What about your online orders?"

"Those have gone up a bit." She expelled a heavy sigh. "On the bright side, several people have told me they don't believe I killed Fiona. So that's good news. Now if we could just convince the deputies."

"We're working on it." I gave her shoulder a squeeze before letting my hand drop to my side.

"That's right." Spence's tone was bracing. "We're not giving up. You can't, either."

"It still upsets me to think that someone was murdered in my store." Jo crossed her arms over her Gator green shirt. Her voice was a whisper. "How can friends, neighbors, employees—customers—ever feel safe here again?"

"Of course they will." And clearing her name would help. The sooner, the better.

The arrival of our lunch order afforded us a brief diversion. Earlier, Jo had taken our soup and salad requests so we could share lunch and catch up on our investigation in the privacy of her office.

"What do we owe you?" I dug through sales receipts

and coffee shop napkins to find my wallet. Once again, it crossed my mind I should clean out my purse.

"It's my treat." Jo paid the delivery woman, then took the food bags from her. "It's the least I can do for all the two of you are going through to help me."

Spence and I protested her generous offer, but Jo remained stubborn. She seemed to ignore us as we followed her to her office toward the center of the bookstore. Her obstinacy was her only flaw—and one of many characteristics we shared.

We gathered around Jo's cozy conversation table for lunch. The air in her office was brisk. I was convinced she kept the temperature down for an excuse to wear her orange-and-green college cardigan.

In my peripheral vision, I noticed Jo had added a few more stress balls to the collection on her desk. A peek at her hands revealed she'd all but decimated her fingernails. While we dug into our soups and sandwiches, we kept our conversation light—delicious food, wonderful weather, weekend plans.

"My big weekend plan is celebrating my parents' fortieth wedding anniversary." A grin stretched my lips. "My brother's going to teleconference me in to the celebration to surprise them."

"Congratulations to your parents." Jo paused with her soup spoon partway to her mouth.

"That's wonderful." Spence sketched a toast with his bottle of iced tea.

"I'm happy for them." I sighed with satisfaction and a tinge of regret for the distance between us. If only I could use some vacation time. "And I'm taking Phoenix to a new vet after work this evening."

"I hope this one can help him." Spence gave me a

look of concern as he finished his Southern-fried fish sandwich.

Jo swallowed a bite of her Southern-style buttermilk fried chicken sandwich. "Has he shown any improvement at all?"

I flexed my shoulders in a restless movement. "A little, but he's still not himself. In Brooklyn, he loved to explore. He was always getting into something. Ever since our move, he's been disinterested in everything."

"Hopefully, the vet will be able to treat Phoenix and he'll make a speedy recovery." Jo set aside the remains of her sandwich, and chicken stew with tomatoes and herbs. Her voice bounced with an optimism I hadn't heard in days.

"I hope so too." Since my favorites—turkey club and New England clam chowder—weren't on the sandwich shop's menu, I'd made do with the turkey-and-cheddar sandwich and chicken noodle soup. I slid a look toward Spence. "Your mother came to see me this morning. She asked me to stop our investigation."

"Really?" Spence sounded amused.

"*Really?*" Jo was horrified.

"Really." I held up my hand to stop Jo as she started to interrupt. "But I was able to change her mind."

Spence took a deep drink of his iced tea. "She gave me a similar lecture about the newspaper and my position in the community."

Startled, I frowned at him. "You could've warned me your mother was opposed to our inquiry."

His smile was unrepentant. "Now where's the fun in that?"

Jo's wide-eyed look of concern swung from him to me and back. "Your mama's a member of the library's board of directors. Is Marvey's job in jeopardy? I don't want her to get in trouble for helping me."

I blinked. "My job isn't in jeopardy. Ms. Holt agreed I could continue our inquiry."

"But, Marvey, *your boss's boss* came to your office." Jo emphasized her words as though willing me to feel her fear. She turned to Spence. "Would your mama fire Marvey for helping me?"

"Don't worry, Jo. My mama won't do that." His tone was somber, but I caught the glint of humor in his dark eyes.

Jo didn't appear convinced. "How do you know?"

"Well, first, my mama's a savvy businesswoman." He set down his sandwich and gave Jo his undivided attention. "And second, she's told me often enough she's impressed by what Marvey's already accomplished for the library in the short time she's been here."

I pinned Jo with a direct look. "Are you satisfied?"

"She's been singing Marvey's praises." Spence collected his sandwich.

I patted his firm arm, which was covered by his pale cream business shirt. "That's enough now, Spence. You're embarrassing me."

"Yes, thank you, Marvey. I'm satisfied." Jo folded her arms across her chest. "I just don't want either of you getting in trouble with Spence's mama any more than I want to lose my store."

A chill crawled through me. What would happen to To Be Read if we weren't able to clear Jo's reputation? What would happen to the community if it didn't have convenient access to a bookstore?

"We're going to prove your innocence." Spence's tone made a believer out of me. "I heard back from Isaiah, our Peach Coast Inn manager. He confirmed Pelt checked in Saturday night, after the deputies would've taken his statement for Fiona's murder."

"Thank you for looking into that for us, Spence." Was it wrong that part of me was disappointed Willy hadn't lied about when he'd gotten into town?

Jo pushed aside her half-eaten sandwich. "Does this mean we have to take him off our list?"

"He's still a person of interest as far as I'm concerned." I finished my soup. "But it would've been easier to build an argument to investigate him if we had proof he'd had time to commit the murder."

"We've been investigating for five days." Jo balanced her elbows on the table and cradled her head in her hands. "Tomorrow will be a week since Fiona's murder, but we don't have any additional information to present to the deputies and they're still focused on me. What are we missing?"

I jerked my chin toward Spence. "We're meeting with Buddy's lawyer Monday. We're going to keep digging, Jo."

Hoping to lighten the mood before going back to work, I redirected our conversation to more casual topics—upcoming new book releases, summer plans, and the weather. We cleared the remnants of our lunch and made our way out of Jo's office. In the store, I faced a view of shelf after shelf after shelf of books. As usual, the sight sent my inner bookworm into a fit of ecstasy.

Without To Be Read, residents would have to drive nineteen point one miles to the nearest bookstore. Granted, the grocery store, general store, pharmacy, and a few other locations had modest literature selections. Jo's store, however, catered to a wide range of literary tastes, and offered events to celebrate books and reading. Losing either the library or the bookstore would be a devastating blow to the Peach Coast community.

I turned to follow Jo and Spence to the front of the store...then did a double take. The sight of a familiar figure in the store's romance section captured my attention.

I called to my friends over my shoulder. "Go ahead without me. I'll catch up with you."

"Where are you going?" Jo's voice trailed after me. I ignored her for now.

I had Zelda Taylor in my sights and was determined to question the writing group president. "Hey, Zelda. I'm so happy to see you at the bookstore."

Startled, she spun to face me. The pleated skirt of her cream cotton dress spun around her. A cloud of her soft, floral perfume embraced me. "Marvey. Hello. I'm happy to see you here too. My, your pendant is lovely."

"Thank you." I touched my *Joy Luck Club* pendant. "There are people in town who are giving Jo's bookstore a wide berth after Fiona's murder."

"Yes, I've heard some of the talk around town." Zelda waved a dismissive hand. The diamonds in her silver charm bracelet glittered under the fluorescent lights. "People are unsettled because of the murder. It's understandable. Once the killer's been caught, everyone will feel better, and things will go back to normal." She dialed down her master-of-ceremonies volume for a more confidential tone. "I've also heard you're doing some amateur sleuthing. What have you learned?"

I released my pendant and folded my hands in front of my hips over my pencil-thin dark blue skirt. "I've learned there was tension between you and Fiona. May I ask the cause of it?"

Zelda straightened as though jerked from behind. A few red strands escaped the pile of hair on top of her head. She touched the short pearl necklace that dressed up the otherwise plain bodice of her dress. "What are you saying? Do you think *I* could've killed Fiona?"

"I'm not trying to find the killer." I spread my arms. "I'm trying to prove my friend's innocence."

"By pointing the finger at someone else? You're very bold."

"I'll let the evidence do the pointing."

Zelda took my measure as though trying to decide how much, if anything, to tell me. I knew she wasn't obligated to speak with me. No one was. But I dared to hope she would, if only to clear suspicion from herself. I held her gaze, reminding myself to breathe.

After a moment, her body relaxed. She shrugged. "Why not? They say confession is good for the soul. There was a time I wanted to hurt Fiona." Zelda's voice was low and intense. "I even fantasized about it. That woman ruined my life."

She wasn't the only one who could make that claim. "How?"

"As I said, those feelings are in the past. I didn't kill Fiona." Zelda's simple gray pumps tapped across the hardwood flooring as she crossed to a pair of overstuffed armchairs.

I followed. "What happened between you?"

Zelda gracefully lowered herself onto one of the floral upholstered armchairs. I sank onto the one beside her. Her white cheeks flushed pink, and she dropped her eyes. "I was a financial manager with Malcovich Savings and Loan. I loved my job. I really loved it, and I enjoyed working for the bank. Over the years, I'd climbed the corporate ladder, and I was looking for my next big move."

"I'm listening." I could hear her excitement as she talked about her previous job. It reminded me of the passion I had for the library and my career.

My empathy was growing for her. Because I knew how the story would end, I took a breath to brace myself and caught the scent of fresh paper and new books. A brief scan of the seating area confirmed we had the space to ourselves. Nearby signage revealed we were in To Be Read's self-help section. I forced myself to look away from the bookshelves.

Zelda folded her arms and crossed legs. I was pretty sure that with her interest in body language, Viv would agree Zelda was feeling defensive. "The bank asked Fiona to do an audit of a product I was in charge of. It was a successful product. They were thinking of expanding it, but wanted an outside review to make sure the numbers were solid. I didn't think anything of it."

"Why would you? I'm sure you did your due diligence to confirm your reports." I sensed we'd come to the part of her story in which bad things were about to happen. Her dream career would become a nightmare.

"Absolutely I did." Zelda sat straighter and gripped the arms of her chair. "I was confident the audit was a formality. The bank would greenlight expanding the product, and I'd get my promotion. I was wrong on all three accounts."

Here it comes. "Fiona found something."

Zelda sighed. It was the sound of someone trying to put the past behind her and to find inner peace. "According to her audit, the formula I programmed for my spreadsheet was wrong. The bank was actually losing money on the project. I was fired on the spot."

I briefly closed my eyes as I imagined the pain, anxiety, and humiliation Zelda must've felt as a result. "I'm so sorry. How devastating."

"You have a way with words." Zelda's tone was dry. "Yes, I was devastated, mortified, and very, very confused."

"Because if the product was losing money, you—or someone—would've realized it sooner."

"That's exactly what I thought." She wiped away tears. "I was certain Fiona had done something to my files to make it seem as though the error had been mine. I was confident my spreadsheet could not have been wrong. I was sure of it. I even confronted her."

Reaching into my purse, I took out a small packet of tissues and offered one to Zelda. "Had Fiona tampered with your files?"

"No, she hadn't." Zelda dried her eyes. Her face was pale and pinched. "The error had been mine. *I* had made the mistake, and it went undiscovered until Fiona's audit. Confronting her just made matters worse. At first, I felt like a failure. Afterward, I also felt like a fool. The whole thing really shook my confidence, you know? I didn't even have the courage to apply for another job."

"I'm so sorry." I waited a beat for her to regain her composure before continuing. "Is that the reason you and Fiona stopped attending your writers group's critique sessions? Because of this bad experience?"

Zelda took a shuttering breath. "I can't speak for her, but that's part of the reason I stopped attending. Seeing her reminded me of my failure. It was bad enough sitting next to her during the meetings. I didn't want to extend my discomfort with the critique sessions."

"I'm truly sorry you had that experience." I considered the other woman. She was smart, professional, personable, and loved books. "I don't mean to pry, but have you found another job? The library is filling entry-level positions. They're only part-time, but you could get a paycheck while looking for something more suitable."

Zelda offered me a weak smile. "Thank you, Marvey, but I already have a part-time job. Fiona hired me." She sighed again. "Instead of being grateful, I was embarrassed. Pride is a sin. I'd been a financial manager for a national bank. Now I'm working part-time for a local accounting firm. Well, it's a paycheck and it's helping to rebuild my confidence."

"Good luck. And thank you for sharing your experiences with me. I know you didn't have to."

"They were right." Zelda squared her shoulders. "Confession is good for the soul. So are you taking me off your list of persons of interest?"

"As far as I'm concerned, you're cleared." I rose from the soft floral armchair. "But if you think of someone who may have had a stronger motive to kill Fiona, could you please let me know?"

She looked up at me. "You know, during that whole ordeal, Fiona never told a soul outside of the bank about my mistake. Not even Nolan. Even after I confronted her. She never told a soul."

"It makes me wonder whether she was the villain people considered her to be."

Zelda stood. "It's been my experience people often aren't what they may seem."

That was only part of the problem.

CHAPTER 27

WE WERE CROSSING NAMES OFF our suspect list quickly. Too quickly? Betty, Bobby, Willy, Nolan, Zelda. Was I too trusting of their protestations of innocence? One of these people must be the killer.

Or am I overlooking someone?

These doubts and second-guesses dogged my footsteps as I rejoined my friends. The only thing I was absolutely clear on was Jo's innocence.

"I just spoke with Zelda Taylor." I found Jo and Spence beside one of the front book displays of new nonfiction releases. I lowered my voice to share what I'd learned.

"Maybe blackmail wasn't her motive." Jo sounded as desperate and frustrated as I felt. "Maybe she had another reason to want to hurt Fiona."

Spence put a comforting hand on Jo's shoulder. "We'll get to the bottom of this."

"Excuse me, Ms. Jo." A bookstore employee bounded forward. Her big brown eyes smiled, and her mass of reddish-gold curls seemed to wave at us before she centered her attention on her employer. "I'm sorry to interrupt y'all. Ms. Jo, I was wondering if you'd seen my jacket? I'm sure I'd left it in the storage room."

The words "storage room" grabbed my attention. A jacket was missing from the crime scene? I gave the store clerk a measuring look. She was about my height—five-foot three—and slender. Our primary suspects probably wouldn't be able to fit into her jacket to cover themselves from the blood. Disappointed, I allowed my thoughts to wander. What was my next move?

"I'm sorry, Blanche. I don't recall seeing a jacket." Jo frowned as though searching her memory. "What did it look like?"

Blanche shook her head, reanimating her curls. "It's actually my boyfriend's. He loaned it to me a little more than a week ago. It's just a plain black spring jacket. It's pretty beat up, but I told him I got cold in the storage room sometimes, and he said I could hold onto it."

Hope revived in my heart. I used the new information about the jacket to tailor my mental image of our suspects' ability to fit into it. "What size is the jacket?"

"Well, he's pretty big." She nodded to emphasize her statement, changing the course of her swinging curls. "His jacket just about swallowed me up. Donny's about six-foot five and about two hundred pounds."

Any of our suspects would fit into that size comfortably. "When was the last time you saw it?"

"I'm not really sure." She angled her head and contemplated the store's white textured ceiling. Waiting for her to finish her sentence was like waiting for ketchup to come out of a bottle. "Well, no, that's not right. I had it on last Saturday morning when we were unpacking the boxes for the book signing." She looked at me again and shrugged a shoulder apologetically. "Donny's a great guy, but he's not The One. You know what I mean? And I'm not getting any younger. I need to move on."

"I understand." Although I wasn't certain I did.

The young woman smiled her appreciation. "Thanks! But I need that jacket." A cloud swept away her smile. "I can't break up with Donny without it. Well, I guess I'll just keep looking. Thanks, y'all!"

Frowning, I tracked Blanche's bounding gait as it carried her briskly across the store. "Now we know how the killer left the store without anyone noticing all that blood."

"I'm so sorry, Phoenix." I freed my tabby from his cat carrier the minute we walked through our front door Friday evening. Our trip to the vet had been enlightening, but still traumatic.

I carried Phoenix to the faux leather sofa, petting and whispering my apology over and over. My hope was to comfort him as well as myself. The vet's diagnosis racked me with guilt: stress.

"I'm so sorry, baby. I don't know why I didn't see it myself." I held him to my shoulder and caressed his back in long, slow strokes.

All the signs had been there for me to see if I'd just paid attention: mood change, weight loss, lack of appetite, lethargy, hiding beneath my bed. Phoenix had been anxious—even more than I'd been—about our move from Brooklyn to Peach Coast. He still was.

"I don't know if I can ever forgive myself." I turned my head, seeking Phoenix's eyes. "Can you ever forgive me?"

He half-closed his eyes as though to say, *Sweetheart, keep petting me, and I'll forgive you for anything.*

I chuckled in response to his expression. It made me feel a little better. Careful to continuing petting him, I rose from the sofa and crossed to the bag I'd left beside the cat carrier. "I need to give you more attention and affection to help you feel comfortable in your new home. I should've realized that without the vet having to tell me."

He purred as though to assure me he wouldn't hold a grudge.

"Thank you." I pulled the small lavender-scented pillow from the bag. I'd also purchased cat food, snacks, and an extra toy. "The vet said lavender is the most calming scent for cats, so this pillow should help soothe your anxieties as you get used to our new home."

Phoenix had probably marked several pieces of furniture in our Brooklyn apartment with his "happy scent," according to the vet. The scent identified places he was familiar and comfortable with. I hadn't realized the significance of this. Before we moved, I'd sold our old second-hand pieces and bought second-hand furniture I'd thought was better suited to our new home. My lack of awareness had sent my poor cat into a spiral of confusion, depression, and anxiety. My inattention because of my new job and the investigation had made matters worse.

"That's going to change." I had to find a way to help both of my friends in need.

On Friday evening, my phone vibrated in the front pocket of my pants. Asleep on my lap, Phoenix never stirred. The lavender-scented pillow must be working.

Slowly, carefully, I rolled my hips and slipped my right hand into the pocket to free my phone. The screen alerted me that the caller was my mother.

"Hi, Mom." My greeting was muted.

"Why are we whispering?" The echo behind her voice indicated she had me on speaker phone.

"Phoenix is sleeping on my lap. I don't want to disturb him." I rubbed my hand over the length of his side. "I think this might be the best sleep he's had since we moved here four months ago."

"Is he sick?" My father's voice boomed his concern across the line.

I hurriedly lowered the volume on the phone. "No, actually, I took him to the vet today. She said Phoenix is suffering from anxiety and stress. He hasn't yet adjusted to our new place or new surroundings."

"Hmmm..." My father's noncommittal noise was his signature sound. It said everything, but even those closest to him weren't always certain what that was.

"You seem to be having trouble adjusting too." My mother's tone was thick with maternal concern.

In the background, I heard the familiar voices of the local news anchors. A sense of nostalgia washed over me. "I like it here, but there's a lot to adjust to. I still get homesick from time to time." Phoenix's breathing lifted and lowered my right hand as it rested on his side.

"Is there something else bothering you besides Phoenix's health?" Dad sounded like he'd moved closer to the phone.

Of course my parents would sense something else was weighing on my mind. Our familial bonds were strong. It was comforting to know distance hadn't changed that. Now the question was, should I tell them I was investigating a homicide? I didn't want to lie to them; however, I was still suffering the emotional effects of Dre's reaction to my helping Jo clear her name.

Time to change the subject. "I really miss you both, and Dre, Kay, and Clay."

"We miss you too." My parents laughed as they echoed each other. I heard the catch in their throats, an indication they were much more emotional than they wanted me to know.

"Our anniversary won't be the same without you here," Mom added.

"Cee, she's already feeling bad." Dad's tone was gently chiding. "Don't make her feel worse."

"It's all right, Dad." I smiled. "I feel the same way. It's your *fortieth* wedding anniversary. I wish I could fly out to be there with you."

Mom sighed. "We understand. With most new jobs, you have to wait a year before you can use your vacation time."

"That's right." I shrugged off my disappointment.

Of course, Dre and I were planning to videoconference me into the celebration Saturday morning. That wouldn't be nearly as good as being in the same room with my parents and giving them a real hug, but it would have to do.

My parents and I chatted a few minutes longer before

saying good night. Moving in slow motion, I returned my phone to my pocket. Thankfully, Phoenix remained asleep. I transferred him—and his new lavender-scented pillow—from my lap to the sofa cushion beside me. Poor little guy. Either he was exhausted, or that pillow was a stronger calming agent than I'd expected.

After reassuring myself Phoenix was out for the count, I jogged upstairs to my office to retrieve my party decorations. I had a celebration to prepare for.

"Marvey!" Mom's screech of joy made me wince and laugh. Her image was sharp and clear on my laptop's monitor Saturday morning.

Phoenix froze on my lap, staring at the screen. His reaction seemed a combination of curiosity and surprise.

"Hi, everyone! Happy anniversary, Mom and Dad." I waved at the gathering of my family—Mom, Dad, Dre, Kay, and Clay—crowded together in front of Dre's tablet.

A videoconference for my parents' anniversary celebration had seemed over-the-top at first. Was I doing it for them or for me? But the grins on my parents' faces rivaled mine and answered the question. The videoconference was for all of us.

Dad wrapped an arm around Mom. "It's great to see you, sweetheart."

I heard the emotion in his voice and swallowed back my own. "It's wonderful to see you too. To see all of you."

They were in the dining room. From memory, I could almost smell the apple potpourri that sat in a glass bowl just out of sight of the computer on the mahogany table. Or was I smelling the potpourri in my own home?

The warm tan wall behind them featured the growing collection of framed family photographs. The images chronicled our history from my parents' wedding to the birth of their first, and so far only, grandchild. In my mind's eye, I could see the tall china cabinet that stood against the left wall and the matching credenza on the right.

Everyone started talking at once. I did my best to keep up with their questions while monitoring Phoenix's movements. He'd bounded onto my dining table and prowled around my laptop. He seemed to be searching for an explanation as to how my family was able to appear in it. I was thrilled by the reemergence of his curiosity.

"Aunt Marvey, I miss you!" My four-year-old nephew leaned closer to the monitor as though trying to make his way to me. "When can I come for a visit?"

"Soon, Clay. And you can bring your parents." I couldn't stop smiling. "I miss you too. You look five inches taller than when I left."

"He's growing like a weed." My sister-in-law, Kay, laughed as she plucked her son away from the laptop and off the table. "You look wonderful, Marvey. Small-town life agrees with you."

I gave her a wry look. "I don't miss the subway. That's a promise."

Empathetic groans and eye rolls echoed the sentiment.

Dre shook his head. "Now you're practically rolling out of bed and walking to work. Must be nice."

"Indeed it is." I smirked. "But today isn't about me.

It's about Mom and Dad. It's time for the toast. I already have my glass."

I drew my champagne flute of sparkling apple cider from behind my computer. Phoenix had found his water bowl, which I'd placed beside it.

My mother's eyes widened as though I'd performed a magic trick. "You kids thought of everything."

"We tried to." I adjusted my laptop to keep Phoenix on the screen.

Mom squeezed my father's hand as it rested beside hers on the table. "This videoconference is so thoughtful of all of you. You make us feel very special."

Dre took two glasses of champagne from Kay. He offered one to Mom. "You and Dad *are* special."

"Very special." I waited while Dad accepted a glass of champagne from Dre. "You taught us the importance of family. That's why I wanted to be with you today, even if it's through this videoconference."

Dre raised his glass. "It's not every day that one's parents celebrate forty years of wedded bliss. Here's to many, many more healthy and happy years together."

"To wedded bliss." I tapped my glass against Phoenix's water bowl.

"And to parental bliss." Dad took a sip of champagne.

"Absolutely." Mom touched her glass to Dad's.

Dad shared a glance with Dre and me. "Parents work hard to secure their children's future. It's rewarding to see our children happy, healthy, and doing well."

Parents work hard to secure their children's future.

Dad's words drew my thoughts to Bobby and his father, Buddy. I felt guilty being distracted during their anniversary celebration, but I couldn't help myself.

People in Peach Coast had told me Buddy and

Bobby had been close. They'd been friends as well as father and son. That was like my relationship with Mom and Dad. My parents were also my friends. Whenever I had news, good or bad, they were the first people I contacted.

Mom and Dad were starting to open their anniversary gifts. Thankfully, my package had arrived in time for me to watch them unwrap it.

My attention drifted again, much to my regret. If Buddy and Bobby had been close, why would Buddy have left Fiona in charge of Bobby's money? He must've known how they felt about each other. If he hadn't thought Bobby was capable of managing money, why hadn't he named Betty to be the executor of the account? As Bobby's mother, it would make sense that she'd manage Bobby's inheritance.

Was it that he didn't trust Betty? What effect would that have had on Betty's attitude toward Fiona? Each question seemed to draw me closer to identifying Betty as Fiona's killer. Or perhaps Betty *and* Bobby?

CHAPTER 28

Q UESTIONING BOBBY ON HIS OWN would be challenge enough. Questioning Bobby and his mother... Well, I'd been hoping for better circumstances.

Right after the videoconference celebration for my parents' anniversary Saturday, I drove to Fenton's Hardware & Repairs, planning to speak with Bobby. I spent a few minutes exploring the metal shelves of tools and gadgets while working up my courage for one last push through Bobby's Sphinx-like demeanor. My goal was to make this latest interview a quick one. I didn't want to leave Phoenix on his own for long. But after spying Betty at the checkout counter with Bobby, hope shriveled and died.

Betty appeared to be in full Helicopter Mama mode. Bobby's strategy for coping with that seemed to be to ignore her. Customer traffic was slow. During the down-time, Bobby cleaned counters and rearranged product displays.

I drew a deep breath, then made my way to the front of the mid-sized store. It smelled of cut wood, construction glue, and turpentine. "Good afternoon, Betty." Her reply was a brusque nod. I turned to Bobby. "Hi, Bobby."

"Afternoon, Ms. Marvey." His expression was inscrutable, but not unfriendly. "How can I help you?"

I tilted my head and added a pleasant smile. "I'm looking for enlightenment."

A smile slowly brightened his hazel brown eyes. "Don't librarians think they can find such things in a book?"

"Good one." Again I suspected he was more of a reader than he let on. "But this particular book raises more questions than it provides answers."

Betty came to life. "What are you talking about?" Her tone was defensive. "Bobby doesn't have time to talk to you. Can't you see he's at work?"

This from the woman who seemed to be under the mistaken impression that today was Bring Your Parent to Work Day. "You appear to be the kind of mother who'd make it her duty to raise her children to be strong and independent."

Betty lifted her chin. "That's right. I raised Bobby to think for himself and to be able to stand on his own two feet."

"Then why won't you let him do that now?" I asked gently.

She gasped, looking at me as though I'd insulted her peach cobbler. "Well, I—"

"It's all right, Mama." Bobby turned back to me. His eyes gleamed with humor. The right corner of his mouth curved upward before he managed to compose his features. "Are you talkin' about Fiona's book?"

Betty bristled. "You have no right to harass—"

"Mama," he interrupted her. "I said I can handle this. Thank you."

Betty's pale cheeks had pinkened.

Ignoring her discomfort, I offered Bobby a smile. "Everyone in Peach Coast says you and your father were close."

A smile softened his inscrutable square features. "We were, especially as I got older."

I chuckled. "That reminds me of a Mark Twain quote."

Bobby returned my smile. "The one about his father gainin' knowledge between the time he was fourteen and twenty-one?"

"That's the one exactly." Bobby had only deepened my suspicion he was more of a reader than he'd let on. Surely, this was a sign we were meant to be friends—provided he wasn't a stone-cold killer.

Betty rolled her eyes at him. "You know, *I* was the one in labor with you for thirty-six hours, *not* your father. Are you done?" Her question, directed to me, was dry and bitter.

My smile faded. "Bobby, if you and your father were so close, why did he appoint Fiona to manage your inheritance? You appear to be a responsible adult—"

Sensing an affront to her child, Betty charged in. "What do you mean, 'appears to be'? Of course he is. He's—"

"Mama." Bobby's voice was tense. "Please let me handle this."

A hapless customer approached the checkout counter at that moment. His appearance helped to distract from some of the tension. Bobby handled the sale with polite efficiency. It was strange the way he managed to remain distant yet approachable at the same time. He'd probably fit in well in New York.

Once the customer had disappeared, Bobby turned back to me. "How'd you hear about my inheritance?"

Stalling tactics. I couldn't blame him. I had a few of those myself, but now wasn't the time. I had a cat waiting at home, and I needed the truth. "Bobby, your father didn't appoint Fiona to manage your inheritance, did he?"

Betty's face filled with heat. "Are you calling my boy a liar? Is that what you're doing? Because if you are—"

"Mama." His tone was sharp. "Be still."

This time, she wasn't the only one shocked by Bobby's curt command. I had the sense the mellow young man didn't often lose his temper.

Bobby expelled a harsh breath. He paced behind the counter, rubbing the back of his neck. When he finally turned toward me, his inscrutable mask was back in place. "Ms. Marvey, you're bound and determined to crawl into my mind and pick apart my thoughts, ain't that right?"

I took his words as a statement of fact rather than an attack. "We're both interested in the truth. I believe the truth is your father didn't leave Fiona in charge of your inheritance, so what really happened to your money?"

Bobby looked toward his mom. "Your lies about Fiona gave the town the wrong ideas about her."

"Bobby!" She shot a panicked look in my direction before giving him a quelling stare.

"It's the truth." Bobby appeared unmoved by Betty's show of temper. He held my gaze. "I cared about Fiona, but I didn't want to contradict my mama."

"That's right." Betty gave a decisive nod, her previous shame forgotten. "I raised my son right."

Bobby rubbed his eyes. I sensed the tension he was battling. It was strong and must've had a grip on him for a very long time. "What you did was wrong and unfair. Worse, I'm your son, and you put me in a bad position."

"Bobby!" She gaped at him.

He ignored her interjection. "Fiona was a good person. She loved my father. He was happier with her than he'd been with my mama. I couldn't resent my father for finding a woman who could love him like that."

"Excuse me?" Betty's tone was strident.

"And he never cheated on Mama." Bobby pointed toward Betty in an almost accusing manner. "You know that's true, Mama."

Again Betty's gaze met mine before slipping away. "Well, I…"

After speaking with Nolan and Zelda, and considering the information the librarians had uncovered about Buddy's finances, I'd begun to suspect Fiona's tattered reputation had been a figment of Betty's imagination. Now Bobby was confirming that realization too.

Bobby turned back to me. "Don't get me wrong. I had my doubts about Daddy and Fiona at first too."

"I understand." How would I feel if my father divorced my mother to marry another woman? It would be a difficult position. I'd want both of my parents to be happy. However, in such a situation, for one to be happy, the other would suffer a broken heart.

Bobby crossed his arms and propped his hips against the counter behind him. "Daddy tried real hard to correct the lies about Fiona. But no one listened. Everyone thought he was a fool." He slid his mother another look. "Doctors said Daddy died of a heart attack. I think he died of a broken heart because of the lies goin' 'round town about Fiona."

Betty seemed to shrivel inside herself, but she maintained her silence. For once, she didn't have anything to say.

My heart ached for Fiona's untenable situation. "It must've been horrible for her. Did she ever say anything to you about it?"

His shrug was restless, impatient. "I asked her about it once. Wanted to know why she didn't call out Mama's lies. She said she'd rather people thought she was spendin' all of Daddy's money than for people to see Daddy as a failed businessman."

I frowned. "She obviously loved your father very much."

Bobby hesitated. "She also didn't want to have me hurt by people sayin' unkind things about Mama."

I glanced at Betty and found her hanging her head as though in shame. I returned my attention to Bobby. "Did you know Fiona was using her own money to prop up your father's real estate business?"

Bobby slid a look at his mom before responding. "Yes, I did. I felt horrible for not defending Fiona. I didn't kill her. I don't think Ms. Jo did, either. But I do want whoever killed her to be caught and punished. Fiona deserves justice. She was a good person. I miss her very much."

The emotion in his voice was sincere. So was the shame and regret in Betty's eyes.

"I do have another question, if you're up for it." My voice was tentative out of respect for Bobby's grief. His sorrow felt as though it had been building for quite some time.

He nodded. "What is it?"

I still hesitated. "What were you arguing about with Willy Pelt in On A Roll last week?"

Bobby's features tightened. Anger flashed in his eyes. "Pelt wants Fiona to be buried in Beaufort. That's not right. She had a plot right here next to my father. That's what she would've wanted."

I thanked Bobby, nodded to Betty, then left the store. Bobby had asserted he hadn't killed Fiona, nor did he believe Jo had. It didn't escape my attention that he hadn't made a similar assertion about his mother.

"Your usual, Marvey?" Anna May's greeting reached me from across On A Roll as I entered the cozy café before work Monday morning.

"Yes, thank you, Anna May. And a slice of your delicious peach cobbler, please."

Even from halfway across the café, I could discern the twinkle in her eyes. I drew an appreciative breath of the fresh-baked sweets and chocolatey pastries. My comfortable cream pumps carried me closer to my café mocha with extra espresso.

"Good morning, Marvey." Etta's smile warmed her dark blue eyes. "I'm enjoying that women's fiction novel you recommended to me. Thank you."

I paused beside the tiny table the retiree shared with her café companion. "I'm so glad. Thank you for letting me know. You might also be interested in the sequel. If you'd like, I can reserve it for you at the library."

Etta leaned toward me. "Oh, that would be wonderful. I'm almost done with this one."

"I'll set it aside for you." I felt the familiar rush that came from spreading book love. Still smiling, I turned to her friend. "Good morning, Dabney. Is there a book you'd like me to hold for you at the library?"

"I don't like *fiction*." He made it sound like a dirty word. "I'd rather keep my feet grounded in reality."

So far, Dabney was my greatest challenge as a librarian. "You know the library also has an extensive selection of nonfiction in a wide variety of subjects. You have an open invitation to stop by and browse through those sections."

Dabney responded with a noncommittal grunt.

Undaunted, I boosted the wattage on my smile. "Enjoy the rest of your day." As I turned toward the counter, I adjusted my *Read, Renew, Return* canvas tote bag on my shoulder, then fished my wallet from my oversized black purse. "How was your weekend?" I had the exact change ready for Anna May as I arrived at her cash register. Her T-shirt read *No Kissing Before the Sipping*.

"Busier than a moth in a mitten."

Since I'd recently heard the phrase, I wasn't as thrown by the imagery as I otherwise would've been. "What's keeping you so busy?"

"The Cobbler Crawl is less than a week away. There's still a lot of baking to get done." Anna May handed me my receipt, then turned to prepare my mocha. "How 'bout yours?"

"It was nice. Thank you."

"But don't you worry now. I'm still making time to

read." She laughed. "Since you moved to town, I'm reading more books now than when I was in school."

"Speaking as a librarian, that doesn't exactly dampen my spirits," I said dryly.

Anna May snorted. "Yeah, well, I picked up one recipe book from the library, then decided to buy it from To Be Read. It came in Saturday."

I was listening, fascinated, to her description of a Coca Cola cake recipe—who knew there was such a thing?—from her new pastry book when Willy joined us.

"Mornin', ladies." He rocked on his heels as he looked from Anna May to me.

Anna May handed me my mocha and the bag with the peach cobbler before turning to frown at Willy. "You look like someone just licked the red off your candy."

My eyebrows stretched up my forehead. I forced myself not to grab my cell phone to add her comment to my Peach Coast translation notes.

"I'm anxious to return home to Beaufort." He sighed gustily. "No offense to your town, but I've got a business to run."

"None taken." Anna May spread her arms to encompass her café. "I run a business of my own. I can understand how you must be feeling. If the deputies held me over for a week, I'd be pitching a hissy fit with a tail on it."

Pitching a hissy fit. That sounded familiar. I dug my cell phone out of my bag, launched my Notes application, and scrolled to the Ps in my Peach Coast to New York Translation List. In context, *pitching a hissy fit with a tail on it* meant *Anna May would've been furious.*

"So, where's your better half?" Willy asked.

Looking up from my phone, I was surprised to find

him watching me. The hint of a smile curved his lips. Curiosity brightened his eyes. Was his question for me? "I don't know what you're talking about."

Willy glanced at Anna May before turning his frown to me. He looked as confused as I felt. "I'm sorry." His laughter was nervous. "I thought you and Spence Holt were dating? You were with him at Fiona's signing, and I've seen you in here with him a couple of times. Am I mistaken?"

Attending a book event with a friend meant we were dating? If we split a peach cobbler, would that mean we were engaged? Things were different in the South.

That was when I noticed the eerie silence surrounding the café. Disconcerted, I scanned the nearby tables. Conversations had stopped. No one was looking at me, yet I sensed I was the center of everyone's attention. Even Anna May, Etta, and Dabney seemed to be holding their breaths.

With a sense of heightened awareness, I returned my attention to Willy. Was this the way reality television show participants felt? I was waiting for a director to yell, "Cut! She needs more makeup. *A lot* more makeup. Don't skimp."

"Spence and I are friends. We're not dating." I detected a collective sigh of disappointment all around me. Was I imagining things?

"I'm sorry. My mistake." Willy didn't look as though he believed me. He shoved his hands into the front pockets of his dark green trousers and rocked back on his heels. "How's your investigation going? Have y'all found any leads?"

I shook my head. "I wish I had some progress

to share with you. Have the deputies given you any updates?"

His shoulders lifted and fell with a sigh. "No, they haven't given me any reason to hope they'll solve this case any time soon. In the meantime, I'm having to leave town without completing the arrangements to have Fiona's body shipped back to Beaufort."

Was the cause of the delay Bobby's opposition to Willy's claim on Fiona's body?

"The deputies will solve the case soon. They haven't found anything yet, but I'm hopeful they will." I didn't know why I felt compelled to defend Peach Coast's finest. The deputies were stubborn and prideful—at least, Jed was.

"Marvey's right." Anna May brought Willy a cup of plain, black coffee and his change. "The deputies may not have much experience investigating murders, but we're lucky to have them. They'll get to the bottom of this just as fast as they can. Don't you worry."

"I'm sure you're right." Willy accepted his coffee and stepped away from the counter. I heard the skepticism in his voice.

"You mentioned you're getting ready to return to South Carolina. When?"

Willy sipped his coffee. "I'm leaving tomorrow. The deputies have finally verified my information, including when I checked into the hotel."

I raised my eyebrows. "I would've thought the deputies would check that information first."

"Me too, but I suppose they've been busy." He shrugged. "And I was trying to arrange transportation for Fiona's body."

I checked my watch. "I'd better get to work. Have a safe trip home."

Willy smiled. "It was nice meeting you, although I wish it'd been under happier circumstances."

"Me too." I exchanged a wave with Anna May, who was waiting on a customer, then turned to leave.

As I made my way to the library, I glanced over my shoulder in the general direction of Willy's hotel. How long would it take to drive from the hotel to the bookstore—and back?

CHAPTER 29

"A S WE WERE BEGINNING TO suspect, Fiona wasn't who we were told she was." I didn't even try to mask my frustration when I joined Jo and Spence for lunch Monday afternoon.

Spence was hosting us at the conversation table in his office at the newspaper. We'd ordered our usual sandwiches, soups, and iced tea. During our meal, I'd caught Jo and Spence up on everything Bobby had told me about him, Betty, and Fiona. They'd been as surprised as I had.

"Betty has a lot to answer for." Jo leaned back on her chair and sipped her iced tea.

"No doubt." I shrugged my eyebrows. "But she's not our main concern right now. You are."

Jo continued, looking from me to Spence and back. "Although, I can't understand what Fiona was thinking. I can't see myself sitting quietly by while someone spreads vicious, hateful rumors about me. She must've been *crazy* in love with Buddy."

Spence set down his glass of iced tea and looked at me. "That's a good point. What would you do for love?"

Confused, I shook my head. "I don't know. I've never been in love."

Jo laughed. "I've fallen in and out of love at least a dozen times."

Spence shifted on his seat at the matching circular table to face her. "You said if you were Fiona, you wouldn't have allowed Betty to spread lies about you."

"No, I would not." Jo sounded quite adamant. "That kind of slander would not only destroy you personally, but it'd damage you professionally."

"That's true." Spence gestured toward her with his bottle of iced tea. "We build our businesses on the backs of our good reputation. If that reputation is tarnished, our business takes a hit."

Jo spread her hands. "Look at how the rumors I killed Fiona are affecting my store. And most people don't believe them. Daily receipts are down almost forty percent. Online sales are down too. People aren't even coming in for a cup of coffee. And that's despite my defending myself."

No wonder Jo looked like she wasn't getting any sleep. I directed my question to Spence. "Do you know whether the gossip about Fiona hurt Nolan and Fiona's accounting firm?"

Spence looked thoughtful as he shook his head. "Nolan's business seems to be doing well. There are only a handful of accounting practices in Peach Coast, but Nolan's is the largest. He's handled my family's accounts for years."

Jo nodded. "Nolan handles my accounts too."

I swept my gaze across Spence's office as I considered what he and Jo had said about Fiona's firm. "Maybe people like the idea of having someone rumored to be obsessed with money handling their finances." My attention settled on the family photos beside Spence's computer. There was one of him with his arms around his parents' shoulders and another with his parents embracing. His mother and father were lost in each other's eyes. "Bobby implied Fiona stayed silent because she loved Buddy and didn't want people to know his business was failing."

Jo made an impatient sound. "I can't understand her not defending herself. There's no way I would've stayed silent. No way."

"I agree with you, but we aren't Fiona." I returned my attention to my friends. "Can we all agree that perhaps the motive wasn't money but love?"

"I can agree to that." Spence drank more of his iced tea.

"So can I," Jo agreed. "Does that leave only Betty with a motive?"

I turned the conversation back to the matter at hand. "What about Willy? He seems to care a great deal about Fiona."

Jo's expression was dubious. "I don't know. Would someone really drive all the way to Peach Coast just to kill someone out of unrequited love?"

"That does seem farfetched." Spence also seemed skeptical. "And we confirmed he didn't check into the inn until after the police took everyone's statement."

Distracted, I wrapped my hand around my book pendant. I'd recreated the original 1994 cover of *Night Song*, a historical romance by Beverly Jenkins.

Jo slumped back on her chair. "We may not have a motive for anyone anymore."

I needed chocolate. "If we don't come up with a motive for Willy soon, we're going to lose our window of opportunity. He's leaving Peach Coast tomorrow."

"Fiona Lyle was the best thing to ever happen to Buddy Hayes. It's a shame that blockhead didn't appreciate her as he should've." Grant Gillis was a plain-spoken person. Someone should've warned me.

A co-founding partner of Gillis & Sweets LLC, Grant had agreed to stay after normal business hours to meet with Spence and me Monday evening. Spence had driven, which was fortunate. First because I didn't have my car since I'd walked to work, and second, if I'd driven, we may have ended up in Florida.

Grant had told us in advance—and repeatedly—that he wouldn't divulge privileged information pertaining to either Buddy's or Fiona's legal or business affairs jointly or separately. Legal speak for he wasn't going to gossip.

The seasoned lawyer's firm stood in the heart of Peach Coast. It was housed in a renovated gray brick building I suspected had been a family home once upon a time not too long ago. Its interior showcased an abundance of dark wood trim, hardwood flooring, and closet space. Vivid area rugs splashed color across the main floor. The firm's executive secretary-cum-receptionist had escorted Spence and me up a winding staircase and down a spacious hallway to the older gentleman's office. After dropping us off, she'd wished Grant a good evening and had gone home.

I took a moment to recover from my surprise at

Grant's directness. "What makes you think Buddy didn't appreciate Fiona?"

Grant angled his head and shared an inquiring look between Spence and me. "Young lady, are you married?"

I bit my tongue to keep from asking why my marital status was relevant to our conversation. "No, sir, I'm not."

Grant gave Spence a pointed look before returning his attention to me. "My wife and I have been married for more than thirty-seven years. She's a saint. Yet I assure you we wouldn't have made it to our second wedding anniversary if I'd had an ex-wife who said even half of the scurrilous things about my wife that Ms. Betty said of Ms. Fiona."

I exchanged a look with Spence. It seems we'd found another Fiona supporter. I turned back to Grant. His executive chair was positioned in front of a large window that let in an abundance of natural light. It overlooked the front of the building, which made me think his office had once been someone's master bedroom. "We understand you were Buddy's lawyer. Did you also work with Fiona on her will?"

Grant arched a thick dark eyebrow. "Yes, I did, young lady. But I will remind you that information falls under attorney-client privilege. I cannot divulge the details of any of my clients' last wills and testaments."

I nodded. "Of course, we understand. It's just that Deputies Whatley and Cole seem overly focused on a friend of ours for Fiona's murder, and we're trying to help clear her name."

Grant spread his hands. "I'll answer any question I can. I also want justice for Fiona. Buddy was a friend. We'd known each other for years. I remember when

Buddy told me he and Fiona were getting married, he'd bragged he'd 'stolen' Fiona from a much younger man."

Spence sat straighter on his black leather visitor's chair. "We understand you can't give us any details about Buddy's or Fiona's wills but, in your personal opinion, how was Fiona's relationship with Bobby?"

A thoughtful expression settled over Grant's classically handsome features. His cream dress shirt, navy suit jacket, and matching tie suggested high-quality tailoring. "Fiona and Bobby seemed to get on very well enough." His words were measured as he rocked back on his chair. "Though they didn't spend much time together. Bobby's very loyal to his mama."

"Well enough" for Fiona to name him in her will?

I searched my mind for a way to dig for more information without implying I wanted Grant to violate his clients' privacy. "You sound as though Fiona was more than a client. You seemed to have known her personally as well."

Grant's smile was faint. "Buddy and Fiona, and my wife and I, did some socializing together. After Buddy died, my wife and I checked on Fiona a few times. She didn't have close friends or family in town. We wanted her to know she wasn't alone. We were here for her."

I was impressed. "That's very kind of you."

Grant spread his broad hands. "That's what friends do."

I smiled at the familiar phrase.

Spence's eyebrows knitted. "You said Fiona didn't have friends or family *in town*. Do you know whether she had any family or friends back in Beaufort or anywhere else?"

Grant cocked his head as he considered his question. "She never mentioned anyone to my wife or me."

That seemed strange. "Is the name Willy Pelt familiar?"

Grant shook his head. "No. Who's that?"

I froze. "Fiona's uncle's lawyer. He's also her friend."

Grant shook his head again, even more certain. "No, she never mentioned him."

Spence and I exchanged a quick look. Willy claimed Fiona had left her uncle's property to him in her will. If that was true, why didn't Grant recognize his name?

"About the Cobbler Crawl." Spence hesitated as he escorted me to my door after our meeting with Grant Gillis Monday evening. "I understand if you want to withdraw. You have a lot on your mind with this investigation."

Surprised, I almost tripped over my feet. Spence steadied me before I planted a facer on my cobblestone walkway. He had one hand on my elbow and the other around my waist.

"Thank you." I stepped back and turned to him. "I have no intention of backing out. You've kept your word to help with this investigation. I'll keep my word to be your partner for the event. But I'm warning you now—eating all that pie during a race might make me sick."

Spence chuckled. "You'll be fine. And thank you."

"No. Thank *you*." I mounted my porch steps. "A good run usually helps clear my mind. It might be just what I need to figure out how to keep the deputies from charging Jo with murder."

"The event's still five days away. You may have solved the case by then." Spence smiled, but his eyes were serious. His faith in me was just the energy boost I needed. It was better than chocolate or caffeine.

"Thank you for saying that, and for seeing me home. Good night." I opened my door, stepped inside.

"Have a good night." Spence inclined his head before turning away.

I watched him get back into his car and drive off before locking my door and setting my alarm. Phoenix greeted me at the entryway. It was just like old times.

I scooped him into my arms and wandered farther into our home. "I'm so happy you're feeling more like your old self." In the kitchen, I was gratified to see his half-empty water bowl and practically clean food bowl. I set him on the ground. "Well, this is wonderful news. Let me know if you'd like any changes that'll help make you feel even more comfortable in our new home. Perhaps you'd prefer to have your bowl moved to the French doors. Or maybe you want your own room upstairs?"

Phoenix turned from his water bowl to give me a look that was a perfect blend of incredulity and conde-scension. I interpreted his expression to mean that if he indeed wanted a change or two to his current setup, he was perfectly capable of handling them himself.

"Point taken, buddy." I crossed to the sink to wash my hands. "All right, let's see if I can find some food for myself. I'm getting weak at the knees." I surveyed my fridge and cupboards for inspiration. "Grilled cheese sandwich and a cup of hot tea it is."

Phoenix and I chatted about our days as I cooked dinner. He wandered closer, executing graceful figure eights around my ankles. Just like old times. He made me smile. Once my dinner was ready, I carried my meal and tea to the dining room table. Phoenix followed me.

"I may have put too many expectations on Buddy and Fiona's lawyer." I settled onto the chair at the head of the table. Phoenix gave a long, luxurious stretch, then laid near my feet to groom himself.

"I should've known better than to have done that. I mean, I knew he wouldn't be able to share any business or legal information with us. Maybe subconsciously, I was hoping he'd let something slip. Well, actually, there's no maybe about it."

I glanced at Phoenix as I took a bite of my sandwich. I suspected he was only half listening to me—typical male—but I continued anyway. "Perhaps I subconsciously thought Grant would share some earth-shattering revelation about Fiona or Buddy—or both—that would break this case wide open. But of course, that only happens in books, movies, and TV."

I took another bite of my sandwich as I mulled over the recent meeting Spence and I had had with Grant. "Grant didn't recognize Willy's name. Maybe Fiona never told him about her past in South Carolina. After all, Corrinne said she was a very private person. But if, as Willy claimed, he was a beneficiary of Fiona's will, then Grant would've recognized his name, wouldn't he? The question, Phoenix, is why would Willy lie about Fiona's will?"

Phoenix's right ear flicked at the sound of his name, but otherwise he still had nothing to contribute to the brainstorming.

I ate in silence for a while, recalling bits and pieces of the evening's conversation with Grant and Spence. Part of me wished I'd thought to record our interview or at the very least had taken notes. Then I recalled something Grant had said about Buddy.

When Buddy told me he and Fiona were getting married, he'd bragged that he'd stolen Fiona from a much younger man.

"What younger man? Had Fiona been engaged to someone when she'd met Buddy? If so, how had this mysterious younger man handled her breaking up with him?" I directed my stream of questions to Phoenix. He aimed a brief and vaguely curious look in my direction before returning to his grooming.

Not wanting to take him away from his toilette, I excused myself from the living room and climbed the stairs to my study. Logging on to my laptop, I did an internet search for "Fiona Lyle Engagement." The screen filled with the query results. The first link took me to an article posted to the electronic platform of Beaufort's local weekly newspaper.

As I waited for the article to upload onto my computer, Phoenix wandered into the room. He gave me an impassive nod of greeting, then proceeded to stalk the study's perimeter. Was he pacing out the space to decide whether to claim this room as his own?

"You look fabulous, Phoenix." I spun my black ergonomic desk chair to track his progress around the study. "Not a hair out of place."

I turned back to my computer. The article had finished uploading. Its headline read, "A Whirlwind Romance in Beaufort." The article's dateline was Beaufort, South Carolina. It ran a little more than two years ago. I was intrigued. It would be fair to refer to Fiona's marriage to Buddy Hayes as a whirlwind romance. She and Buddy had married six months after his divorce from Betty.

"Okay, Fiona, whose heart had you broken?" I used the touchpad to scroll down the screen. Slowly, a small photo came into view between the headline and the story.

My hand froze.

The image showed a tall, slender woman in her late-thirties/early forties. She posed in a rose, knee-length, center-fold sheath dress she'd accessorized with pearl jewelry. Waves of honey-blond hair framed her strong porcelain features. Her green eyes were serious as they returned the camera's stare. Fiona. She didn't look like someone in a whirlwind romance in Beaufort or any-where else. She seemed like someone announcing a business deal.

But it was the man beside her who'd caused my mind to stutter and my hand to stiffen above my key-board. I recognized that tall, lanky man with the pierc-ing gray eyes and shock of red hair.

"Willy hadn't been Fiona's *friend*. He'd been her *fian-cé*. And she'd dumped him. To marry Buddy." I swung my chair to face Phoenix again. "Question—how had he handled their breakup?"

CHAPTER 30

"**F**IONA HAD DUMPED WILLY TO marry Buddy?" Jo sounded scandalized. I'd called her Monday evening, right after discussing this latest development with Phoenix. "It must've been love at first sight. I wonder how she broke the news to Willy?"

I shook my head at the tangent Jo had taken. I needed to keep her focused on Fiona's murder rather than the deceased woman's romantic entanglements. "I don't think we've given Willy as much attention as we should've during our inquiry."

"But I thought we'd agreed he wouldn't have driven all the way from Beaufort just to kill Fiona." Jo's voice kept raising and dropping in volume as though she'd left her cell phone on a table as she wondered around a room. Did she have me on speaker phone?

"It's a distance." I made the concession reluctantly. "It's a two-and-a-half-hour drive. Willy said he'd made the trip in less than two hours, though. And if he could make the trip in less than two hours, don't you think it's strange he's never visited Fiona before?"

Jo hesitated as though considering my question. "I don't know. I haven't thought about that."

I rose from my desk. "Remember the morning we went to retrieve Bobby's trash?"

"You mean the day we went dumpster diving before dawn? Yes. What about it?"

I rolled my eyes at my friend's dramatics. "Stella Lowry was going to drive five hours to Tampa to cheer up a friend. Willy knew Betty was giving Fiona a hard time, but he never came to visit, even though he's less than two hours away. Isn't that strange? Neither did he come to comfort his friend while she was grieving her husband's death. Also strange."

"But still, to drive all that way just to kill someone?" Jo's voice drew closer to her phone. She definitely had me on speaker. "Wouldn't his temper have cooled off by the time he arrived in Peach Coast?"

"But Willy hadn't come to Peach Coast to *kill* Fiona. He'd come because of her book signing. Or at least that's what he said." Holding my phone with my left hand, I collected Phoenix with my right and returned to my living room downstairs. "Remember the coroner said the description of the scene fits a crime of passion. The killer probably hadn't *planned* to kill Fiona."

Jo was silent for several long seconds. As I gave her time to draw her own conclusions, I fiddled with my book pendant and paced my living room.

Finally, Jo came to a decision. "All right, let's say we investigate Willy. He's leaving tomorrow. That doesn't give us much time. Where do we even start? There's no way he's keeping the murder weapon or his incriminating clothes in that hotel room."

"You're right. Housekeeping would've stumbled across them by now."

Jo gasped. "We're not going to go dumpster-diving in the hotel's trash, are we? I thought Bobby's trash was bad. I can only imagine the hotel's would be a million times worse."

I could hear her gag reflex over the phone. "Willy wouldn't have put such incriminating evidence in the hotel's dumpster. They would've been discovered."

She breathed a gusty sigh of relief. "Okay, so if not his hotel room or the hotel's trash, where do you think we should search for the box cutter and Willy's bloody clothes?"

"Fiona's uncle's property."

Although seemingly not as enthusiastic over my response as I was, Jo at least sounded like she was considering the possibility. "What makes you think that?"

"I'm glad you asked." I allowed my pacing to carry me out of the living room and around the dining room table. Certainty flowed through me like a superpower. "First, Willy seems familiar with the property."

"And second?"

"He lied about Fiona leaving the property to him in her will."

"How do you know that?" Jo's question and tone were cautious, but I could sense my argument winning her over.

"I strongly suspect it, because Grant Gillis drew up Fiona's will." I stopped pacing, standing still in the space between the living and dining rooms. "Spence and I spoke with him this evening. When I asked him about Willy Pelt, he didn't recognize Willy's name. Surely, if you'd recently written a will that named Willy Pelt as a beneficiary, you would've recognized his name."

"Let's do it."

"I'll pick you up, but first, I need to make a call."

"Dumpster diving. Breaking and entering. I didn't realize I'd have to commit crimes in order to clear myself of suspicion of one." Jo's low hissing sounded more like nervous chatter than endless complaints. Either way, I did my best to tune it out as we crept closer to Fiona's uncle's property. Or, rather, Fiona's property. Well, whoever-owned-it-now's property.

"Dumpster diving isn't a crime." I felt compelled to point that out. "And we're not exactly breaking and entering."

"Are you sure?" Her low hissing became a stage whisper. "Because it feels like breaking and entering."

"We're *inquiring*," I whispered back.

Jo absorbed that in silence. "So, it feels like breaking and entering to you too?"

"A little." I scanned the area as I adjusted the gloves I wore to prevent leaving my fingerprints behind. Jo wore gloves also. Perhaps they were a bit much. "But the cabin's empty, and we're not going to take anything. We're just going to have a look around. Floyd said it's at the end of this dirt path."

"It's a road."

"It's not much of a road." I gave her a sharp look. The Brooklynite in me was sure I was being pranked. The path wasn't wide enough for a bicycle.

We'd opted to leave my car a distance away and approach the—hopefully empty—cabin on foot. Parking in front of the structure hadn't been an option. That would've been tantamount to shining a spotlight on our borderline illegal activities and alerting any neighborhood patrol, the deputies, not to mention the killer to our presence.

Before picking up Jo, I'd called Floyd. As I suspected, he knew how to get to the cabin. The grumpy Saint Nick really was a treasure trove of local information. In fact, he'd driven out here several times. He'd said something about enjoying the solitude, and that the nearby lake was a good fishing spot.

His familiarity with the location enabled him to provide vivid and detailed instructions for the directionally challenged. *Turn right onto Squirrel's Hunt, which means you'll turn toward the weathered black-and-white cabin that's seen better days. About half a mile after that, you'll see three fat Sugar Maples. They should be on your right. Once you've past the Jesus Saves sign on your left, take the next left.* I'd only made one wrong turn. Instead of turning left at the Jesus Saves sign, I'd turned right. Fortunately, our course correction had been quick.

"Oh, this is beautiful." Mesmerized, I stopped in my tracks as Fiona's family's cabin appeared before us. "Did you know it was this beautiful?"

"No, I'd never seen it before." Jo sounded equally enchanted.

I don't know what I'd been expecting, but this wasn't it. The two-story cabin was perhaps fifteen hundred square feet, built from live edge cedar. Three steps led from a graveled walkway to a front porch with a couple of chairs and a pine log swing. To the right was a masonry chimney covered in live river rock. To the left was an empty cedar carport spacious enough to accommodate two cars.

"How should we approach this?" Jo's whisper prompted me from my scrutiny of Fiona's cabin in the woods.

In addition to being charming in a rustic nature sort of way, the cabin also seemed well-maintained, as though Fiona had been preparing to either move into the home or sell it. My hope it would be a dilapidated shack we could get into without much effort was quickly laid to rest.

"Let's try the back." I led the way to the rear of the cabin.

It was well after six PM. The evening sun cast longer shadows now, but we had almost three hours of daylight left. We could see clearly, but others could see us too. We moved fast, trying to act as natural as possible so we didn't draw attention to ourselves. The last thing we needed was for a vigilant neighbor to report our admittedly suspicious activity to the sheriff's department. I didn't want to have to explain our trespassing to Jed or Errol. I checked over my shoulder again before Jo and I ducked behind the cabin.

"There are four windows." She pointed toward the cabin.

Five steps led to the cedar deck, which was a little bigger than mine. Four windows were set, two each on either side of the backdoor.

"Let's hope one of these windows is open." I climbed the steps to the deck.

This time, my wish came through. The first three windows were locked. But the fourth, offset from the deck, gave when we pushed up on the windowpane. It didn't open all the way, just enough for a smaller person to attempt to wiggle through.

Jo gave me an expectant look. I wasn't happy about it, but I capitulated without a word.

I turned to face the deck railing. "This reminds me of all the times Dre and I forgot our house keys. After school, if Mom and Dad were still at work, I'd have to crawl through the window and let him into the house."

Jo probably had the tougher job, though. I needed her to help balance me as I climbed over the deck railing and into the window. My not-breaking-and-entering landed me in the cabin's kitchen. Gaining my feet, I pulled my gloves snug again before rushing toward the backdoor. My elbow knocked against something—a wooden rolling pin—on the corner of the kitchen counter. That was a weird place for a rolling pin. Why wasn't it in a drawer? I steadied it as it started to topple over, then opened the backdoor for Jo.

"Are you okay?" Jo looked me over.

"Yes, thanks."

She did a visual sweep of the interior. "Do you want to split up?"

I heard an ominous "click" right before Willy Pelt stepped out from behind the wall that separated the kitchen from the great room. My gaze dropped to the gun he pointed at us.

Willy's voice was flat; his face expressionless. "Y'all want to go right back out that door."

CHAPTER 31

I N MY PERIPHERAL VISION, I saw Jo raise her hands. I followed suit and tried to ignore how badly my legs were shaking. "What happens after we leave? Will you let us go, or will you follow us?"

Jo inhaled sharply. All the color had leeched from her face. Her eyes were as wide as saucers. Even her hair was motionless.

Willy's eyes narrowed. "D'y'all think I'm stupid? I'm going to follow you, of course."

His response was barely audible over the pounding of my heart. I was so scared. It was a toss-up as to what would happen first. I would either pass out, throw up, or wet myself. I struggled to slow my breathing. I needed to think. My mind was screaming, *Keep him talking! Just keep him talking!*

"And then what?" My voice wobbled as though I was crying.

"And then you and Ms. Jolene will disappear." Willy's voice was as cold and heartless as his words.

Jo cut off a sob. My attention shifted to her. If she fell apart, so would I. I wanted to use our silent communication to urge her to be strong. But my gaze dropped to the rolling pin lying on the kitchen counter behind her. When I'd opened the door for her, we'd inadvertently switched positions. Now she was within grabbing distance of the rolling pin.

I returned my attention to Willy as my mind raced to form a plan. "We can't just disappear. We have friends, family, and coworkers. Jo has a business." I caught her gaze and used mine to direct her to the rolling pin behind her before meeting Willy's eyes again. "People would search for us."

"So what?" He waved the gun dangerously. "I'll be long gone and forgotten by then. They haven't connected me to Fiona's murder. Why would they connect me to yours?"

"So you did kill her?" I needed to move. I needed to keep Willy's attention on me and away from Jo to create an opportunity for her to act. But I was too scared to convince my legs to work.

I glanced at Jo and read my terror in her eyes. *Marvey, I can't.*

I dug deep, trying to find even a drop of courage for both of us. *Please, Jo, please take this chance with me.*

Willy responded to my question with a question of his own. "How did you figure it out?"

"Buddy told someone he'd 'stolen' Fiona away from a younger man. *You* were that man. You and Fiona were going to be married, but then Fiona met Buddy." I forced my legs to step away from Jo and the door, drawing Willy's attention with me.

"I begged her not to break our engagement." He kept his gun trained on me. "Buddy Hayes wasn't good enough for her. He was a failed businessman with no ambition."

"But Fiona was in love with him. She wasn't in love with you." I took another, larger step away from Jo and the door. Willy's back was almost completely turned toward her.

"What are you doing?" He waved the gun. "Get back to the door."

I held his gaze. "Your engagement was a business arrangement. You didn't love her and she knew it. You wanted to marry Fiona for the money and property she'd inherited from her uncle, your biggest client." I stepped back, further angling him away from Jo.

"Stop. Moving." Willy raised his voice.

"Killing Fiona was a crime of passion." I was counting on his "passionate" nature to keep him blinded to everything except me, giving Jo the opportunity to strike him with the rolling pin. "You proposed to her again, didn't you? At the bookstore. How did you know she was a widow?"

Willy's lips curled in disdain. "I read about Hayes's death on the internet months ago and immediately proposed."

That probably hadn't been a good idea. "Of course, because in your mind, she was free to marry you."

"And she said no!" He was shouting now, almost out of control in his anger. The gun was still pointed at me. "She kept saying no every time I asked her. When I found out about her book signing, I decided to come to Peach Coast and ask her again, in person." Willy's back was to Jo now. He couldn't see her. He was so angry, I didn't think he could see me, either. But the gun was still on me. "I got so mad. I shoved her. She fell."

This was Jo's opportunity.

"Then I was stabbing her—" Suddenly he crumbled. The gun dropped from his hand and he fell, unconscious, to the ground.

Jo stood over him, her eyes wide, one hand covering her mouth, the other clutching the rolling pin. "My God, Marvey. Have I killed him?"

I crossed to her on shaky legs and kicked the gun out of Willy's reach. I kneeled beside him, searching for a pulse in his neck. "No, he's alive." I looked up at her. "And so are we, thanks to you."

"No." The rolling pin clattered on the ground as she dropped down beside me and wrapped her arms around me. "It was all thanks to you."

"Okay, then we did it together." I tightened my hold on her. "And now that we've closed our investigation, let's never do this again."

Our first call was to Spence—after we'd tied up Willy to the best of our ability. Spence called the deputies. Although he drove separately, and Jed and Errol used their lights and sirens to speed through town to the crime scene, Spence arrived at the same time as them.

Jo and I spotted his car pulling up behind the deputies' cruisers at the end of the walkway. He'd barely stepped from his sedan when we raced toward him, throwing ourselves into his embrace. The three of us stood in a silent group hug, giving and taking strength from each other.

CHAPTER 32

"'C OBBLER CRAWL' IS APTLY NAMED." I braced my hands on my knees as I fought off a wave of nausea after the fifth annual Peach Coast Cobbler Crawl late Saturday morning. "I almost ended the race that way, by crawling."

Conversely, Spence, my race partner, stood beside me, looking like he could run another three-and-a-half-mile event. Jo, Corrinne, Floyd, Viv, and Adrian had gathered around us to offer their congratulations.

"But, Marvey, you and Spence won." In my current mood, Jo's laughter seemed to be in poor taste, since I wasn't convinced I wouldn't soon be revisiting at least one of those servings of cobbler.

"Not bad for our first Cobbler Crawl." Spence had already started plans to defend our title at next year's event.

I had to nip that in the bud. "Our first and last." I cautiously straightened, then waited to make sure the nausea had passed.

Jo shook her head in mock chastisement. "This from the woman who faced down an armed gunman."

It had been five days since Jo and I had put our lives in danger to clear her name and had caught Fiona Lyle-Hayes's killer in the process. Willy Pelt had confessed to killing Fiona and attempting to kill us.

He'd also set off my motion sensors during his prowl around my home, booby-trapped my chair, invited the snake into my car, and tried to run me over with a car he'd rented to direct suspicion away from himself. All of those acts had been attempts to frame Bobby for Fiona's murder.

After reading the account of Willy's capture and my role in it in their online version of *The Peach Coast Crier*, my parents and my brother had called in a panic. Understandably. Almost a week later, I was still trying to calm them down.

I'd assured them in a dozen different ways that I wasn't going to do anything like this again, but my words weren't having any effect. That was why Phoenix and I were preparing for a surprise family visit any day now.

I scowled. "Jed and Errol still owe you an apology."

"Marvey, they did apologize." Jo spread her arms, drawing attention to her Florida Gator tattoo, which matched the image screened onto her bright orange T-shirt. "And customer traffic in To Be Read is getting back to normal. Slowly."

"Humph." I wiped the sweat from my eyes with the back of my right wrist. "If they hadn't been so focused on you, they would've found the truth before things got out of hand."

Spence and I chugged bottles of water as Jo and the librarians led us through the crowd to the event parking lot. It looked like all of Peach Coast had come to either participate in or cheer on the fundraising event, which started and ended at the Mathilda Taylor Beasley Park & Recreational Center. It was a beautiful day for the event and a lovely venue in which to hold it. The sun was smiling brilliantly. A cool breeze played tag with the Sugar Maples. The sky was a warm azure with only wisps of clouds sailing past.

Corrinne turned to catch my eye. "Actually, Marvey, they should thank you. If it wasn't for you, they would've committed a miscarriage of justice and a murderer would've gone free."

I swallowed a drink of water as I shook my head. "You're giving me too much credit, Corrinne." I swept my arm to indicate her, Spence, Jo, Floyd, Viv, and Adrian. "Everyone contributed something to this inquiry's success."

Jo looked around the group with a shaky smile. "I really can't thank everyone enough. This tragedy could have become a personal nightmare."

Floyd gestured toward Jo with the box of peach cobbler he was carrying away from the event. "Just remember us when you get the library donor package in the mail next month."

Spence opened another bottle of water. "Jo, we have a dinner party to plan."

"Oh, that's right." She grinned, clapping her hands.

I laughed, remembering her disappointment from being excluded from our librarians' dinner party and that Spence had cheered her up by promising to host a special dinner party once we cleared Jo's name.

"Uh-oh." Adrian did his best impersonation of a subdued warning system. "Here comes Ms. Delores Polly at ten o'clock."

I was so surprised my water went down the wrong pipe, which triggered a coughing fit. Six sets of arms tried to assist by pounding on my back. I was fortunate enough to wiggle free before their caring bruised me. I dried my eyes and caught my breath in time to see Delores march up to Jo.

"Jolene Gomez." The older woman stood a few inches below Jo's five-foot-eight-inch height, but still seemed to be scowling down on her.

"Yes, Ms. Delores." Jo sounded understandably wary. "How can I help you, ma'am?"

"By accepting my apology." Delores didn't even crack a smile. "When I'm wrong, I admit it."

Around me, I sensed a collective sigh of relief from the group. During the inquiry, I'd shared with them Delores's assertion—based on Betty's word—Betty and Bobby were innocent, and Jo was guilty.

Delores continued. "I allowed myself to be duped by someone I considered to be a friend. This person led me to believe the worst about you, and for that I sincerely apologize. I've since had some strong words with this person. I've made it quite clear she'll have to do much better if our friendship is to continue."

Jo's smile was warm and full of joy. It lit up her face and brought a smile to those of us around her. She stepped forward and wrapped her arms around Delores. For a moment, the other woman seemed startled by Jo's reaction, then she returned the embrace.

Their image filled my heart. "Oh, I love happy endings."

Beside me, Spence rested an arm around my shoulder, sharing the moment.

"Congratulations, Mr. Spence." Mayor Byron Flowers's booming voice came from behind us.

Spence turned, still with his arm on my shoulders, so we both faced the mayor. "Good morning, Mayor Flowers, and thank you. The congratulations aren't just for me, though. My partner deserves them as well."

The mayor's cheeks pinkened. "Yes, yes. Of course. Congratulations, Ms. Marvey. So happy you were able to come out today to support this community fundraiser for a worthy cause. The money will help fund our hospital's critical services."

I smiled, taking in the public official's tan carpenter shorts and navy Izod shirt. "Thank you, Mayor. I'm happy to support our hospital. May I ask you a question?"

"Yes, of course."

"Do you have a library card?"

THE END

CLASSIC PEACH COBBLER

A Hallmark Original Recipe

In *Murder By Page One*, peach cobbler is the dessert of choice for the people of Peach Coast, Georgia. They even have the Cobbler Crawl, a town fundraiser that centers around the tasty treat. Marvey, a librarian turned amateur sleuth, orders some with her mocha each morning before she goes to work. Our Classic Peach Cobbler is perfect for solving the mystery of what to serve for dessert; it's easy to make, and so delicious, people will always come back for seconds.

Prep Time: 10 minutes
Cook Time: 30-35 minutes
Serves: 10

Ingredients

- 1/2 cup sugar
- 1 tablespoon cornstarch
- 1 tablespoon lemon juice
- 4 cups ½-inch sliced peaches
- 3 cups Bisquick™
- 3 tablespoons butter, melted
- 2/3 cup orange juice
- 1/2 cup sugar

Preparation

1. Preheat oven to 350°F.
2. Toss together 1/2 cup sugar, cornstarch, lemon juice and peaches. Portion into 4 (5'x5') ramekins.
3. Combine Baking Mix, 1/2 cup sugar, butter and orange juice in bowl; mix until it forms a batter. Pour batter evenly over peaches.
4. Bake 30 to 35 minutes or until bubbly and golden brown.

Thanks so much for reading
Murder by Page One. We hope you enjoyed it!

You might like these other books
from Hallmark Publishing:

Dead-End Detective: A Piper and Porter Mystery
Out of the Picture: A Shepherd Sisters Mystery
Behind the Frame: A Shepherd Sisters Mystery

For information about our new releases and
exclusive offers, sign up for our free newsletter at
hallmarkchannel.com/hallmark-publishing-newsletter

You can also connect with us here:

Facebook.com/HallmarkPublishing

Twitter.com/HallmarkPublish

Turn the page for a sneak peek of

Behind the Frame

A Shepherd Sisters Mystery
from Hallmark Publishing

TRACY GARDNER

J ESSAMINA CARSON'S HEAD WAS MISSING.

Savanna took an involuntary step back, away from the defaced, century-old statue, taking in the scene. What in the world?

The head of the statue lay several yards away on the ground, scattered debris littering the grass between the base of the statue and the eerily severed concrete head. Across the base of the statue, from one side to the other, spanned large, red spray-painted words, *NEVER CARSON.*

Savanna whirled around at a sound behind her, hands up defensively—a reflex, considering what she'd just stumbled onto. Her friend Britt was walking toward her, his eyes wide and his short, white-blond hair making him look paler than Savanna felt.

"Savanna? What is this? What happened?"

She shook her head. "I have no idea." She turned in a circle, searching the park for any sign of the person who'd done this. No one. The park was deserted.

Britt stood, hands on his hips, looking the statue up and down, gaze coming to rest on the ugly words. "Well, I'd say someone has a problem with your town."

Savanna stared at him. This made no sense at all. She moved closer to the statue, reaching out and gingerly touching the top of the red "C" with one finger. "It's dry. Whoever did this is long gone—look how thick the paint is. I have to call the police."

She paused, phone in hand. If she called 911, this wouldn't be considered an emergency. She guessed they'd send someone whenever they had a chance, to check things out. But this was a threat. Against Carson. And on the morning of the Art in the Park planning banquet. *Ugh.* She groaned.

"Savanna?" Britt was looking at her, concerned.

She frowned up at him. "Mrs. Kingsley is on her way here now. She's sure to tell the rest of the committee about this. What if they cancel the whole event? Award it instead to the runner-up?"

He nodded. "I see your point. But what can we do?"

"We need help. Now," she said. "I'm calling Detective Jordan."

"Sure, good idea. Call Detective Jordan. Who is Detective Jordan?"

Savanna looked at him, phone to her ear. "I know him through Skylar," she whispered. "He handled the case last year at the Carson mansion."

Nick Jordan finally picked up. "Savanna?"

"Hi, Detective. I'm so sorry to bother you at home. On a weekend," she added, cringing.

"Don't worry about it. What's up?" His voice sounded dry. She could never tell if he was irritated or if this was just always his tone.

Britt motioned to her, pointing toward the parking area. "John's here, I'll go tell him," he whispered loudly before heading toward the councilman just getting out of his car.

Savanna groaned inwardly. John Bellamy was here now, and Mrs. Kingsley would arrive any minute. She had to find a way to direct attention away from the statue. She followed Britt, not keeping up at all with his long-legged stride as she spoke into the phone. "I'm in the park, and someone has vandalized the statue. It's bad. And the banquet is tonight, to kick things off for the Art in the Park event, and the state committee is coming, and I really think you need to see Jessamina. This wasn't random. It's awful. Will you please come?"

She heard Nick Jordan sigh heavily. She supposed maybe he was at home with his wife, enjoying a leisurely Saturday morning...or maybe she'd woken him up. Savanna had a pang of guilt.

"I'll be there in ten minutes." Jordan hung up.

Savanna stared at the phone in her hand before dropping it into her purse. She jogged a little to join the councilman and Britt. Councilman Bellamy wore a suit, as he did every single time she'd ever seen him. It seemed out of place today, a seventy-degree day in the park, but Bellamy had just announced his candidacy for Carson mayor against longtime incumbent Mayor Greenwood. Midterm elections were only three months away. John Bellamy was obviously intent on making good impressions no matter where he went.

"Let's sit for a minute while we wait for Mrs. Kingsley." Savanna directed her little group to a row of park benches under a large maple tree. Each bench back bore a colorful ad for a local business or service, something Savanna had just started noticing around town. She chose a pink-and-yellow bench that declared *Let us pamper you,* depicting a woman relaxing with cucumber slices over her eyes, for Carson's new day spa. The adjacent few benches advertised Skylar's law office, a property development company called Better Living, and a fishing charter company, Lake Michigan Expeditions.

John Bellamy stared toward the statue. "Oh, no. What happened?"

"We don't know. We found her like that. I'd really like to avoid Mrs. Kingsley seeing the vandalism up close, if possible. We need to keep this festival in Carson. I don't want her to get spooked. Things like this just don't happen here!"

———

Read the rest!
Behind the Frame is available now!